THE FIRST BITE

Eric moved me toward one of the curtained-off areas. He lifted me easily and laid me across the couch, and then pulled the curtain closed. He hadn't released my left hand and now he lifted my arm and licked the inside of my wrist. I literally shivered with pleasure, even though he was barely touching me. I closed my eyes and felt his lips touch my cheek, cold enough to cause me to flinch, but warming almost instantly. His kisses moved lightly across my face to my neck. I breathed in his scent and it flowed through me like a drug, swept away my inhibitions, all my conscious thoughts. His hands slipped under my dress and moved everywhere, bringing the nerves to life all over my body.

"Angela, surrender yourself to me, and I will fulfill all your dreams." His voice seemed to come from someplace deep inside me. *Did he really say that?*

"Yes, yes, God, yes . . ." *Did I really say that?*

His lips caressed my face, my arms, my neck. I felt his teeth against my skin like tiny shards of glass scraping and burning, but the pain was the same as the pleasure, and my body reached out to receive him. I was overwhelmed by a yearning to be closer to him, to merge with him so that nothing could ever separate us.

Then came a sudden pinch of pain, exquisitely sharp . . .

BOOK YOUR PLACE ON OUR WEBSITE AND MAKE THE READING CONNECTION!

We've created a customized website just for our very special readers, where you can get the inside scoop on everything that's going on with Zebra, Pinnacle and Kensington books.

When you come online, you'll have the exciting opportunity to:

- View covers of upcoming books
- Read sample chapters
- Learn about our future publishing schedule (listed by publication month *and author*)
- Find out when your favorite authors will be visiting a city near you
- Search for and order backlist books from our online catalog
- Check out author bios and background information
- Send e-mail to your favorite authors
- Meet the Kensington staff online
- Join us in weekly chats with authors, readers and other guests
- Get writing guidelines
- AND MUCH MORE!

**Visit our website at
http://www.kensingtonbooks.com**

ONCE BITTEN

CLARE WILLIS

ZEBRA BOOKS
KENSINGTON PUBLISHING CORP.
http://www.kensingtonbooks.com

ZEBRA BOOKS are published by

Kensington Publishing Corp.
119 West 40th Street
New York, NY 10018

All Kensington titles, imprints, and distributed lines are
available at special quantity discounts for bulk purchases for
sales promotion, premiums, fund-raising, educational, or insti-
tutional use.

Special book excerpts or customized printings can also be
created to fit specific needs. For details, write or phone the
office of the Kensington Special Sales Manager: Attn. Special
Sales Department. Kensington Publishing Corp., 119 West
40th Street, New York, NY 10018. Phone: 1-800-221-2647.

Zebra and the Z logo Reg. U.S. Pat. & TM Off.

ISBN-13: 978-1-4201-0871-2
ISBN-10: 1-4201-0871-9

First Printing: December 2009

10 9 8 7 6 5 4 3 2 1

Printed in the United States of America

ACKNOWLEDGMENTS

I owe a debt of gratitude to my agents, Joanna MacKenzie and Danielle Egan-Miller, and my editor, John Scognamiglio, for making my dream of being published come true; to my writing group (Joe, Amy, Yang, Susan, John, and Bill) for holding my feet to the fire; to Mom and Dad for passing on the writing gene; and to Vail for his unconditional support. I'd also like to thank Kevin Collins and Jane Willis for their advice on the technical aspects of advertising.

Chapter 1

I met my vampire lover on a Wednesday.

I almost missed my destiny that day by oversleeping, but if I had missed it, wouldn't *that* have been my destiny instead? Usually I take the bus to work, but since I was late I drove my Mini to the lot next to our building in downtown San Francisco, resigning myself to the hemorrhagic rate of three dollars every twenty minutes. At lunchtime I'd move to a cheaper lot. After parking in a half-space that could only have accommodated my elfin vehicle, I stopped to watch a sailboat glide under the Bay Bridge. Sun sparkled on the water, the boat, the bridge, and the bikini-clad woman lying on the sailboat's deck—a picture worth framing. It was the second Wednesday in October, the time when savvy tourists come to San Francisco because they know it's when we have our best weather. Since playing hooky on a sailboat was not an option, I consoled myself with the promise of lunch at an outdoor café. Little did I know it would be the last time I'd be enjoying sunlight for quite a while.

I revolved through the door of 555 Battery and waved to Clive, the silent security guard. The elevator was packed like the Tokyo subway, so I opted to walk the three flights to my office. Letters etched into a wavy glass wall in the lobby proclaimed the owner of my labor as Hall, Fitch, and Berg, Advertising. We were also known informally as HFB (and sometimes as Heel, Fetch, and Beg due to our reputation for doing anything to acquire an account). If a jingle pops into your head spontaneously while you're cruising the supermarket aisle for soda pop or laundry detergent, it's probably ours.

The administrative assistant, Theresa, was standing outside her cubicle nibbling a fingernail. She ran to meet me, her three-inch heels clicking on the polished concrete floor.

"Oh good, Angie, you're here. The clients will be here in fifteen minutes, Lucy's still not here, and Kimberley and Les are in Dick's office waiting for *you*."

"Lucy's still not here?"

My boss, Lucy Weston, had missed the last two days of work without notifying anyone. This was out of character for her, but not unheard of at HFB. Last year, one overworked account supervisor had gone out for coffee and sent her resignation from Puerto Vallarta two weeks later. So no one had taken much time to worry about Lucy, as we were all busy trying to make her absence invisible to the clients. I had been in the office until 11 o'clock the night before, working on the Unicorn Pulp and Paper account, which was why I had overslept.

Theresa shook her head. "No, nobody's heard from her."

"So is somebody going to call the police today?"

"Mary from HR is going to do it, but she's trying to find any friends or family to call first, to see if Lucy told anyone where she was going."

I was harboring a secret hope that I'd get to do something around a client besides play stagehand for Lucy, so I had to admit to being somewhat grateful for her absence.

"Which room are we using?" I walked toward my office with Theresa following in my wake.

"Nobody told me anything," she answered. "Lucy usually arranges the rooms with me."

"What rooms are available?"

"Hammett is being used. Kerouac and Ferlinghetti are open."

"Kerouac will do. Pull down the projection screen and set up some snacks in there, okay?"

"What do you think they want to drink?"

I couldn't resist the obvious answer. "How about some fresh blood?"

Theresa laughed dutifully and veered off toward the Kerouac Room.

I made this quip because our new clients were vampires. Macabre Factor consisted of a twenty-something Goth couple who were into the vampire club scene in San Francisco. They started out creating makeup that they used on themselves; chalk-white base tinged with blue, fine-tipped red liner to outline the veins in the neck, and fake fingernails in shades of green, gray, and blue. But when they showed up with real fangs and topaz eyes friends and admirers began clamoring to buy their products. Thus a business was born, with cosmetics manufactured in Sweden, contact lenses from China, and a dentist in Los Angeles with an exclusive contract to manufacture custom fangs that attached to your canines like dental crowns.

I rushed down the hall to my office. All of the assistant account executives have real offices, as opposed to cubicles, which makes us feel very grown up, but every door has a narrow glass window next to it so our bosses can check up on us as they walk by.

For two years Macabre Factor concentrated on selling only to their own kind through their website. But they had recently decided to expand their client base, and with many of the highest rated shows on TV this season featuring an undead creature of one sort or another, the market research showed that they had picked the perfect time. I wasn't sure where the capital was coming from, since Macabre Factor was a small company, but it was going to be a big launch.

This morning we were going to pitch our preliminary ideas for their campaign. Had Lucy been here this morning my job would have been to show up early and set up my computer as a backup in case Lucy's went on the fritz, follow along as she gave the pitch and supply any details she might have forgotten, and make sure everyone's coffee cup was full. But I had done a lot of the background work on this account, so with Lucy absent I was hoping Dick might let me manage the meeting. It occurred to me that if anything bad had happened to Lucy I was to feel awfully guilty. In fact I already did.

I threw my coat over the Aeron chair and shoved aside the pile of illustrations that I had been going over last night. The logo for Unicorn Pulp and Paper was a unicorn surfing on a ream of copy paper and we'd been choosing a personality for the new iteration. There was a classical unicorn, a chubby unicorn, a mean-looking unicorn with a drill-like horn, and an angelic unicorn whose horn resembled an upturned ice cream cone. In my dreams last night the mean unicorn had skewered the angelic unicorn like a shish kebab.

When I turned on my computer the screen was cluttered with files, just like my desk, and the floor behind my chair, so I wasn't surprised when I couldn't immediately locate Macabre Factor. But after I did a search for it and turned up empty-handed, that was when I really began to panic. I'd spent five years working as an actor before starvation drove me to the ad business and one of my biggest fears then was forgetting my lines, imagining myself staring into the footlights like a stroke victim. This was the ad agency equivalent.

I opened my email and began searching through

the two hundred and eighty three messages in my inbox. We'd emailed the Macabre Factor illustrations back and forth dozens of times between Accounts and Creative but my email showed no evidence of it. At this point I started having another creeping feeling. This one was suspicion. I allowed myself to use a curse word that I was raised never to utter, but I was alone and in this case it was justified.

I might have accidentally deleted a file, I could admit to that. But I did not go through two hundred and eighty three emails and trash every one pertaining to Macabre Factor. No, it was clear I had been sabotaged.

Dick Partridge's office was three doors down from mine. I knocked and went in without waiting for an answer, since I was already late. As VP of Consumer Product Advertising Dick had earned a large corner office with windows facing the turning cogs of progress in buildings across the street. It wasn't a view of San Francisco Bay, but it was much nicer than my blank wall. He also had space for a round table and four chairs, which was where I found Dick, Les, and Kimberley.

"Good morning, Angie," Dick said, looking at his watch conspicuously. "I trust you have a good reason for your dilatory behavior, so let's leave it at that, shall we?"

We'd have to, since I had no idea what he was talking about.

Dick Partridge talked like he had cotton balls in his nose and a stick up his you-know-what, using the longest words he could find to express the simplest ideas. Today he'd made the unfortunate choice of wearing a pink Oxford shirt. He looked like a pimple ready to burst.

Next to him, writing industriously, was Kimberley Bennett, my fellow assistant account executive. She was also my roommate, although we never came to work together because Kimberley kept earlier hours than I think is healthy. Kimberley looked like Hollywood's idea of an advertising executive: blond hair (fake, but not so you'd know) to her shoulders, big blue eyes, and an hourglass figure. To complete the image she wore skirts so short and heels so high she looked like she was on stilts. The black A-line skirt I was wearing ended sensibly at mid-calf, grazing the tops of my black leather boots. No sense competing when the game is fixed.

Les Banks, the graphic artist, looked up from his BlackBerry to give me a nod and a smile. Because Les was a "creative," he was allowed a laxity of attire that would never be tolerated in the account executives, who are known as the "suits." Today he was wearing black jeans and a black T-shirt adorned with a grinning skull. His buzz-cut brown hair revealed a perfectly oval head, both ears sported gold hoop earrings, and he had a tiny rectangle of facial hair under the lower lip which, when I first saw it, I thought was the result of neglectful shaving but later realized was a fashion statement. I secretly thought Les was quite good looking. In boring meetings I would sometimes fantasize about what his half-inch-long hair would feel like rubbing over my stomach. I managed a smile for Les, despite my misery.

"What did I miss?" I tried to sound peppy.

"We just convened," said Dick. "As you are all aware, the clients are arriving instantaneously. We probably should have postponed, but of course nobody could have apprehended Lucy's absence. Speaking of which, I'm sure no one wishes to arrogate her duties, but if she's not back by tomorrow we're going to have to discuss an emergency distribution of her clients. I've already set a meeting for ten o'clock in the Ferlinghetti Room. Which we'll cancel if Lucy surfaces, as we trust she will. So, Kimberley and Angie, I guess this will be your chance to fly solo. Are you ready?"

Kimberley jumped in before I'd even opened my mouth. "Oh, yes, Dick, the presentation is completely ready."

"Well, I would certainly like to attend, but my presence is required by a major client," Dick said. "So you three are going to handle Macabre Factor this morning."

Kimberley batted her eyelashes at Dick. "Dick, since Lucy isn't here, someone is going to have to take the lead. I'd like to volunteer. I coordinated the market research and I'm the most familiar with the account. And I've got the presentation right here on my laptop, ready to go."

Kimberley was the most familiar with the account? I cursed silently, but I couldn't really blame her. We had both been laboring in Lucy's chain gang for months; of course she would be plotting a break out as well. The only difference was that she didn't care if there was collateral damage. But there was nothing I could do without making myself look like a faker, a whiner, or a tattletale.

I looked at Les, expecting him to be claiming his free ticket to the ladies' mud wrestling show that was about to begin, but he was busy digging dirt out of his fingernail with the cap of his pen. I made a mental note to myself to stop fantasizing about him.

Dick didn't miss a beat. "I suggest you handle the presentation conjunctively. Two heads are better than one." He waved the backs of his hands at us. "Well, go ahead. Mustn't keep the clients waiting. Although since they're vampires, I suppose they are *immutable*." His arch delivery indicated a joke, so we all laughed. Kimberley grabbed her laptop and rushed out the door.

In the hall I saw Les walking in the wrong direction, to the Creative Department rather than the Kerouac room.

"Les, aren't you coming?"

He turned around. "Listen, Angie, I'm swamped with another account. Do you think you could do this one without me?"

His expression was plaintive. I had never noticed before that his hazel eyes were flecked with dark stripes, like a cat's, but with him staring so intently at me I couldn't miss it. Most of the people in Creative were chronically behind, the mark of an artist being asked to work in a widget factory. Les, however, had never asked me for special favors. I wondered why he was starting now.

"Yes, all right, but only if you promise to keep your phone on in case they have any questions that only you can answer. Is that fair?"

"I owe you one. And Angie, please don't tell Dick I didn't show, okay?"

"Okay."

He surprised me with a brief hug before dashing down the hall.

When I arrived at the meeting Kimberley and the founders of Macabre Factor were already there, chatting amiably under a photograph of a cloud of cigarette smoke with Jack Kerouac inside it. Although I knew their legal names from the various contracts we had signed, Douglas and Marie Claire Paquin, they insisted on being called by their *noms de sang*, Suleiman and Moravia. These vampires didn't seem to be the daylight avoiding type. Even though it was 9:00 A.M. they were as bright-eyed as game show contestants.

"Good morning, Suleiman, Moravia," I hurried to say. "I'm so sorry to be late."

"No, please, do not worry about it," Suleiman answered, as he bowed over my hand. "Theresa made us very comfortable."

Suleiman's accent was British plus something else, possibly Indian. His black hair was slicked back from his slightly receding hairline with a shiny hair gel, probably the one from their line called "Sleek." His eyes were dark and thick-lashed and his skin was olive-toned. His outfit was straight out of *Hedda Gabler*: a pinstriped cutaway frock coat, paisley vest, and a red silk cravat secured with a pearl tie tack. He was unusual without being over the top, and despite my better judgment I was intrigued. I also wanted to know where he bought his clothes.

Once, when Lucy had referred to the clients as "the vampires," Moravia had corrected her.

"We don't say 'vampires,' we refer to those *in the vampire lifestyle.*"

Since then we always used the politically correct term, at least to their faces. I assumed the vampire lifestyle meant dressing in black, frequenting night clubs, listening to Goth music, and drinking Bloody Marys. Although I'd never been to a vampire club, I felt I understood something about their chosen lifestyle. Taking on an unusual persona gives you an entrée into a world that is glamorous and different from your own mundane life. You can easily recognize who belongs and who doesn't. I can't count the number of late-night, coffee-driven conversations I've had with other actors about how much

different (and better) our world was compared to
the nine-to-five one. Of course, I recanted those
statements when I couldn't make my car payments,
but I still understood that need to feel special.

"Will Lucy be joining us this morning?" Moravia's breathy voice interrupted my reverie.

Human Resources had already told us yesterday
that until we had some definitive answer about
Lucy's whereabouts we were to simply say Lucy was
"unavoidably delayed."

"Lucy was unavoidably delayed this morning,"
Kimberley answered. "But Angie and I can't wait
to show you the great concepts we've prepared
for you."

Moravia nodded and leaned back in her chair,
giving me a view of the tops of her breasts, perfectly
round and the size of small cantaloupes. Her cleav-
age could support a pencil upright. She bore a
close resemblance to Elvira, Mistress of the Night,
who appears in display ads (not ours) in liquor
stores every Halloween. Her long black hair was
parted in the middle and worn loose down her
back. Her face was an artful display of all of her
company's wares, with translucent white skin, black-
rimmed eyes that could give Cleopatra a run for
her money, and juicy red lips. Moravia might have
been plain if you caught her just out of the shower,
but then you probably wouldn't be looking at her
face. The two were the perfect spokesmodels for
their brand, and that was the pitch.

Kimberley projected the first illustration, of

Suleiman and Moravia in a red Ferrari convertible driving out of a Transylvanian-style castle on a mountain. Suleiman was smiling at Moravia while she laughed with her head thrown back, her hair blowing in the wind. Both were wearing sunglasses and had visible fangs. Moravia's dress was classic Vampira, with jagged-edged sleeves, while they'd put Suleiman in a playboy smoking jacket. The caption under the picture read: "You're going to live forever. Make sure you look good." Below that the words "Macabre Factor Cosmetics" dripped down the page in a spidery Gothic font.

The rest of the illustrations had the same combination of style and campy humor: the couple at a Hollywood-style party, toasting each other with glasses of red liquid; skiing down a mountain dressed in bright parkas, red lips sparkling against the snow; in the stands at the horse races, shielded from the sun in huge hats. Kimberley ran down the campaign logistics—the magazines, the websites and blogs, the rollout in select cosmetic and department stores—and I helped her the same way I helped Lucy, filling in relevant details and statistics.

Finally it was over and we were silent. Now was the moment of truth.

Chapter 2

Neither Suleiman nor Moravia spoke for a long time. Finally Suleiman took a deep breath. "Well, you certainly made us look attractive. But I don't think this quite gets at what we're after. After all, it makes us look like we're trying to join *their* society, instead of vice versa. I think people might be attracted a little more to the dark side. The seductive lure of the vampire, so to speak."

Moravia chimed in. "Yes, Sully's right. We don't really see our target audience as the debutante ball, Junior League types. Frankly, most of us don't go skiing. Too much risk of sunburn."

I got up to close the projection screen, using the motions to cover my discomfort. How could Lucy have been working with these people for the last month and not know what they wanted? I consoled myself by thinking that if she had let me talk to them we wouldn't be having this problem, but I knew that wasn't necessarily true. Sometimes clients have to see a pitch to realize what they *don't* want, and it helps them clarify their desires. It's awkward, however, and a little embarrassing.

Kimberley cleared her throat. "You know, I totally agree with you," she said. "Angie and I were pushing for something a little more, uh, edgy, but *Lucy* felt sure you would love this. We've got some other great ideas for you, though, in that vein." She giggled at her own joke.

I kept my head down. Kimberley was now insulting Lucy in front of the clients. If Lucy caught wind of it when she came back I didn't want her to think I'd been involved.

Suleiman jumped in, his voice enthusiastic. "I think it would be a great idea if you both came to the club and soaked in the scene, met some of our friends. I bet some of them would even be willing to be part of the campaign. Why don't you come tonight?"

Moravia leaned across the table like she wanted to confide something. Her bosom threatened to pop out of her dress. "There's just one thing. If Lucy comes back today, well, if you could possibly keep tonight's date between us . . . It's not that we don't like Lucy, not at all, but we think you two deserve a chance with this."

Suleiman nodded. "We see how things are with her," he said pointedly.

There's something we call account executive telepathy, which is a subtle form of body language we use to communicate around clients. I tried to silently ascertain what Kimberley thought of their proposition, but she seemed to have turned off her radar.

"Well, we'll certainly try to come," I said, "if not tonight, then another time. We'll just have to check our calendars. Why don't you write down the address?"

Suleiman pointed at Kimberley, who was stacking pens on a legal pad.

"Ask Kimberley, she's been there before."

Kimberley and I saw Suleiman and Moravia to the reception area. All the way back up in the elevator and down the hall I waited for Kimberley to speak. I'd already imagined the scenario—Kimberley's tearful confession followed by my generous forgiveness. Lucy had kept us both on a short leash, but her absence had set us free. Kimberley had decided on a Machiavellian approach to career enhancement. I, on the other hand, had been raised by an Eagle Scout and a Sunday school teacher, and wasn't capable of taking two newspapers out of the kiosk when I had only paid for one. If I were Kimberley I'd be riddled with guilt and waiting for the first opportunity to unburden myself. But Kimberley didn't seem to feel any such obligation. When we reached her office she walked in without another word to me. Before the door had shut I followed her inside.

"So you've been to the House of Usher before?" I asked. "What's it like?"

"I'm not sure." She brushed a stray golden hair from her eye. "It was dark."

"When did you go? Was it with Lucy?"

"Yeah, I guess it must have been. Anyway, what about going to the club tonight? It seems like Suleiman and Moravia want to give us a chance to manage their account."

"I don't know, Kimberley. It doesn't seem right, with Lucy not here. We should probably put them off and wait until she shows up to decide on our next move."

"Angie, Angie, Angie." Kimberley shook her head. "That's why I like you, you're so . . . nice. Can't you smell an opportunity here?"

She moved closer. "You and I both know that Lucy was never going to let us get ahead. I hope she's all right, and I'm sure she is, but this is our chance."

I was sure she wanted to say "*my* chance," but I let her go on.

"If we show some initiative I'm sure Dick will take notice. Then maybe we can go over Lucy's head to get a little more responsibility."

The gleam in her eye was that of a cat who'd just spied a lame mouse. I loved the way she kept saying "we." I could tell she felt she couldn't go to the House of Usher by herself, since the invitation had been to both of us. But given the events of this morning, I figured she'd try to find some way to leave me on the highway with a flat tire.

"Okay, we'll go," I said. "Then if someone wants to suck our blood, we can defend each other."

"Whatever." Kimberley rolled her eyes.

"By the way," I tried to make it sound like an afterthought, "about this morning, what you said to Dick . . ."

She brushed an imaginary lint fleck from her jacket.

"I know we've both been feeling a little controlled by Lucy, and it seemed like a good chance to show your stuff, but really, what you did was out of line."

Kimberley knitted her perfect eyebrows and tilted her head as if she were trying to understand a foreign language. "It seems like you're accusing me of something, Angie."

"Someone deleted all my Macabre Factor files and emails." I summoned my acting prowess in an attempt to look menacing and accusatory.

"Someone? Are you saying I did it? How would I know your password?"

"It's my birthday." My twenty-eighth birthday had just passed. Theresa had brought out a cake at the end of the day and everyone sang *Happy Birthday*, then the men ate cake while the women drank Diet Coke.

"Theresa told me neither you nor Lucy were here this morning, so I got ready to handle things by myself. And when you did show up you weren't prepared. As for your computer, if it's organized like your office or your bedroom, it's no wonder you lost the files." She smiled and twitched her head like a bird. "I'm going to do you a favor and forget we had this conversation. By the way, I'm house-sitting at my parents' for a few days, so I won't be at the apartment. Why don't we just meet at the House of Usher, say about eleven o'clock? I bet things get started late."

"How are you going to change clothes?"

"I have clothes at my parents'. And there's my mom's closet as well."

"Okay, then. I'll see you at the club." I left, closing her door gently behind me. I didn't know what to think. Maybe I'd been wrong about Kimberley, maybe the loss of the files was a computer glitch or a big, stupid mistake on my part. And even if I'd had the presentation ready on my laptop I wasn't sure I would have been able to take over the way Kimberley had, without any concern about other people's feelings. Kimberley had me beat in the ambition department and now I could see my ruthlessness wasn't up to par either.

Back in my office, I organized my email files until the blue screen of my desktop was as clear as the Tahitian ocean. Then I sorted through every piece of paper that was on my desk. I never found the Macabre Factor files, however, so I ruefully sent Kimberley an email asking for copies. That killed most of the morning, and I decided to leave a little early to move the car and have the *alfresco* lunch I'd promised myself.

In the ground floor lobby I ran into Steve Blomfelt, in an impeccable charcoal gray suit and white shirt so starched it looked like it was made of paper. While other men just tied their ties, Steve actually knew the difference between a Windsor knot and a four-in-hand and alternated them depending on the fabric.

"Leaving already?" he asked. "Did one of the other kids steal your crayons?"

Steve was a master of the split personality—starched and serious with clients and a riotously bitchy queen with friends and colleagues. He was also the closest thing to a friend that I had at this house of mirrors we called an office. Steve was thirty-five, seven years older than I, but he'd been in the advertising business for only two years. Before that he worked as a travel agent booking gay tours, until the Internet made his job obsolete. We also had that in common—we both wanted to be doing something else but hadn't been able to make a living at it.

"Hey, Steve, I'm glad I ran into you. I want to ask you a favor. You know my clients, Macabre Factor?"

"You mean Lucy's clients, don't you?" Steve grinned evilly.

"Lucy's still not back yet, Steve. No one's seen her yet today."

The smile turned to concern. "That *is* strange. I hope she's all right."

"Yeah, me too," I said, and immediately felt guilty.

"Your clients, Angie?" Steve prompted.

"They rejected the preliminary ideas. It appears they want normal people to see themselves in the vampire lifestyle, not Suleiman and Moravia in the normal one. They want Kimberley and me to come out tonight to a club. Their idea is that they'll use people from the club as models."

"It could work. At least in New York and LA. I don't know about Paducah, Kentucky." Steve patted his wavy black hair, but it was already perfect. "Actually I take that back. All the teenagers in Paducah will move here when they see the ads."

"The weird thing is that they said Kimberley had been to this club with them, but she never mentioned it to me, though, or anyone else."

"I guess it wasn't worth mentioning. I've certainly been to some strange places to schmooze a client. Me, at a baseball game?" He shuddered. "Clients are fickle, Angie. You know that. They wake up one morning and decide that dancing bears are the best way to sell their product. Go to this club with them. Maybe you'll see something that Kimberley didn't."

"Can you come with me?"

"Tonight? No, sorry, I have a date. What about Kimberley?"

"Oh, *she's* going. You wouldn't believe what she did this morning, Steve. It's like Lucy being gone has made her crazy."

I took a step closer and lowered my voice. "I

swear she got into my computer and deleted my Macabre Factor files. Then she asked Dick to let her make the pitch this morning."

"What did she say when you confronted her?" He paused and narrowed his eyes. "You *did* say something, didn't you?"

"Yes, I confronted her. She denied everything, of course."

"So all you know is that she tried to take the lead at the presentation? That's not crazy, Miss Angie. That's what we call ambitious. Maybe you could learn something from Kimberley's, um, initiative?"

"Steve, the thing I hated about acting was that every time you got a gig you had to screw someone, one way or the other. I intend to do things the honorable way."

Steve rolled his eyes so vigorously the irises practically disappeared. "Angie, you really are too sweet to live. Let's go get some lunch before I have to take a shot of insulin."

I grabbed Steve by the sleeve. "Steve, do you think I should be nervous about going?"

"To lunch?"

I punched him in the arm. "No, to the club."

"Why?"

"Well, Lucy is missing. And these guys are, they're . . ."

"Posers." He sniffed. "Honey, Lucy's fine, I'm sure of it. She could have just decided she was tired of the advertising biz and was going to raise

goats in Mendocino. I'd be out of here too, if not
for my indentured servitude to Master Card and
Mistress Visa. Besides, this club is a public place,
there'll be lots of people there. Go, have fun. Just
don't let them show you the crypt."

I knew one thing: even if I didn't go, Kimberley would. She would steal the account out from
under me and I'd only have my naïveté to blame.

I checked with Theresa on my way out that night.
No one had heard from Lucy. Mary in HR had
called the police, who drove over to Lucy's house in
the outer reaches of the city by the ocean. They had
looked in the windows and seen no signs of distur-
bance. Since no one except us had called them they
were going to contact her sister in St. Louis before
breaking in.

When I arrived home I flopped down on the
living room couch in front of the window. I could
never look at this view without thinking how lucky
I was to have an apartment in Pacific Heights, the
nicest neighborhood in San Francisco. The view of
Angel and Alcatraz Islands was like looking into a
jewelry case, emeralds tossed on the blue velvet
background of the San Francisco Bay, framed by
the Golden Gate Bridge.

Before I became Kimberley's roommate I had
been living alone in the converted attic of a dilapidated three-story Victorian in the Excelsior district, between a check-cashing store and a Popeye's

Chicken. At night the flashing red Popeye's sign punctuated my dreams at two-second intervals.

Despite the obvious charms of this urban lifestyle, when I read a notice on the company's electronic bulletin board saying that someone wanted to share a two-bedroom apartment in Pacific Heights for $800 a month I thought I'd died and gone to heaven. Or at least to Kansas, where apartments probably still cost less than $2,000 a month, the going rate for a studio in San Francisco. It took me a while to figure out why the rent was so cheap, but when I did, it still seemed like a sweet deal.

It turned out that Kimberley's father, Edward Bennett, a plastic surgeon, owned the building, as well as several others. Kimberley's mother was high society, from an old San Francisco family, the Prestons. Trudi Preston Bennett's people had come west in the Gold Rush of 1849. Edward Preston's roots were not nearly so deep, but that didn't keep the family out of the *Chronicle*'s society pages. San Francisco's "in crowd" was not nearly so persnickety about pedigree as their East Coast counterparts. They couldn't afford to be, since a hundred and fifty years ago the whole town was up to its neck in mud.

The Bennetts didn't like their precious girl living alone; in fact they wanted her to live with them in the family home, a colonnaded Georgian Revival mansion at the top of Pacific Heights. The compromise was that she was allowed to live nearby, as long as she had a roommate for security. I wasn't sure why she picked me, since I offered all the security of a Chihuahua puppy. Not to mention the fact that we are about as different as two people can get.

All of Kimberley's clothes were sorted by color and arranged from light to dark in her closet. Her shoes were stacked neatly with a photo of each pair pasted to the box. My clothes arrange themselves when I throw them on the floor, and I often search for ten minutes to find the mate to a shoe I want to wear. But as long as I confined the mess to my room our arrangement worked out.

Three months after I moved in Kimberley was transferred from High Tech to my department, Consumer Products, with Lucy as her boss. This created a little more togetherness than either one of us would have chosen, but we seemed to be making the best of it, at least until today's show-down. Macabre Factor was the only account we shared, thank goodness.

I made a sandwich and a bag of microwave popcorn, the mainstay of my diet. "We" don't eat in the living room, so I flipped through Kimberley's fashion magazines in the kitchen. Then I watched TV until 10:00, took a shower, and headed to my room to find something to wear to the club.

I plowed through my closet, pulling things out, looking at them, and then dropping them into piles that I fully intended to pick up later. Anything that wasn't black wouldn't do. Luckily that didn't eliminate much of my wardrobe, since most my clothing was black, the preferred palette of both actors and advertising account executives. A lot of my stuff was also vintage, which didn't work too well in a business that worshipped the new, but would be great for mixing with folks who favored floor-length gowns and cut-away frock coats. In the back of my closet I hit pay dirt: a beautiful Victorian silk mourning dress with long narrow sleeves that closed with a dozen tiny buttons, even a little train falling from a slight bustle in the back. I had found it a year ago in a used clothing shop on Haight Street and had paid two hundred dollars for it without argument. The silk was worn and there were a few tears at the stress points but that just added to its appeal. It was so *Arsenic and Old Lace* that I couldn't resist it. I hung it reverently in my closet but never imagined there'd be an occasion to wear it.

Now makeup. I had some Macabre Factor products: white base makeup, black eyeliner, a lipstick called "Coagulate," and some greenish-black fingernail polish. But really, how far was I going to take this? Normally I wear just enough makeup to ease the contrast between my pale skin and dark freckles. I powdered my face with my own powder, lined my eyes with the Macabre Factor eye pencil, put mascara on my lashes. Finally I dabbed on a little Coagulate lipstick, which was red with a disturbing blue undertone.

My hair was looking pretty good, thanks to

the three products I'd applied to tame my curls. The McCaffrey hair, inherited from grandfather Seamus, is what an advertiser would term "irrepressible," and what my mother called unruly. When I was a child my hair stood up on my head like a frizzy auburn halo, when it wasn't arranged in braids so tight my teeth hurt. I used to pray every night that I'd wake up with straight hair. God never changed my hair, but He did eventually send me antifrizz crème. Stepping back from the mirror I surveyed my handiwork. I still looked a little too sanguineous to pass for a vampire, but I was pleased with the results.

At eleven o'clock I was in Hayes Valley, driving down Divisadero Street. Home to many of the loveliest Victorian homes in San Francisco, the neighborhood had started out rich, then turned working class and African-American for dozens of years. During that time many blocks fell under the axe of urban renewal, replaced with ugly high-rise apartment houses. The remaining Victorians, old-fashioned and cheap, provided shelter to cash-poor but culture-rich music clubs, theaters, and cafés. Now that San Francisco's property values were sky high there wasn't a neighborhood in the city that wasn't experiencing gentrification and this one was no exception. Victorians restored to their nineteenth-century glory with BMWs in their driveways shared walls with Dollar Stores and aromatic barbeque joints.

I identified the House of Usher not by the address, but by the line of people in front who looked like they had slithered out of *Nosferatu*, the black-and-white version. They were waiting to enter a narrow nondescript door in the side of an Italianate Victorian with faded multicolored paint and a sagging colonnaded front porch. I parked a block down and scurried back to the club.

The bouncer—a typically large man with an absurdly small bowler hat perched on his bald head—was turning people away right and left, checking everyone's name on a clipboard he held in his hammy hand.

Uh-oh, Suleiman and Moravia didn't mention anything about a guest list.

Chapter 3

I tapped the shoulder of the woman in front of me. She had so much eyeliner on she looked like a raccoon.

"Is there a guest list?" I asked.

She nodded. "It's a private club. You have to be on the guest list if you're not a member."

"Well, I'm sure my friends put me on it."

Raccoon girl smiled at me pityingly.

The 200-pound gorilla quickly dispatched the line. "Name," he grunted at me.

I choked out my name.

"Angie, okay, you're in." The behemoth stamped my hand with a tiny bat in iridescent purple ink. I waved casually to raccoon girl, whose name didn't appear to be on the list, and headed inside.

A dark hallway ended in a steep, narrow stairway, probably the servants' stairs. Spine-crushingly loud music exploded from the rooms above. I could barely hear myself think and I wasn't even upstairs yet. People pushed around me to get in, and I let myself be swept along in their tide, trying to gawk and simultaneously appear as if I knew where I was going.

The House of Usher's main vestibule seemed virtually unchanged from its heyday as a Victorian mansion. A large circular velvet couch sat in the center of a room dimly illuminated by gaslights in a crystal chandelier. Twelve-foot high walls were topped with ornate moldings. Wide doorways led in five directions. To the left were the bathrooms and a coat check. The chambers were marked Girls and Boys but men and women ignored the signs and entered indiscriminately. I made a mental note to try the Boys' room later just for the novelty.

To the right were a tiny poolroom and a long ornate wooden bar arrayed with backlit bottles of booze that glowed like lava lamps. The largest doorway opened onto an auditorium filled with people swaying to the deafening music, smoking, or yelling into each other's ears. Directly in front of the stage a small but intrepid portion of the audience was dancing with wild abandon.

The band members didn't seem particularly vampiresque, except for the fact that they were all pale as an alligator's underbelly. The guitarist, wearing black leather pants and naked to the waist, was pounding three chords for all he was worth. The front man was a whirl of long black hair and a costume that seemed to be made entirely of rags.

He crouched low and slunk across the stage, screaming lyrics at an indecipherable speed and decibel level. I put a finger into my ear, and then checked it for blood.

I passed into another room, separated from the stage by a heavy door so the noise level was almost tolerable. White-clothed tables topped with flickering candles created an aura of genteel elegance. Most of the people in the room looked like what you might expect at any hip nightclub. Lots of black clothing and leather jackets, red lipstick, and everyone smoking. I guess if you think about it it's kind of hard to tell a vampire from a typical night-living poet or musician. Same pale skin, same dark circles under the eyes, same intense faces peering through wafting cigarette smoke.

I glimpsed Suleiman and Moravia sitting at the back of the room. Kimberley was between them, looking like Casper the Friendly Ghost in a white sleeveless dress. She couldn't have been more conspicuous, but I knew she'd done it on purpose. Kimberley never made a fashion mistake. I walked over to the table.

There was a woman on the other side of Moravia: painfully thin, with a face that was all sharp angles and lines, but her blue eyes were huge and long-lashed. Her nose, her right eyebrow, and the spot just below her lower lip were pierced with gold studs and rings of varying sizes.

Suleiman stood up and made his customary bow. "Angie, I'm glad you decided to come. Please, have a seat." He pulled out the chair next to the thin woman for me. Kimberley smiled and raised her champagne glass, as if to toast me for making it this far.

Moravia was concentrating on her martini, staring into it like she was reading her fortune. She didn't seem to be drinking so much as inhaling. A female wraith in a black leather corset took my order for a cosmopolitan. I usually drink wine but I felt like I needed some liquid courage.

Suleiman introduced the blond woman as Lilith. She offered me a hand that felt like twigs in a silk bag. She twirled a hank of her bleached blond hair nervously around her other hand. If you were into Dickensian street urchins, you would find Lilith very attractive. I was searching for something to say to her when a man materialized out of the smoky darkness and pulled out the chair next to mine. When I looked at him I got gooseflesh. No, it was more than that. It felt like my skin was trying to slide off my bones in an attempt to get closer to him.

His long reddish-blond hair was tied behind his head, framing a face with a slender nose, square jaw, and sumptuous lips. His eyes were such a light blue they seemed to glow in the dark. He was what I imagined a French prince of the eighteenth century would look like if there had been no inbreeding. The suit he was wearing was right out of Jane Austen, a soft midnight blue velvet that you only see in women's lingerie nowadays, but on him it looked as masculine as a leather jacket and a cowboy hat.

This man was not just handsome. I had seen the Mona Lisa in person on a high school chorus trip, and like her, he made you want to stare until your eyes dried out. His gaze enveloped and then stripped you, literally and figuratively. It seemed he already knew your every hope, dream, fear, and crime; there was nothing you could say that would surprise him. With his lips lifted in that same tiny smile as Mona, he seemed both amused and slightly impatient with the antics of normal humans.

I heard a noise, like a fly buzzing on a window, which turned out to be Suleiman speaking to us. "Eric, nice of you to join us. I'd like you to meet Kimberley Bennett and Angie McCaffrey. They're the ones I told you about from the ad agency. Ladies, may I present Eric Taylor."

Eric Taylor? He should have been named something exotic and unpronounceable. But when he took my hand and put it to his lips I forgot his name anyway, giving myself up to a brief but blissful sexual thrill. He kissed Kimberley's hand as well, but she didn't seem as moved. He sat down between us, but turned to me.

"That is a beautiful dress you have on. You look like you fit right in." A slight accent, maybe French, rolled the *r* in dress.

"Is that a nice way of saying I'm obviously not a regular?" I responded. When I'm nervous I tend to get a little uppity.

"No, of course not, I was just teasing. There's nothing to be obvious about. This is just a night-club. Most of the people here have nothing to do with the lifestyle anyway, except that they like to wear black and go to clubs. No, Suleiman told me about you. He mentioned that you were fascinated by us."

"Really, now." I was all the more indignant be-cause it was true. "I don't believe the word fasci-nated ever crossed my lips."

Eric leaned into me so that his lips were about two inches from mine. A rich sweet scent rose from him, something I thought I recognized but couldn't quite place, definitely not cologne but almost an internal perfume.

"But you are fascinated, aren't you, Angela?" he whispered, his voice low and caressing.

I closed my eyes and took a deep breath, trying to get a grip on myself. But when I inhaled my head spun like I'd had three cosmos. With my eyes still closed I leaned closer, forgetting for a second who and where I was, wanting to enter the smell, want-ing to kiss the lips . . . then somehow my cerebrum came back and took over from my cerebellum. I leaned back and opened my eyes, mentally pinched myself. I took a big slug of my drink. Eric sat back in his seat so that he was facing the whole table.

"So, Eric, what do you do for a living?" Kimber-ley asked.

"Hmm, for a living, an interesting expression. I live, for a living. But if you mean what do I do that involves money, I dabble in this and that. The stock market, venture capital, real estate development."

I looked for a smile to see if he was kidding, but his expression was serious. I figured that if he were lying he'd at least have the smarts to pick just one of those areas, instead of claiming all three.

"And I'm a model," Lilith interjected.

This woman did have the sunken cheeks, acne-ravaged skin, and dark circled eyes that most models display when you see them up close, but a steady diet of coffee, cigarettes, and blow did not mean she made her money on the catwalk. As with actors, most of the people who claimed to be models didn't have the W2 forms to back it up.

"Really, what was your last job?" I asked, not wanting to be mean, but unable to stop myself.

"French *Vogue*." Lilith smiled. She had me there. It would take quite a bit of effort to check that one.

"You should give me your card," I parried. "My agency hires a lot of models. I might be able to get you a job sometime."

I looked at Eric and wondered if Lilith and I were sparring over him and I hadn't even realized it. His self-assured smile told me that was what he thought.

"Do you live in San Francisco, Eric?" I asked.

He shook his head. "Alas, no. It is a lovely city, but I'm here on business."

I felt a not-so-little stab of disappointment. "Where do you live?" I asked, hoping he'd say somewhere close, but with the sinking feeling that the answer would be Paris, Tangier, or Burkina Faso.

Suleiman interrupted before Eric could answer, leaning forward to speak to both Kimberley and me. "Eric and Lilith are two of the people I had in mind for the ad campaign. I just love the way both of them look, don't you?"

Well, one of them, yes, indeed.

"Lilith is a model, so she already has experience," Suleiman said. Lilith gave me an "I told you so" smile.

"Show them your teeth, both of you," Suleiman said.

Lilith drew back her upper lip and I let out a gasp. She had perfect little fangs, about a half-inch long, the color blended exactly with the rest of her teeth. They looked as real as the ones on the tiger in the San Francisco Zoo.

Suleiman said, "We did those for her about a year ago. I don't know where Eric got his, but they're even better. Show her yours, Eric."

Eric's eyes glinted in the candlelight. "Maybe later," he said, and smiled without opening his lips.

I suddenly felt the need to change the subject. "So, Eric, where do you know Suleiman and Moravia from?"

"Oh, Sully and I are friends from way back. But let's talk about you," Eric said, moving toward me again. I leaned back. I wasn't ready yet for another whiff of his magic spell.

"Sully tells me you're doing the advertising for Macabre Factor. What are some of the other companies you're working with?"

I picked some of HFB's "household name" brands. "Strevichnaya vodka? You've seen those big billboards with the naked lady in the bottle, like a ship in a bottle?" Eric nodded, gazing at me with those translucent eyes. "Um, Comet toothpaste, you guys probably use a lot of toothpaste, we do their advertising. Tangento, they're a big company, have a lot of subsidiaries you might know, Adonis athletic wear, Venus lingerie. Unicorn Pulp and Paper, they make, uh, paper products."

Oh my God, I'm babbling.

Eric smiled. "Not at all. I am aware of all these companies. Very high profile."

I wondered about his saying "not at all," an obvious non sequitur. It almost seemed like he had read my mind.

"You must be very good at what you do," Eric continued, "but you don't seem like the type."

"And what 'type' would that be?" I replied. I felt like he was toying with me, but I didn't want him to stop.

"The business type, the nine-to-five type. You seem like an artist to me."

"Well, I was an actor. Majored in drama in college."

Eric nodded knowingly. "Yes, an actress, that's what I would have said. Why did you leave it?"

"The usual three reasons. Food, clothes, and a roof over my head."

Eric put his hand on mine. His touch was ice cold, but he had just put down a frosty glass. "Would you care to dance?" he asked.

Although I'd had years of physical training for the theater, my dancing was still strictly character actor. I thought up a quick excuse. "I don't think so. The sledgehammer is not my favorite instrument."

Eric laughed. "Not there," he answered. "We insiders know a much better place."

Still holding my hand, he helped me stand up. "We're going to dance," he announced.

"Have a good time!" Kimberley trilled, like a mother sending her daughter to the prom. Before we walked away I saw her pull her chair closer to Suleiman. I knew I should stay and chat with the clients, but ever since Eric had appeared I didn't really care about the usual things anymore. Lilith was busy trying to light a cigarette and didn't acknowledge our departure. We went to the back of the room and through a door with a sign reading MEMBERS ONLY.

The new room was designed like a Victorian opium den. The walls were draped with velvet curtains of indeterminate color. A group of tables, all of them set for two, lined one curtained wall. The rest of the room was divided into curtained-off areas, some open to display couches, although I suppose chaise lounge is the correct term for long sofas with one high back and side. Several couples were dancing to music that could not have been more different from the alligator underbellies. It had a slow hypnotic beat topped by the softly keening sounds of a woman singing in a language I had never heard before.

In front of us a woman with long dark hair danced with her back to another woman. Her head was leaning on her partner's shoulder, eyes closed, an expression of ecstasy on her face. The other woman swayed in time to the music, stroking the dark-haired woman's body rhythmically, nuzzling her neck. And all around me was that sweet indefinable odor. I thought I was going to faint. I stumbled and Eric grabbed my arm.

"What do you think?" His voice seemed to come from inside my head.

"I had heard that some of the bars in San Francisco have make-out rooms but this is something else."

I tried to joke, but I wasn't feeling very funny. In fact, I couldn't tell exactly how I was feeling, but I knew I didn't want it to end. Eric swept me into the circle of dancers. He held me away from him, as if we were in dancing school. His left hand held my arm aloft and his right hand gripped the small of my back, subtly directing me to move with him. Even though I had no idea how to waltz I was doing it, and feeling graceful besides. I realized I'd never danced with a man who really knew how to lead a partner. While we danced he gazed into my eyes, the Mona Lisa smile gracing his lips. The attraction I felt was so intense I wanted to look away, if only to catch my breath, but I couldn't tear my eyes from him.

The music's tempo became quicker. With one move Eric pulled me close, simultaneously angling me so that I was pressed against his right hip. His arm tightened around me and I felt each of his fingers separately through the thin silk of my dress. He pressed his cheek against mine and just like that we were doing the tango. His skin was soft and silky, but hard underneath, like marble wrapped in velvet. His breath was cool and dry but had the same rich, heady sweetness that seemed to seep from his pores. His scent was what perfume makers had been trying to capture for thousands of years: the distilled essence of attraction, indefinable but irresistible.

As the music morphed into a mesmerizing Middle Eastern tune, Eric moved me toward one of the curtained-off areas. He lifted me easily and laid me across the couch, and then pulled the curtain closed. He hadn't released my left hand and now he lifted my arm and licked the inside of my wrist. I literally shivered with pleasure, even though he was barely touching me. I closed my eyes and felt his lips touch my cheek, cold enough to cause me to flinch, but warming almost instantly. His kisses moved lightly across my face to my neck. I breathed in his scent and it flowed through me like a drug, swept away my inhibitions, all my conscious thoughts. His hands slipped under my dress and moved everywhere, bringing the nerves to life all over my body.

"Angela, surrender yourself to me, and I will fulfill all your dreams." His voice seemed to come from someplace deep inside me. *Did he really say that?*

"Yes, yes, God, yes . . ." *Did I really say that?*

His lips caressed my face, my arms, my neck. I felt his teeth against my skin like tiny shards of glass scraping and burning, but the pain was the same as the pleasure, and my body reached out to receive him. I was overwhelmed by a yearning to be closer to him, to merge with him so that nothing could ever separate us.

Then came a sudden pinch of pain, exquisitely sharp.

Chapter 4

Instinct told me to pull away, but my body wanted something else. It yielded itself up to him, pressing closer, offering every vulnerable inch of skin to his ravishment. I saw colors on the insides of my eyelids as if a bright light were shining on them, twisted vines of red against a pink sky. At each beat of my heart waves of blood crashed against my skin. I could no longer hear the music or feel the couch I was lying on. Everything was Eric.

Then the world went black.

I woke up sprawled on the couch with Eric smoothing my hair off my face. I heard his voice before I opened my eyes.

"Angela, are you awake?"

I heard myself mumble, "Yeah, okay, must have been the drink, not used to hard liquor. I think I need to go to the bathroom, wash my face . . ."

He tried to stop me, telling me to lie still and rest, but I slid off the couch and stumbled away.

Kimberley and the Macabre Factor people were
no longer in the bar, thank goodness, so I was able
to get to the women's room without being seen by
anyone who knew me. I went into a stall and sat on
the toilet without lifting my dress. The fog had
cleared a bit but my memory was still very fuzzy. I
was fully clothed, down to my bra and black stockings. My body had the shuddery, slippery feeling
of postcoital release but there was no evidence
that sex had happened. At least not sex as I had
thought of it previously. *Something* had happened,
something powerful and earthshaking, and I felt
excited, happy, and desperate to touch Eric again.
Also scared by his power over me, embarrassed
that I didn't remember the consummation, and
worried that I'd let everything move too fast.

I smacked myself on both cheeks and told myself
to snap out of it. A plan had to be formulated. I
firmly believed my mother's admonitions against
being "loose," not because I wanted to save anything
for my husband, but because the few hook-ups I'd
had were humiliating wastes of time and body fluids.
The guys involved treated me like a piece of chewed-
up bubblegum afterward. I wanted, no, needed, to
see Eric again, for him to want to see me. I didn't
regret our encounter, far from it, but I felt I had to
exert some control over the situation.

I stood up, straightened my stockings and dress,
and left the stall. I couldn't use any of the mirrors
because they were all occupied, one by a woman so
beautiful you would never guess she wasn't female

until you saw her big hands, another by a pair of huge breasts topped by an insignificant head, and the last by a skinny man applying black eyeliner onto the eye that wasn't covered by a pirate patch.

In a lounge filled with threadbare velvet chairs two women were snorting cocaine off a glass coffee table. One of them held a straw out to me, but I shook my head.

"I think I've had enough," I said.

Eric was where I had left him, arrayed casually on the velvet couch, knees crossed, arms spread. In the dim light his face and hair gave off a faint glow, like a candle glimpsed through a curtain. He stood when I approached and made a little bow, then handed me my purse.

"You forgot this."

As I received it our eyes met and I felt dizzy again. The current pulling me toward him was frightening in its intensity. I forced my gaze down to the tie tack in his cravat, a coiled golden snake with a ruby eye.

"So, I need to be going, I'm feeling a little unwell, but, um . . ." I fumbled in my purse and took out a business card, "but I'd really like to see you again, if you're thinking about doing any advertising for your businesses . . ." *Oh, shut up, already!* I handed him the card.

He smiled and put it in his breast pocket. "Are you sure you don't want to stay?"

"No, I mean, yes." This was really embarrassing. "I really should go."

He reached out and smoothed some hair off

my cheek, letting his fingers glide around my chin and down my neck, leaving everywhere he touched tingling.

"Could I have your card?" I whispered. Propriety be damned, I couldn't take the chance of not being able to find him again.

He took out a wallet and handed me a card that was square and thick, nothing like a regular business card. I held it under the light of the candle.

M. ERIC TAYLOR
HARBINGER, INTERNATIONAL

I looked up. "There are no numbers on here."

He shrugged. "I prefer more traditional methods of communication."

What could be more traditional than the telephone, I wondered.

"Ink and paper has been used for two thousand years. The telephone is barely one hundred."

There it was again, another comment that sounded like he was reading my mind.

He laughed, which was another non sequitur—unless we were having a separate conversation from the verbal one.

"Let me see you to your car." Eric held out his arm with the elbow bent, a gesture I hadn't seen since my father asked me to dance at my sister's wedding.

I shook my head. "No, please don't." I couldn't trust myself if he took me to my car. What if he asked to come home with me? I turned and left the room without looking back.

It wasn't until I was in my car, checking my face in the rearview mirror, that I saw the dried blood on my neck, glowing purple in the street lamp's fluorescent light.

Morning again, and the shifting clouds cast bands of light and shadow across my bed. I had forgotten to close the blinds last night, in fact I hardly remembered getting home. The black dress lay in a heap on the floor, next to my purse, keys, and pantyhose. My head throbbed, my tongue and teeth felt fuzzy, and one of my eyes was partly glued shut. My muscles ached like I'd slept on a bed of rocks. The light from the window was killing my eyes, so I pulled the covers over my head.

I tried to go back to sleep, but my thoughts kept jostling each other like kids at an ice cream truck. Maybe I did get drunk last night and blacked out, I thought. How else to explain the gaps in memory and the hangover? I only recalled having one drink, but I rarely drank, so I didn't have much experience with its effects. My behavior had been unlike me in so many ways—the drinking, leaving clients unattended, not to mention making out with a guy I just met. And then feeling like I would jump off a cliff if I couldn't see him again. All these things—not like me at all.

Just the thought of Eric reignited an eagerness

I hadn't experienced since junior high, when I still believed in love at first sight. Being with him had been a breathtaking experience, literally. Was it possible to pass out from sheer excitement? I closed my eyes and remembered the sweet scent, the luminous blue eyes . . .

Time for another symbolic slap on the cheek. And a reality check. *What the hell happened last night?*

Telling myself to be clinical, I touched my body from face to knees, with each part trying to remember exactly what had happened. I was remarkably unsuccessful. The encounter with Eric remained a glorious blur. There had been kissing, I recalled the velvety feel of his lips and tongue against mine. There had been touching, from what felt like a dozen hands at once, all over my body. Yet I had come out of it wearing all my clothes. Was it possible to have had the greatest sex in my life without actually having sex? It reminded me of my mother's favorite movie, *Ghost*, which she watched on DVD at least twice a year. In it the woman's boyfriend is killed but he comes back and makes love to her, except he has no body, so it's all in her head, or all spiritual, or something like that, but it's staggeringly sexy.

But Eric had been undeniably corporeal. And I did have one clear memory, from the car, while looking in the rearview mirror.

I went to the bathroom and examined my neck, standing on my tiptoes to lean in close. There were a few rusty smudges still, so I wet a washcloth and wiped them off. Sully and Moravia had never mentioned that those in the vampire lifestyle actually used those faux fangs to suck each other's blood, but then why would they? I would never think of telling them what I do in bed (of course there would be precious little to tell). I cleaned my neck but kept scrubbing because I was sure there was a wound somewhere, but there wasn't.

I walked past Kimberley's room. Her four-poster bed with the fluffy white duvet and pink pillows was neatly made, and for a moment I wondered whether she had met someone at the club as well. Then I remembered that she was staying at her parents' house while they were on vacation in Bermuda.

In the kitchen I poured a glass of orange juice and toasted a slice of bread. My stomach was churning and the last thing I wanted to do was eat, but I knew it would be good for me. The juice tasted strange, a little metallic. I checked the expiration date but it was fine. The toast seemed gritty and I wondered if Kimberley had changed to a health food brand, but the bag was the same.

After breakfast I went to my closet and put on a sober black pantsuit with a crisp tuxedo-tailored white cotton blouse, hoping the conservative attire would counteract my feeling of being a crazy vampire-chasing slut.

* * *

I had just sat down at my desk when a knock came at my office door. Steve sauntered in, wearing a gray three-buttoned suit with a blue pin-striped shirt and a silvery gray tie. A matching pocket square peeked out of his breast pocket.

"So, the Empress of the Night arises from her coffin. How were the nocturnal festivities?"

The smile on his bronzed face was wry and his dark eyes twinkled with mischief. The thought occurred to me, not for the first time, that I was glad he was gay, because otherwise his handsomeness would make me too nervous to be his friend.

"Steve, you're not going to believe what happened to me last night."

Before I knew it the whole story came pouring out, of my tryst with Eric Taylor, the vampire capitalist. The whole story—except the part about the blood on my neck. Steve, who usually interrupts all the time, listened with his mouth open. When I finished I waited, hoping he would say something reassuring.

"Well, I sure wish I still smoked, because now would be a good time for a cigarette. So, are you going to see him again?"

"The prudent answer would be no, but to be honest, I just can't say that. There was something about him that was so . . ." I couldn't think of a word that would do him justice.

"Say no more, honey. If he was half as good looking as you say he was, I'd have let him suck my . . ."

I interrupted him. ". . . your blood, I know."

Steve sat down and crossed his legs, revealing lavender socks and shiny black loafers. "Let's get serious for a moment here. Did you say you passed out?"

"Yeah, I think so, but I'm not sure."

"How much did you have to drink?"

"One drink, I think."

Steve wagged a finger at me. "I saw this on *Oprah*. The guy drugged you with that date rape drug, Rohypnol."

"Oh, come on, Steve." I laughed, but the idea wasn't that farfetched. It would explain the hangover.

"I should have gone with you last night. I blame myself. Where was Kimberley while this villain was manhandling you?"

"Where I should have been. Talking to the clients," I answered guiltily.

"But at least you're okay, right? Nothing happened?"

Nothing except I can't stop thinking about the guy.

"We exchanged cards."

Steve leaned closer and squinted at me. "This was no date rape. You liked him, didn't you, princess?"

"How would I know, I just met him. Anyway, it's almost time for the meeting and I need to check my voicemail. Let's talk about this later."

He didn't move.

"Steve, I need a little time to myself."

"To call this guy? Don't do it, it's too soon. You've got to wait forty-eight hours."

"Get out."

He sighed heavily but obeyed my command, flashing a four and an eight with his fingers before he left the doorway.

I listened to my voicemail while skimming my email for my new love's name, the only dull thing about him. He had said he preferred traditional methods, but I was too addicted to electronic communication to believe that anyone in this day and age who was younger than ninety wouldn't use them. My palm was sweating on the mouse as I scrolled through my inbox.

The first voicemail was from Les Banks, the graphic artist, asking me to call him back, not saying about what. The call had been placed last night at 5:45, after I left the office. I saved it and made a note to call him later. The second message was from my mother, made at 9:02 this morning.

"Honey, I know you're really busy, but your father and I haven't laid eyes on you in weeks. Could you come over for dinner this Sunday? I'm making your favorite meatloaf . . ."

Normally, the way to my heart is through my stomach, but the way I was feeling this morning, eating was the last thing on my mind. Still, I saved that one and made another note to call Mom back.

The last message was a guy obviously reading a script, inviting me to a conference on online marketing in Austin, Texas. I deleted that one.

* * *

The emergency meeting was in the Ferlinghetti Room, which overlooked the Bay and was decorated with photographs of the author and poet standing in front of City Lights, the bookstore he founded in North Beach in the 1950s. When I got there everyone was already seated. Dick Partridge was at the head of the table, tapping his pen and looking at his watch.

On his right was Kimberley, looking like she had suffered no ill effects from her late night. She was dressed in a more somber than usual blue suit with a short-sleeved jacket, in deference, I supposed, to the unfortunate circumstances of the meeting. Around her neck was a necklace bearing a cashew-sized, presumably real, diamond pendant.

To Dick's left was Lakshmi Roy, the other Consumer Products account executive, so small she looked like she should be sitting in a booster seat. A native of India, she was the classic American success story. By the age of thirty she had gone to Yale and worked in Hollywood and had already amassed credentials as grand as she was little. According to Steve, who worked for her, Lakshmi's managerial style was as different as night and day from Lucy's. Lakshmi was kind and fair, open to suggestions and gave credit where it was due. On her left was my pal Steve, watching me closely like he was expecting me to fall down at any moment from the after-effects of Rohypnol.

Next to Steve was Lakshmi's other AAE, Chase Johnson, a recently graduated frat boy whom Steve referred to as "the human beer keg." Theresa was also there, with her laptop open, ready to take notes. Her silky red shirt plunged to reveal two prominent collarbones and not much else. I took a seat next to Webster Northrup, manager of the Creative department. Web tried to bridge the sartorial gap between Creative and Accounts by dressing in Levi's Dockers and button-down shirts with the sleeves rolled up. In his mid-thirties, he had a round, pleasant face with brown eyes, thick dark hair, and a bit of a belly. Also in attendance were a copywriter and a media coordinator.

"Now that Angie is here, we can commence," said Dick. "As you all know, Lucy Weston has not been at work since last Friday. She hasn't called in or answered her phone at home. We apprised the authorities yesterday and they are looking into the situation. Naturally we hope for the best. Our task now is to reassign the more pressing duties to ensure that our clients do not experience any discontinuity of service."

Lakshmi gave me a smile from across the table without moving her lips. She was the reigning mistress of account executive telepathy.

"Our clients at Macabre Factor called me this morning. They were very pleased with the presentation. I would like to offer my commendations to Angie and Kimberley, who stepped in and took over that meeting at a moment's notice yesterday. Laudable work, ladies." He smiled thinly at each of us. "They have specifically asked for Angie to manage their account, even when Lucy returns. Whatever you did in there, Angie, it was well-received."

I looked down at the table to hide my confusion. Why in the world was Macabre Factor giving me their account? I hadn't taken the lead on the presentation, they didn't like the pitch anyway, and it was Kimberley who hung out with them at the House of Usher while I was off hooking up with their top vampire model. The only person I'd impressed last night was Eric, and I wasn't even sure how successful I'd been at that. As I raised my head my eyes collided with Kimberley. The look she was giving me was one of sheer malevolence. I wondered if I'd find the locks changed when I got home.

Chapter 5

"Let's go over Lucy's accounts and get an update on when the next client contact is occurring." Dick checked his notes. "Unicorn Pulp and Paper Products. Angie, I think you've been working with Lucy on Unicorn?"

"Yes, Dick, and we've got a presentation coming up next Monday."

"Very well," Dick answered, "who are you working with in Creative?"

"Me." Dave was our newest copywriter. Normally he had iPod earphones growing out of his ears, but in deference to Dick he'd removed one.

"I'd rather have you work with someone a little more senior on that. Web, can you take over for Dave?"

"Sure, no problem, Dick." Web made a few marks on his notepad. Dave smiled at me, looking a little wistful, and I remembered that at our last brainstorming meeting he'd told me that my sweater was pretty.

"Miss Minnie's Muffins?" Dick said it like he was taking an elocution test. "That's yours, Kimberley?" She nodded.

"Deadlines coming up this week?" Dick asked.

"No, not until next month. They're working on new flavors." Kimberley's tone was subdued.

"Plump n' Tasty Chicken?"

I raised my hand. "A week from Friday, I think."

"Okay, check in with Lakshmi on that by next Wednesday at the latest."

Dick looked around the room. "And last, but certainly not least, we have Tangento. I believe you were working with Lucy on that also, Kimberley?"

Tangento was one of the company's most high profile accounts. They spent millions a year on their advertising and everybody at HFB wanted a piece of them. Although few people were familiar with the parent company, as I'd said to Eric last night, their subsidiaries were some of the most common names in apparel. Adonis sportswear. Venus lingerie. Their Proteus line of basketball sneakers had the dubious distinction of being the ones over which ghetto youth shot each other.

Kimberley was saying, "Yes, Dick, we just finished working with the Research department, doing focus groups on Venus and Adonis."

Dick paused and coughed into his hand. "Kimberley, I'd like to have Angie parley with Tangento for the time being. I'd like her to act as account manager, with your capable assistance, of course."

Dead silence took over the room. Kimberley looked down, her cheeks glowing red. Dick looked at his notes, either not knowing what he had just done or not caring. I felt a painful mixture of confusion, pleasure, and guilt.

"Each of you should dispatch an email by the end of the day apprising me of the status of each account. Thank you all for your attendance." Dick tried to make a decisive gesture with his pen, but it flew out of his hand and hit Dave in the chest.

Kimberley walked over to Les and Web and started talking, her back to Dick. She walked out the door with them, and Lakshmi and Theresa soon followed.

I made my way over to Dick, planning to jettison Tangento. Sure, I had wanted to manage some accounts, but because I deserved them, not because my boss was MIA. I also needed to be able to live with Kimberley. At least until I could afford my own place.

"Dick, if I could just speak to you for a minute."

"Yes, certainly, Angie."

"I'm not sure I really have the time to give Tangento the superior service that they deserve. And also Kimberley is so much more familiar with the account than I am . . ."

He held up his hand. "With Lucy gone we are in a staffing quandary. There are issues here that I am not at liberty to discuss, but rest assured that I have complete confidence in your ability, Angie. If you would like me to relieve you from some of your other duties in order to free up time for Tangento, we can delegate Macabre Factor to someone else."

And throw away my chance of running into Eric again?

"No, no, that's okay, Dick, you don't have to do that. I can handle things for now." Whether I was going to be able to handle them with Kimberley was another story.

I saw the envelope immediately when I walked into my office, maybe because I had cleaned up my desk the day before or maybe because I was looking for something like it. It was cream-colored, made of thick, cottony paper, addressed in an ornate calligraphic hand, like a wedding invitation, but it had no stamp or return address. I grabbed it and ran down the hall to Theresa's desk. She looked alarmed as I approached so I slowed to a walk.

"When did this come?" I asked, waving the letter.

"Early this morning. A courier brought it."

I took the letter back to my office and closed the door. My heart pounded painfully as I opened it.

My dear Angela,
    I apologize if I frightened you last night. That was certainly not my intention. If you don't want to see me again, then please accept my apology. But if

*you do, I hope you will do me the honor of meeting
me tonight at 10 P.M. on the terrace behind the
Ocean House.*

I knew I shouldn't go. The guy lived far away,
dressed like Oscar Wilde, and had sexual proclivities
that were, well, strange would be putting it mildly.
Why couldn't I meet a nice guy who I wouldn't be
ashamed to take home to meet the folks? *Maybe I
should meet Eric one more time to get him out of my system,*
I thought. Away from the ambience of the club he'll
look like a run-of-the-mill weirdo and I can forget
about him. Then all I'll have to deal with is the disappearance of my boss, which Lord knows is enough.

Nice rationalization, Steve would say if he could
hear my thoughts. Now, what are you going to wear
on your date tonight?

In the hopes that the hangover I was still feeling
could be cured by a little caffeine, I went out to
get a latte. Leaving the climate-controlled environment of HFB was like opening an oven door. The
day had turned San Francisco schizophrenic,
foggy morning segueing into blazing midday. I
took off my jacket and rolled up the sleeves of my
blouse. The sunlight seemed inordinately bright,
like the earth had moved closer to the sun while I
wasn't looking. I told myself it was because I'd
been in the office all morning and ducked quickly
into the café.

Everyone in San Francisco professes to hate chain stores and love the independent guys, but whenever I went into Starbucks there was always a line. Lakshmi was standing near the cash register. From behind it looked like a ten-year-old was ordering a grande latte.

"Excuse me, can I see your ID?" Steve and I had gotten into the habit of teasing Lakshmi because, unlike my own boss, she had a sense of humor.

"What are you, the coffee police?" she asked with a mock scowl.

"Did you know Coca-Cola actually used to have cocaine in it?" I asked. "Now all we've got is coffee. How are we supposed to maintain our productivity?"

"Yes, don't you hate it when your country won't let you become a drug-addled drain on society?"

"You immigrants, always sticking up for the government. You need to exercise your democratic right to bitch and moan!"

Lakshmi reached the head of the line and beckoned me to order on her tab. We both ordered a grande latte and I followed her to one of the tiny tables.

"So, that was quite a coup this morning," said Lakshmi, looking at me expectantly. "Macabre Factor and Tangento. Are you taking steroids or something?"

I took a sip and burned my tongue. The coffee had a metallic aftertaste, just like the orange juice. I wondered if one of my fillings was leaching metal.

"I don't know what Dick was thinking. I don't

know what the Macabre people were thinking, either. They hated the ideas we gave them."

Lakshmi shook her head. "But obviously they didn't hate *you*. They want to give you another chance."

"Yeah, not sure why they want that, actually."

"Angie, you really don't know how good you are, do you?" Lakshmi laughed. "Actually, that's one of the charming things about you. You're about the only person I've met in this business who isn't always tooting their own horn. But you're sharp. Those ideas you had on Spreckels Cereal and New Freedom tampons, they were great. And the way you handle clients is terrific. But your light is shining in a barrel right now. I hope Lucy's fine, but really, you're lucky she's gone. I'm sure she had you in her sights, right after Kimberley."

I wanted to bask in her compliments, but the last two sentences had me confused. "What do you mean, had me in her sights?"

Lakshmi wiped a dab of foam from her upper lip. "Lucy had it in for Kimberley. She was trying to get her fired, quietly, of course."

"Why?"

Lakshmi looked around, probably to make sure there were no other HFB employees lurking nearby. "Well, depending on which gossip you listen to, either Kimberley was trying to usurp Lucy and take credit for work she didn't do, or Lucy was an impossible manager who wouldn't let Kimberley sharpen a pencil without sending her a memo about it and was trying to fire Kimberley because she refused to knuckle under."

"Wow. Well, I could see both of those scenarios being true." I started to tell Lakshmi about Kimberley deleting my Macabre Factor emails, but decided that I shouldn't go spreading rumors unless I had proof.

"Kimberley might deserve to be fired, and after all, Lucy *is* her supervisor, but you should still watch your back. I wouldn't put it past Lucy to fire someone because she finds them threatening."

"Oh come on now, Lakshmi, who would find me threatening?"

Lakshmi patted my hand. "I'm just telling you how I see it, Angie. I'm only going to be around for another couple of months, so I figure I've got nothing to lose by telling the truth. Dick is going to have to watch out for me. I might start correcting his vocabulary gaffes."

"What do you mean, are you leaving?"

"I'm getting married." Lakshmi said it in such a nonchalant tone I expected her to finish the sentence . . . and then I'm going to pick up my shirts at the dry cleaner.

"I didn't even know you had a boyfriend," I said.

"I didn't, really. It's an arranged thing, between our parents, mostly. He's a postdoc at MIT, so I'll be moving to Boston soon."

I didn't know such things went on in the twenty-first century. I imagined a gift-wrapped Lakshmi being handed over to a bald man in his sixties. "Have you met the guy?" I asked.

"Oh sure, we've met several times. I told my parents I had to approve of the man before I'd agree."

"I see," I said. The man in my mind changed to a broad-shouldered hunk in bicycle shorts. "So you're in love with him?"

"Love comes later, Angie. It's something that grows, from knowing a person, building a life together." Lakshmi looked at her watch. "Oops, I've got to get back." She swallowed the last of her latte and headed out.

I sat for a while longer, pondering. I had dated guys before, one in college for over two years. My parents had loved Andy and hinted broadly about our getting married, but after graduation Andy wanted to be on Broadway, or at least Off-Broadway, and I wanted to see if I could make a go of it in San Francisco. We did the long distance thing for a while, but then Andy got a role in a play in which he and his costar appeared naked. By the second performance he was cheating on me. It felt silly to be angry when I hadn't seen him in six months, so I just officially called it quits. Since then it had been one long dry spell, punctuated by brief showers, and now I had a hurricane on my hands.

What should you trust, your heart or your head? Do you find a partner society considers appropriate and settle down to a life of TV reruns and potpies? Or chase down blatantly inappropriate, not to say sinister, men because they make you feel like a firecracker on the Fourth of July?

At one o'clock I walked to the Azure Sea to meet Steve and the Toothpaste Kings. The foyer was subtly nautical, all dark wood and ship memorabilia in glass cases. The hostess, a young woman dressed in a decidedly non-nautical cashmere sweater set, led me back to our table. The building had once housed an exclusive men's club and the dining room was the former swimming pool. The vaulted ceiling sported a gorgeous WPA-era mosaic of fishermen casting their nets into San Francisco Bay during the days when Fisherman's Wharf was a working pier, not just a mecca for tourists and scammers.

Steve had scored us an excellent table on a raised platform that ran along the side of the dining room, the "see and be seen" area. He was already sitting with the clients, Steve in the best seat, facing out into the crowd, with the two men on either side of him. I was sure Tweedledum and Tweedledee hadn't noticed that Steve had taken the catbird seat. The Tweedle on my left, Stanford "Stan" Ruckheiser, stood up, catching his belly on the edge of the table, and pulled out my chair for me. My right hand was then enclosed in the clammy handshake of Jacob White, who I had secretly nicknamed "Jake the Snake" because he was long, sinewy, bald, *and* he talked like a rattlesnake, a breathy whisper with a sibilant "*s*."

"Sssso, Angie, Ssssteve tells us you have the best recommendations for what plays we might want to sssee tonight," Jake hissed at me.

"Yesss, that'sss right." Steve looked right at Jake as he spoke. "Angie always knows what's a go and what's a missss."

I choked back a laugh. Steve had recently attended a conference called Neurolinguistic Programming for Salespeople, where they taught him to mirror the client's mannerisms, accents, and speech patterns to create instant rapport. I wondered how long it was going to take Jake to catch on and ssstrike Steve across the face.

"I hear *Beach Blanket Babylon* is fun," Stan said.

I groaned silently. *Beach Blanket Babylon*? I was about to take his question seriously and lay out an array of theater choices that was unrivaled on the West Coast, in my humble opinion. Molière at the American Conservatory Theater, Sam Shepard at Berkeley Rep, why, the Fringe Festival was going on right now! He could see twenty new plays a day for the next week! And instead he wanted a 30-year-old cabaret show whose big gimmick was a woman wearing a hat longer than a car with the entire skyline of San Francisco arrayed on it? Next he'd ask us to take him to Hooters on Fisherman's Wharf.

I must have betrayed my disgust, because Steve actually kicked me under the table. "Yes, Stan,

Beach Blanket Babylon is fun!" he said cheerily. "We'd be happy to supply you with tickets. Just let me know how many you need."

Stan and Jake brightened at that news and we turned our attention to the menu. Our two guests from landlocked Fresno were suitably impressed by the variety of fish on offer, while I scoured the list for something vegetarian. I'm not a strict veggie, but I hate all fish. The smell and texture reminds me of something gone rotten. People are always telling me what I'm missing, so I periodically try a scallop or a bite of salmon, thinking that maybe I'll change my mind, but it always tastes like flesh Jell-O to me. I decided on a Caesar salad. Steve, who is always watching his weight, ordered shrimp salad. Our two guests, mindful that lunch was on HFB's tab, ordered appetizers and soft-shell crabs for Stan, lobster for Jake. I steeled myself for a long stinky lunch.

Often our client lunches don't involve any business talk at all. Although I'm sure HFB still takes a hefty tax write-off on them, their purpose is simply to oil the gears of commerce. This lunch appeared to be of that ilk, as the appetizers were consumed and Steve regaled our clients with hilarious stories of the zany citizens of San Francisco, such as the man who kept sixty-one dogs in his mansion in an upscale neighborhood.

"People complained about the stench for eight years before the city did anything about it. Can you believe that?" Steve popped another shrimp into his mouth and smiled brightly.

"Speaking of stench," Stan replied, with a conspiratorial wink at Jake, "I hear you all have Tangento as clients. You don't have any problem with that little brouhaha in Asia, huh?"

Chapter 6

Steve and I looked at each other, desperately trying to communicate via account executive telepathy. Which one of us knew what he was talking about, so we could act like we knew what we were doing? It seemed neither of us had heard anything, but we couldn't let on to that.

"Oh, yes," I answered. "Last we checked it seemed like a flash in the pan. What have you been hearing?"

"I figured you guys would know more than me," Stan answered, looking smug. "This was a piece I saw in the *Economist*."

Steve and I exchanged surprised looks. Stan was reading the *Economist*?

"There was an item a few weeks back," Stan continued. "Slave labor, wasn't it, Jake? Can't really remember, but I thought you'd all be running like chickens with your heads cut off to make sure it didn't come out here."

The waiter brought our entrées then and discussion ceased as shells were cracked and flesh sucked. I rearranged the lettuce and croutons on my plate while filing a mental note to myself to find out what Stan had been talking about. Public relations snafus, even in far away countries, were the nightmares that kept advertising agencies up at night.

On the way out I stopped at the restroom and splashed my face with water. I was still feeling very nauseated, and the smell of fish at lunch hadn't helped.

After lunch I dug around in my office for some hand-drawn art that Creative had done for the Plump n' Tasty Chicken account. I couldn't find the pieces anywhere, and I thought it was my organizational system again, until I remembered I'd handed them to Lucy last week. I went over to her office to retrieve them.

I stood in the doorway for a minute, feeling weird. Everything was just as she'd left it. There was even a sweater hanging over the back of her chair, as if she'd just gotten up to go to the bathroom.

"Lucy, where are you?" I said under my breath.

I opened her file drawer and looked under the Ps. Lucy's workspace was arranged like the Library of Congress, but there was no file for Plump n' Tasty Chicken. I finally found it in the Cs, but the illustrations I was looking for were not in the file.

I picked up Lucy's phone and dialed Web's

extension. He answered on the first ring. "This is Web."

"Hi, Web, it's Angie."

"Angie! What can I do for you?" He made it sound like he had nothing else to do but talk to me, an admirable quality in a coworker.

"Do you remember those pieces you did for the Plump n' Tasty Chicken account?"

"Amish chickens driving horse-drawn wagons? How could I forget? It was actually Les who did those."

"Do you know where they are right now?"

"Lucy had them, last I saw. We went over them on Friday."

"She must have taken them home with her over the weekend. Damn, I really need them. Can I access them on the server?"

"The concept was to have a really old-fashioned, Norman Rockwell feel, so they were hand-drawn. I'm sure there are copies, but I don't know where they are offhand, and Les went home sick." Web sounded very apologetic. "But . . ."

"What?" I asked.

"I live near Lucy and a couple of months ago I took care of her plants when she went out of town on a business trip. She keeps a spare key in the front yard under a little plaster gnome. I guess I could go over there after work."

"I'll do it."

"Really?"

"You know, Web, no one has looked inside her house. Don't you think someone should?"

"Yeah, I guess you're right."

"And I really need those drawings."

Lucy lived in the Richmond District, almost at Ocean Beach. She was as far away as possible from HFB while still being in the city, so I took the bus home to pick up my car. As I drove toward the ocean the temperature gauge dropped block by block. It had been 78 degrees downtown and it was 62 degrees here, with enough mist in the air to require windshield wipers. Although there was still an hour left of daylight on this October day, the fog had rolled in and created artificial twilight. Puffs of fog kept wafting past, as if a giant were smoking a cigar. I opened the window and sucked in deep breaths of the cold, wet air. For the first time all day my head felt clear and my stomach was calm.

The Ocean House, where Eric wanted me to meet him, was only a few blocks away from here. I still hadn't consciously decided whether I was going to meet him or not, but he hadn't been far from my thoughts at any time during the day. I had pondered what Steve said about the date rape drug, Rohypnol. It was very easy to say Eric wasn't the type, but I didn't really know *what* type he was, did I? I couldn't discount the idea, considering the symptoms I'd had, but *why* would he have drugged me? So he could rape me? That didn't make a lot of sense, since I went with him willingly and probably would have had sex with him if I hadn't lost consciousness, given the reckless abandon I was feeling while I was with him.

There were, of course, other implications to the malaise I was experiencing, but those implications were ridiculous, impossible. The only thing I could concede was that perhaps there was a drug I'd never heard of that mimicked the effects of . . . that made one lose one's appetite and want to avoid the sun. But maybe I was getting the flu, and that was why I was feeling so terrible. October was the traditional start of flu season.

All my convoluted reasoning, all my contorted logic, was leading me nowhere. I had to admit that I was not capable of thinking clearly about the man, since I wanted so desperately to see him again. Luckily I had reached Lucy's house, so I could turn my mind to other things for a while. She lived on Seal Rock Drive, which is as far west as you can go in San Francisco without falling into the ocean. The fog here smelled of salt and seaweed, and I could hear the barking of the seals on the distant promontory that gave the street its name.

The house was a 1950s beige stucco box with a front window flanked by black shutters. All the houses on the block matched, but Lucy had done some nice things to hers. The shutters and an ornamental iron balcony under the window gave the house a pre-Katrina New Orleans flair. Clipped hedges bordered a front lawn about eight feet square, but the vegetation was struggling in the marine environment. The fog was so ubiquitous here that most of the houses were coated with a film of green mold, like they'd been sitting in a fish tank.

The front door was reached through a tunnel entry so overgrown with ferns and spider plants that I thought if Lucy ever came in that way she'd have to use a machete. I was pushing the plants around, looking for the gnome, when someone tapped me on the shoulder. I literally jumped with surprise and let out a little shriek.

"Excuse me, are you a friend of Lucy's?"

I turned around to find the gnome's twin sister, an old woman about four-and-a-half feet tall, dressed in a bright green sweat suit. She had circles of pink blush on her wrinkled cheeks and a halo of dyed red hair. She was holding a newspaper, still in its plastic bag.

"I'm Ida, Lucy's next-door neighbor. I've been picking up her newspapers for her. You have to remember to cancel your newspaper when you go on vacation, or it's a dead giveaway to thieves. I've told her that before."

"Okay, thanks, Ida, I'll take it for her." I took the newspaper.

"The rest of them are by the front door. When is Lucy coming back, by the way?"

This elderly lady didn't need to be worried

needlessly. "I think within the next few days, Ida. I'll tell her you were asking about her."

"Okay," she said over her shoulder as she left, "don't forget the newspapers. They're a dead give-away to thieves."

Another minute of searching revealed the gnome, replete with stocking cap and insouciant expression.

As I put the key in the lock I had a revelation. I wasn't coming over just to get the Plump n' Tasty Chicken graphics. I was hoping to solve the mystery of Lucy's disappearance. I wanted to find a clue, something that would happily explain a sudden exit, like a winning lottery ticket, a note from a boyfriend none of us knew about, or an offer of a new job in New Zealand. Then I could be free from the guilt I felt at being fast-tracked at work.

I opened the door and put the key on an old roll-top desk next to the front door. To my right was the living room, and to the left were two doors I assumed to be bedrooms. The bathroom was in front of me. I turned right.

The living room was very modern—taupe walls, Eames chairs, a boxy sofa, two pieces of abstract art in black and white, and a flat screen TV mounted over the fireplace. Lucy obviously made more money than I, a lot more, if she owned this house rather than rented. Everything was in strict, Lucy-like order, except that the Sunday paper was spread out on the coffee table, with two used coffee cups on top of it. I checked the newspapers in my hand. Four of them, Monday through Thursday. Presumably Lucy had left sometime on Sunday. I put the newspapers on the table and shivered. It was cold in the house, even colder than outside.

There was a sour smell in the kitchen. A few Cheerios sat in a bowl of milk that had turned rancid. I opened a few of the cupboards, feeling strange, but doing it anyway. They contained shiny black dishes, all square, including the bowls. Then I noticed Lucy's BlackBerry sitting on the counter, and my stomach lurched. Lucy never went anywhere without her CrackBerry. I picked it up and, with only a tiny measure of guilt, listened to her messages. She had three saved messages and fourteen new ones.

The date on the first saved message was October 4, 10:12 A.M. "Hi Lucy, this is Henley at the salon, reminding you that you have an eleven o'clock appointment on October 6th with Sasha, for a full leg wax."

The next message was from a voice I recognized, breathy and low-pitched. "Hi Lucy, this is Moravia. I know you were planning to come to the club tomorrow, but I think it might be better if you didn't. Sully and I would like to talk to you first. Please call me as soon as you get this." That message came in on Thursday at 7:45 P.M., almost exactly a week ago.

The next message had come in on Saturday, October 6, at 9:15 A.M.

"Lucy, it's Les. Are you there? Pick up the phone, please! We need to talk, I need to talk to you, please call me. I love you."

Whoa! There was a revelation. Les and Lucy, in love? I hadn't seen a hint of it at work. I listened to the message again, noting the desperation in Les's voice. A hint of jealousy arose out of some unexamined region of my brain. I imagined Les's sinewy back, covered in tattoos, his face contorted in wild abandon, while Lucy checked her Black-Berry behind his head.

The new messages were from various people at HFB wondering where Lucy was, starting with Dick at 10 o'clock on Monday morning. Among the others who called were Kimberley, Web, Theresa, and Mary from Human Resources.

I heard a noise at the front door and went into the living room, still holding the BlackBerry. Someone was putting a key in the lock. Thinking it was Lucy, I raced to open the door. There stood Les, as if my imagining had somehow magically summoned him. He quickly stuck the key in his pocket.

"What are you doing here?" I asked him, in what I'm sure was not a polite voice. "I thought you were sick."

"I heard you were coming, and it didn't seem like you should be here by yourself, so I thought I should come and make sure you were all right."

It was Les who wasn't acting all right. He was

nervous, bouncing on the balls of his feet. He looked pale and his eyes were bloodshot.

"So Web told you I was coming down here. Can you help me find them, then?"

"Find what?" Les seemed to be having trouble concentrating.

"The Plump n' Tasty graphics, remember?"

"I don't know where those are."

"I'll go look myself. Her office is probably back here." If Les wanted to pretend he'd never been here before who was I to stop him?

I went to the rear of the house while Les went toward the kitchen. The first door revealed Lucy's office, dominated by an L-shaped oak desk. The top of the desk had nothing on it but a mouse pad and an electrical cord, presumably for Lucy's laptop. The file drawer in the desk appeared to contain only personal business. A row of fluorescent file folders were neatly labeled with titles such as "Insurance: Auto," "Insurance: Health," and "Tax Related."

I started to go back to the kitchen to tell Les I couldn't find the drawings, when I heard sounds in the adjacent room. What was Les doing in her bedroom? I crossed the hall and opened the bedroom door. The small room was almost entirely filled by an oak four-poster bed. Lucy was lying on top of the pale blue bedspread, dressed in a full-length white silk nightgown. Her pale body gleamed like a firefly on a summer night.

Chapter 7

I didn't have to touch her to know she was dead. Her skin was bluish-gray and appeared to have thickened and solidified over her bones, like a thin layer of candle wax had been dripped over her. Her facial angles, pleasantly round in life, had sharpened, and her head looked like a skull with skin on it. But her body was relaxed, her hands lying loosely at her sides. A slight smile rested on Lucy's lips, as if she were having a pleasant dream. A window was open and it was quite cold in the room, but there was still an odor of putrefaction. I put my hand up to my face and stifled the urge to gag and scream at the same time.

Les was on his knees at the side of the bed, his head in his hands, making a noise that was half groaning, half crying. I put my hand on his shoulder. Like I'd given him an electric shock, Les jumped to his feet. He gave me one quick look and then ran over to Lucy's closet. He pulled the door open and started rummaging around in Lucy's clothes.

"Les, what are you doing?" I stammered.

He responded by pulling out several shirts and making a bundle of them. One was a distinctive red and orange tie-dye T-shirt I'd seen Les wearing at work.

"What are you going to do with those? You're not supposed to take anything out of here."

Les didn't seem to hear me. He went over to the wastebasket by the bed and looked in. He lifted the bedskirt and checked under the bed. He took a Kleenex and used it to open Lucy's bedside table. He pulled out a handful of condoms and put them in his back pocket. Then he used the Kleenex to rub the surface of the nightstand.

"Les, are you crazy? This is a crime scene. We should be calling 911!"

Les grabbed me by the arm and dragged me into the living room. He sat me rather roughly on the couch. When I looked at his face he had tears in his eyes. Then I realized I was in tears myself.

"Angie, you've got to believe me, I know how this looks. But I didn't kill Lucy, I didn't even know she was dead. I just came over to get some of my stuff."

"But, I didn't even know you were friends with Lucy!" I felt like I was going to faint. I lowered my head and Les's voice was filtered through my knees.

"We were dating, sort of. Lucy didn't want anyone at work to know about it."

I lifted my head. "All right, but that doesn't explain why you're trying to take evidence away."

"I was over here on Friday night. We had a fight and she threw me out."

"What were you fighting about?"

"She was into this vampire stuff. Blood drinking and a bunch of other freaky shit. She tried to get me into it but I said no. I told her it was dangerous, but she just laughed."

Les rubbed his nose with the back of his hand. "That night, she told me she'd met someone else and she wanted to break up. She said he was a 'real vampire,' not like the posers she'd been with before. Naturally I was upset. I might have said some things I shouldn't have. When she didn't come back to work I thought it was because of me. She said she never wanted to see me again." He looked at me imploringly.

"Did you think that maybe something like this could have happened?" I waved my hand toward the bedroom.

"Yes, of course!" Les was shouting. "But what could I do? If she was into supernatural shit, what was I going to do to stop it?"

I was taking deep breaths to stay calm. I looked up at Les. He looked genuinely distraught, but everything he was telling me could have been a lie to cover for his own crime.

I made my voice very calm. "Les, we need to call the police."

Les jumped toward me and grabbed my hand. I

forced myself not to snatch it away. I didn't want to do anything to upset him further.

"Angie, you've got to let me get out of here. I swear I didn't have anything to do with this. But if the police find out I was here I'm not going to be able to explain things. I know how it works. They'll find a way to pin it on me, even though I didn't do it."

"It's not going to happen like that."

"No one but you knows we were dating, so if I just take my stuff and go home they won't waste their time talking to me. Please, Angie, let me go."

"Les, I have to call the police."

Les let go of my hand and clenched his fists. For a moment I thought he was going to hit me.

"Please, just let me put this stuff in the car and then we'll call." Les didn't wait for my answer but instead grabbed the bundle of clothes he'd taken out of Lucy's room and ran for the front door. Moments later I heard the sound of an engine. When I looked out the front window I saw a car speeding away.

I went outside and called 911. Ghosts made of mist and fog swirled around me while I waited for the cops to come.

Within minutes the paramedics and the police arrived. The paramedics left after certifying what I already knew about Lucy's condition. The police dispersed a small crowd of neighbors who had gathered, and then asked me to sit in a squad car until the homicide inspectors arrived. I watched them wrap yellow tape around the front entrance. Eventually two men approached. They were the first I'd seen wearing civilian clothes, so I assumed they were the homicide guys. I stepped out of the car to greet them.

They were the classic odd couple. One was a handsome Hispanic man in his mid-thirties dressed in a nicely tailored suit, probably not Armani, but a mighty good knock-off. His immoveable, black Ken doll hair reminded me of Steve's. The white man standing beside him had been handsome in his youth, but had let time slip by him with a vengeance. He appeared to be in his mid-sixties, with thinning red hair tinged gray, sunken blue eyes, and the jowls of a bulldog. The tarnished gold buttons of a ratty blue sport coat strained over his formidable belly.

Bulldog shook my hand with what felt like a baseball mitt. "I'm Inspector Sansome of the San Francisco Police Department and this is Inspector Trujillo. We'd like to ask you some questions."

At that moment one of the uniformed officers came up to the Inspectors. Trujillo said a few words to him and left me with Sansome, who said, "Perhaps you'd be more comfortable in the squad car?" I nodded.

Inspector Sansome unbuttoned his coat before sliding into the back seat. Suddenly I was wondering if I should have called a lawyer. Being questioned in the back seat of a cop car had triggered some latent guilt complex. But Sansome smiled at me encouragingly, then gazed out the window.

"Mighty foggy out here. I don't know how people stand it. Me, I prefer the hottest weather I can get. Live in the Mission District myself, and when I retire I plan to go to the desert, Arizona. I know this must be very upsetting for you, Ma'am, but we need to get some basic information. Your full name, please."

"Angela Margaret McCaffrey."

Sansome smiled. "A good Irish name. Did you grow up in San Francisco?"

"Yes. I was named after Angel Island."

People are usually amused when I tell them that I am named for Angel Island, a small, green, undeveloped rock in the Bay between San Francisco and Marin. Accessible only by ferry, it was first an immigration and quarantine station for Asian immigrants. After World War II the Parks Department took it over and people began coming for picnics and hikes. My parents grew up in the Irish working-class neighborhood of Noe Valley, where big families were packed into railroad car Victorian houses with two bedrooms and one bathroom. My mother was one of five children and my father one of seven, so when they were courting as teenagers there weren't many places for them to go to be alone. They would take the ferry to Angel Island and be gone for hours, "walking."

My mother found out she was pregnant a week

before her graduation from Mission High School. I
don't know if theirs could be called a shotgun wedding, but being the good Catholics that they were,
there probably weren't a lot of other viable options.
Mom and Dad graduated from high school and
went straight into full adulthood, with my sister
Thea coming eleven months after me (Irish twins,
as siblings like us were called in the neighborhood).
So I was named after the place that gave my parents
what were probably the only moments of carefree
happiness in their lives. Sansome, with his faded
blue eyes and a ring of copper hair around his
otherwise bald head, looked like he would probably
understand this story, maybe even have lived a similar one.

"Really, that's nice, a local girl. I'm from North
Beach myself," he said, naming an Italian neighborhood just north of downtown. "Boy, was I a fish
out of water in school." He pointed to his hair,
which was probably carrot orange in his youth. I
could imagine him standing out in a classroom
full of dark heads.

"Well, I guess we better get to these questions."
He seemed regretful, and I realized that making
small talk was probably part of the interview process,
intended to make me feel comfortable with him
before getting to the real questions. It had worked,
though. I felt an unexpected camaraderie with
the guy.

He took out his notebook and a ballpoint pen,
unconsciously licking the point of the pen before

poising it over the paper. He reached up and flicked on the car's interior light.

"How did you know the deceased, Ms. Weston?"

"We worked together at Hall, Fitch and Berg. It's an ad agency."

"Did you work directly with Ms. Weston?"

"She was my boss. I'm an assistant account executive, AAE, as we say. She's an account executive." After I said it I noticed I had slipped back into the present tense.

Sansome nodded and wrote in his notebook. "When was the last time you saw Ms. Weston alive?"

"I saw her on Friday, at work. But her Sunday paper was open on her coffee table. And her neighbor, Ida, had collected the other newspapers. Doesn't that mean she died on Sunday?"

"Would you like a job on the police force, Ms. McCaffrey?" Sansome smiled indulgently. "That's good detective work, but I'd say Ms. Weston has only been where she is for a day or so. I'm not the coroner, of course, but I've been doing this job for twenty-two years."

"What do you mean, how do you know that?"

Suddenly Sansome was looking at the thumbnail of his left hand, not at me.

"How long were you in the apartment before you found Ms. Weston?"

"Maybe twenty minutes."

He looked at me without speaking for what seemed like a long time. He was succeeding in making me nervous, if that was his intent.

"Were you two friends, Ms. McCaffrey?"

"No, not really. Work friends, I guess you could say." I paused and thought about it. "Lucy didn't seem to have any friends. No family, either, except for a sister in St. Louis. Human Resources was having trouble finding anyone when she didn't show up on Monday."

Sansome wrote down my answer. "Why did you come here tonight?"

"To get some papers that she brought from the office. Some illustrations." I neglected to mention that I had also come to assuage my guilt.

"Uh huh," said Sansome. "Did anyone else know you were coming?"

"Yes, I told Web Northrup, from the Creative department. He told me where the key was, he'd watered her plants for her before."

It was time to tell Sansome about Les. I felt bad for him, but I wasn't about to lie to the police.

"While I was in the house, someone else came. Les Banks, a graphic artist from HFB. Lucy was dating him, I guess. It was news to me, he just told me now. He showed up a few minutes after I got here. He said he came over to make sure I was all right."

"To make sure *you* were all right?"

"Yes. He seemed shocked when we found the, um, body. But he took some things, his shirts and other stuff, so you wouldn't know he'd been dating her. He said you wouldn't understand."

Sansome didn't give me any indication of what

he thought of this news. He just nodded calmly and asked, "Did he say anything else? Had he and Ms. Weston had a fight?"

"Yes, he said they did have a fight, on Friday night. She said she never wanted to see him again, that she had a new boyfriend. He said he thought that was why she didn't come to work, because she was trying to avoid him."

Sansome wrote, the pen disappearing in his big hand.

"Ms. McCaffrey, as far as you know, was Ms. Weston having any conflicts with anyone else at work?"

I paused again. "I did hear some gossip today that she might have been having a conflict with another AAE, Kimberley Bennett. But it was just gossip."

"Who told it to you?"

"Lakshmi Roy."

"Could you spell that for me?"

When we were done Sansome handed me a business card, white with a little gold embossed shield on it.

"Well, thank you very much, Ms. McCaffrey. I imagine we'll have some more questions for you tomorrow or the next day. You seem to have landed right in the middle of things. And by the way, it might be better if you didn't mention anything to your work colleagues about Lucy dating Les. If it's a secret it might be useful for us to find out who knew and who didn't."

He let himself out of the car, came around to my side and opened the door.

I just couldn't leave without asking one question. "Uh, Inspector Sansome, do you have any idea what happened to Lucy? How she—" I couldn't bring myself to say the word died.

Sansome's face was a mask of professional neutrality. "We won't know that until the autopsy reports are in, and that might take a while."

In the car driving home I thought about the fact that I had said nothing to the police about the "real vampire" Lucy had told Les about. I told myself that I had just forgotten, that I would call Inspector Sansome when I got home. It wasn't until later that I realized that I was already lying to protect Eric.

It was past dinnertime when I got back from Lucy's house. I wasn't hungry but I felt dirty, tired, and miserable. I took a shower and put on my pajamas, consciously telling myself that I was *not* going to meet Eric that night. I climbed into bed and fell asleep, but at exactly 9:30 my eyes sprang open and wouldn't shut again. I lay still and listened to the electric whir of my alarm clock in the silent room. Something huge and horrible had just happened to me. I wanted to crawl into someone's lap, be sheltered by a protective arm and told that everything was all right and I was safe. It was not the first time that I'd lain in bed and felt the sheer depth of my loneliness, but it was the first time that the image of somebody appeared in the darkness, somebody whose arms could protect me from anything.

I got up and went to my closet. If there had been an earthquake that night I would have crawled out of the rubble of the apartment building and dragged myself to the Ocean House on two broken legs, so there was no use trying to convince myself otherwise. I just needed to figure out what to wear. Eric hadn't said what we were going to do or where we were going. By coincidence, the place where I was meeting Eric was almost back at Lucy's house, so I knew that the weather was cold and foggy. I decided going casual would serve two functions: I'd stay warm, plus I might look more nonchalant about our rendezvous than I felt. Enveloped in a soft down parka and my favorite jeans and leather boots I headed west again.

The Ocean House is visible for miles as you wind your way up the Great Highway from the south. For the last mile it's hard to remember you're in the city, with the ocean on your left and the dense greenery of Golden Gate Park on your right. The road runs flat along Ocean Beach then up the cliffs to turn right and disappear into the Richmond District. Right at the top of the hill, clinging improbably to the steep terrain like a baby monkey to its mother, is the restaurant, known more for its beautiful views than for its food. I'd lived in San Francisco all my life and could count on one hand the number of times I'd been there, but I'd always admired the restaurant's strange tenacity. Three different buildings, ornate Victorian affairs with multiple towers and verandas, had burned down between 1865 and 1907. The present Ocean House didn't have anywhere near the same architectural distinction, but it did have the same ocean views as its predecessor. Still, it was an odd place to meet a date. It was probably the last place a real San Franciscan would go to eat, but Eric was a tourist, wasn't he?

And *were* we going to eat? Eric had asked me to meet him, not in the restaurant, but behind it. I circled past the front door and down a flight of concrete stairs to come out on a large outdoor terrace, perched directly over the water facing the seal island. It's outfitted with a few of those binoculars on a platform where you put in a quarter, blink, and it's over. There was no view in the dark, except for the twinkling lights of a passing freighter, so Eric was the only person on the terrace. But even if it had been crowded with people I would have recognized him. His back was to me as he gazed out toward the sleeping seals but his hair was unmistakable. He had taken it out of its fastener and it flowed like liquid copper over the back of his black leather jacket.

Chapter 8

Even though it seemed like I was still too far away for him to hear me, Eric turned and watched my approach. I sucked in my stomach and tried to walk gracefully. I tried on several different expressions and then dropped each one. Every time I had walked into an audition room when I was an actor I felt this same mix of thrill, anticipation, and sheer terror—the feeling that this could be the meeting that changes your life.

I tried a trick that I had used going into auditions to calm my nerves. You are the Queen, I whispered. This man is your subject and you rule over him. He is here at your behest.

The psyching out worked, because by the time I reached Eric I'd pulled myself up to my full five-feet six-and-a-half inches, straightened my shoulders, lengthened my neck, and calmed my fluttering heart. I held my hand out to him, palm down, and he took it and bowed as if we'd rehearsed this little play. But my equilibrium faltered when he pressed his lips to my hand and little bolts of electricity raced up my arm.

He wore a gold signet ring on his pinkie finger. The ring looked old, holding a red stone so worn down it had the opacity of beach glass. His nails were perfectly manicured ovals, perhaps slightly too long for the average man, but they looked like they could give a mean back scratch.

Still holding my hand, he moved in closer and looked at my face as if he were searching for something. His eyes, that light, light blue, were glowing.

"Angela, tell me what happened."

I stepped back, confused. "What do you mean?"

"I see it in your eyes. A tragedy has occurred."

I blinked back sudden tears. "I went to my boss's house today. She was there, but she was . . ." I swallowed hard, ". . . dead."

"Ah, Lucy Weston. I am so sorry."

"Wait a minute. How do you know her?"

"You mentioned her to me last night. I had also met her through Suleiman and Moravia. She occasionally came to the club. This is very sad." Eric seemed distracted. He gazed out toward the ocean. A seal barked in the darkness and another one answered. "Have the police arrested anyone?"

"They might be looking for a guy from our office, Les. He was dating her, but no one in the office knew it."

Eric was holding my hand against his chest. I could feel his heart beating, so strong it was like a fist knocking on a door. "Why do you think the police might want him?"

"He followed me to her house and he was acting really strange. He was trying to hide all the evidence that they had known each other. He also told me they had been fighting, that she had broken up with him. She told him she had met someone new."

"And had she?"

I shrugged. "How would I know? I didn't know about Les, and it was right under my nose."

"These things are always difficult, no matter how many times you experience them."

I looked up at him. "What do you mean? I've never experienced this before. Well, my grandmother. But that was different."

"Yes, of course. But at least they have caught this Les, the one they suspect?"

"No, I don't think so. He ran away from Lucy's house when I told him I wouldn't lie. Oh God, Eric, what if I made a mistake? What if he didn't do it and I've put the police on his trail?" My body began to shake with unexpressed sobs.

Eric pulled me close and I hid my face in the shelter of his arms. There was a brisk breeze blowing off the ocean, but still his sweet fragrance overwhelmed me. I smelled sandalwood, lilies, ocean air, sugar cookies, cumin, and fresh snow. As soon as my mind identified a scent it slipped away, replaced by something richer and more evocative.

I heard his voice in my ear. "You did the right

thing for your friend. Those who have committed the crime will pay the price."

"I guess so," I answered, thinking what an old-fashioned thing that was to say, but how much I liked the sentiment.

Eric stepped back and took my face in his hands. "Angela, I think you need some distraction." He smiled. "Do you like to ride motorcycles?"

At the entrance to the restaurant a disheveled but stylish older couple stood in front of the menu, looking confused. When the man saw Eric he immediately began speaking to him in French. The woman chimed in, Eric answered, and they engaged in a brief conversation punctuated with lots of gesticulation. When Eric shook the woman's hand she gazed at him like a teenager meeting her favorite movie star.

When we were a short distance away I asked, "How did they know you speak French?"

His face took on an expression (lips pursed, eyebrows knitted) that even I recognized as uniquely Gallic.

"Never mind."

The motorcycle Eric had mentioned was parked down the hill. The silver and black chassis gleamed like it was brand new. Suddenly Eric's black leather jacket and heavy boots made sense, just like his blue velvet suit at the House of Usher. He liked costumes. Tonight he was playing the part of a Hell's Angel.

"Yes, it's new," he said. "I saw a guy riding one

and I decided I just had to try it. And believe me, it's as fun as it looks. Would you like to take a ride with me?"

Suddenly I saw my mother's disembodied face floating above me, saying, "Are you crazy? I don't see any helmets, the man has practically admitted he doesn't know how to ride, it's the middle of the night, and you're going to get on a motorcycle with him?"

I brushed the air in front of my face like there was a mosquito bothering me. "Sure, let's do it."

Eric climbed on and held the bike while I slid onto the seat behind him. I put my arms around his waist and pressed my cheek against his leather-covered shoulder. My feet were barely on the footrests before the bike surged underneath us. I had a moment of raw fear as we plunged down the dark hill, like diving into hell with my arms around the Devil. I shut my eyes and took a deep breath. When I didn't die immediately I opened them and looked west. The moon was almost full and the ocean was a deep black bucket full of silver crescents. The beach gleamed silver gray.

What an intimate thing it is to ride on a motor-cycle with a man. My chest was pressed against his broad back, my legs encircling his hips, my arms linked around his slim waist. The silky strands of his hair blew around my face as if it were my own. I wanted to move my hands to feel his chest, but I didn't dare, mainly because we were driving so fast I was afraid to let go for an instant.

The road seemed to move under us, the air split open and we drove through the seam. I couldn't look forward without the skin of my face pulling back and my eyes feeling dried out and pushed into their sockets. We passed a couple of cars in the right lane like they weren't moving at all. One of them honked and the horn blared after us like thunder trying to catch up to its lightning bolt. I looked over Eric's shoulder, trying to catch a glimpse of the speedometer and confirm my suspicion that we were going five miles over the speed of light. That's when I saw it.

The deer was standing in the middle of the road, transfixed by the sound and lights bearing down. We were so close I could see it was a doe, with soft white fur inside the cups of her ears and shiny black eyes. My feet pressed downwards, looking for brakes I didn't have. My arms squeezed Eric's waist as if I could will myself to stay on the motorcycle after the collision. I didn't scream, just waited for the impact.

Then I heard Eric's voice, not in my ear, but inside my head, like it was my own voice.

Don't worry, I won't let anything happen to you.

Just as the last word echoed in my brain we veered around the deer. The pull of gravity toward the ocean was irresistible. The turn was so deep that my leg actually touched the road. I imagined us spinning like a dreidel toward the sea, until the deep sand arrested our movement. But at the moment when we were almost parallel to the road,

Eric pulled the bike back up. I felt like I had just witnessed a miracle.

He steered us to the side of the road and stopped. The deer unfroze and disappeared into the brush. I had never felt so alive. I was exhilarated, thrilled to my very core. This must be why people skydive, I thought. Cheating death makes you appreciate life.

Eric turned partly around and before it became a conscious thought I was kissing him on the lips. He seemed startled, but then he kissed me back. When I opened my eyes, he was smiling.

"You *are* brave, Angela. Just as I'd hoped."

"Let's keep going," I said. "Do you feel like driving to Half Moon Bay?"

If you've ever driven on Highway One, California's coastal highway, you know that it is the brainchild of a madman. The freeway is a narrow lip carved out of sheer cliffs rising hundreds of feet above the Pacific Ocean. Chunks of the road drop into the ocean with astonishing regularity during the rainy season. Highway One had always made me nail-bitingly nervous, but tonight I felt invincible, and all I could see was its beauty.

Eric stopped the motorcycle on a small gravel overlook above Half Moon Bay. Beyond the crescent-shaped beach the almost full moon cast a silver trail across the ocean that looked sturdy enough to walk on. From the horizon it would be only a little hop up to the moon.

Eric took my hands in his. "Your hands are freezing. You should have told me."

"Oh. I didn't even notice." His hands weren't doing anything to warm mine up. After twenty minutes on the handlebars of the motorcycle they were like blocks of ice.

"Is there a place around here we could go to warm up?" he asked. "I'm afraid I'm not familiar with this area."

I remembered a place my father used to take us after church on Sundays. We'd change out of our scratchy Sunday clothes in the car, go tide pooling in the shallow reefs at Moss Beach, then have hamburgers and french fries at Half Moon Brewery before heading home. Those days were some of the best of my childhood.

I directed Eric to drive down the highway another couple of miles, then squeezed his arm to indicate he should turn into the sandy parking lot. There were only two cars parked in front of the wood-and-glass building overlooking the small cove of Moss Beach. A bartender was washing glasses behind the old-fashioned wooden bar in the main room.

"Are you still open?" I asked.

"Sure, unless it's already 2 A.M." The bartender warily sized up Eric's black leather outfit.

"You know, I used to come here when I was a kid, and we would sit out on a porch with swings. There were blankets that everyone would wrap up in."

The bartender appeared to relax a little. "Yeah, we still have that downstairs. It's closed now, but seeing as how you're our only guests, feel free to take your drinks on down there."

Eric picked up the menu. On the back cover was the story of the resident ghost, a woman who had died in a car accident while on a rendezvous with her lover, a piano player at the bar. Ever since then her ghostly figure had been glimpsed from time to time, usually by the restaurant's staff after hours. I had loved the story as a child.

Eric read it and then looked at me. "Do you believe in ghosts, Angela?"

"Not even the Holy Ghost, much to my parents' chagrin," I answered. "If I can't see it with my own eyes, don't bother trying to get me to believe in it."

Eric just nodded and put down the menu.

I ordered an Irish coffee and Eric a type of Scotch I'd never heard of. We took a winding staircase down to a terrace overlooking the beach. It was just like I remembered it, Adirondack chairs covered with thick woolen blankets. There was one wooden swing, which I remembered my sister and brother and me fighting over endlessly. I sat in it and pulled a blanket up to my shoulders, then started the swing rocking gently.

"I haven't been here since I was ten years old. And I've never been here at night," I said. "It's magical."

"Yes," Eric agreed. "Magical."

I couldn't believe he was staring at me as he said this. With my windblown hair and chapped face, wrapped in the plaid blanket, I felt I must look like some giant newborn baby.

"You look beautiful," Eric answered my unspoken thought and set my heart racing.

"Can you read my mind?" I asked, then realized I was only half joking.

"Only when you want me to."

"Then I guess you know what I'm hoping for next."

Eric came over and opened the blanket, then wrapped it around both of us. I took a deep breath of the scents of ocean, leather, and Eric that enveloped me. His lips touched mine gently, then more hungrily. My vision began to get blurry around the edges, as if the fog had suddenly come up off the ocean and surrounded us. I closed my eyes, the better to experience the swirl of sensation. I had the strangest feeling that every part of me improved under Eric's touch. As his hand slid down my arm my skin seemed to become softer, more yielding. The hair that he stroked seemed to fall more smoothly, brushed across my cheek like silk. I was starting to feel beautiful.

Eric's lips alighted on my neck like butterfly wings. I slipped my hands under his jacket and felt the hard muscles of his chest under crisp cotton. I undid one button and put my hand over his heart, caressing his supple skin. His arms tightened, he pulled me against his body and I melted. The normal separations that people feel, even during intimate moments, no longer existed. We were two molten metals, flowing together to create something entirely new. All I wanted was for it never to end. So when he clamped onto my neck I moved into it, like a moth flying into a flame. My blood pulsed in waves that matched the ocean pounding the beach below us.

Did I think about dying? Honestly, the thought never occurred to me, and I couldn't tell you even now whether that was because I trusted Eric, or because I didn't care about paltry things like life and death anymore. When he pulled away from me I clutched at him, trying to draw him back, but his hands on my shoulders were like iron.

"What's wrong?" I whispered. I was absurdly frightened that I'd disappointed him in some way.

"No, you didn't. But it's enough." He sat up straight and brushed the hair back from his shoulders. With two slender fingers he fastened the one button I'd undone on his shirt.

Tears pricked at my eyes and I turned from him to briskly rub them away. I wasn't going to let him see me acting like a little girl. But then he gently turned me back and kissed me on the forehead. I heard his words in my head while his lips were pressed against my skin.

Be careful what you wish for, Angela, because it might come true.

Before I could ask Eric what he meant the

bartender appeared at the door to announce that it was closing time.

We said our good-byes and headed out into the parking lot. By the bright light of the moon we could see a guy sitting on Eric's motorcycle, with another man standing next to him with something in his hand, monkeying around near the handle-bars. The next moment we heard the loud roar of the engine starting.

"I'd better go stop him," Eric said.

Chapter 9

I grabbed his arm. "Are you crazy? There's two of them. We'll go back in and call the police."

Eric ignored me and ran toward the men. I watched in disbelief as he grabbed the man on the bike and pulled him to the ground. The other man, who was about seven feet tall and built like a tree trunk, grabbed Eric from behind. The man on the ground picked himself up and hit Eric in the face with a sickening crunch I heard all the way across the parking lot. I felt as if I'd been dropped into a bad kung fu movie. I started running toward them, then stopped short. Eric was moving so quickly that all I could see was a blur of arms and legs. Tree Trunk toppled to the ground with a thud. The other man backed away from Eric with his hands up, then turned and ran up the road, leaving his friend to meet his fate.

I walked over on unsteady legs. Tree Trunk had

rolled himself into a fetal position and was groaning quietly.

"He'll be all right," Eric said. "I hardly touched him." He pulled a handkerchief out of his jacket pocket, but before he covered it up I saw that his nose looked like a squashed cupcake and blood was flowing freely out of his nostrils. Even his cheekbone looked askew.

"Eric, they broke your nose!" I gasped.

Eric turned to the motorcycle, which was lying on its side in the dirt. With one hand still on his face he picked it up and set it on its kickstand.

"Eric, we've got to get to a hospital. Your nose . . ." I fluttered around him, pulling at the handkerchief. Eric grabbed my shoulder to steady me.

"Angela, I'm fine, really. Nothing's broken. Just a little bloody nose, that's it. All part of the game."

He removed the cloth and smiled at me. Sure enough, his nose and cheek looked completely normal, except for a little blood under one nostril.

I blinked hard and looked at him again, but nothing had changed. "Eric, your nose was broken. I know it was."

"My nose is fine, you can see that. Only believe what your eyes see, isn't that what you said, Angela?"

Eric dropped me off at the Ocean House so I could pick up my car, and then followed me home to make sure I got there safely. I hoped we would get to say good-bye again, but after he watched me back into a spot in front of the building he waved and took off. I got out of the car and sniffed the breeze, certain that I could detect molecules of that maddeningly delicious odor. He had said nothing about seeing me again, so I was left once more at his mercy. *At his mercy.* I shivered at my choice of expression.

I went to bed but couldn't sleep, so I sat in the living room until the sunrise paid its compliments to the Golden Gate Bridge. The day's memories flipped through my mind like a slide show. Lucy looking like Sleeping Beauty in her white nightgown. Les telling me she had met a "real vampire." Sansome smiling in the back of the squad car. Eric's copper hair creating a curtain around me as we sped down the highway. The scrape of something sharp against my neck. A broken nose magically healed. When the slide show ended I waited for the explanation that would answer all of my questions, but none came. Certain words skittered at the edge of my consciousness, but I refused to acknowledge them. Guilt and fear mixed freely with excitement and happiness to create a cul-de-sac where all my emotions bottlenecked. I couldn't think any further than the next five minutes.

When the sun filled the room I closed the blinds. Then I went to bed and slept until a police siren bore into my consciousness. I checked the clock. I was going to be late for work again, that made three days in a row. I considered taking a sick day, since I was certainly feeling ill, but being at work seemed preferable to moping around the house. I didn't have any client meetings, and Dick let us observe Casual Friday if we weren't going in front of the public, so I put on a pair of nice jeans, flat shoes, and a beaded cashmere twin set from the 1970s. Even with two layers of sweater I was still cold, so I topped everything with a heavy black wool coat.

The first thing I did when I got to the office was google Eric Taylor and Harbinger, International. There was a professor of chemistry at Tulane University named Eric Taylor who had written way too many articles in obscure (to me) science journals. There was a corporate lawyer in New York specializing in public finance. There was a major league baseball player. There was a musician who was going to be playing at the Freight and Salvage on Saturday night. I looked up that guy's photo to make sure he wasn't the Eric I had in mind, and he wasn't. There were Harbinger, Internationals in Hong Kong and Bangladesh, one making computer parts and the other a textile manufacturer. It was starting to look like Eric Taylor had managed to avoid the octopus tentacles of the Internet. Finally I tried googling Harbinger, International and San Francisco. One entry came up describing a company that dealt in "international real estate investment and management."

There was a phone number and a downtown address listed. When I called an intelligent sounding female voice said that Mr. Taylor was in a meeting and could she take a message. I said no and hung up. The address was on California Street, only a few blocks from HFB. I checked my watch. I could be there and back in under an hour, unless the job required stalking.

In the reception area I ran into Dick, who was coming from the conference rooms. He blocked my way, shifting awkwardly from foot to foot and looking miserable. I could tell he knew what had happened yesterday and was searching for something to say to me. Finally he reached for my hand and shook it. I understood that this was as close as he could get to a hug.

"Angie, the police called me last night, they informed me that you found Lucy. I'm very sorry that you, well, I'm very sorry. How are you faring?" Dick wiped his cheek, his eyes moist, his Rudolph nose glowing.

"Thanks, Dick, I'm all right." I didn't feel all right, but it seemed like that was the response everyone wanted from me.

"Lucy was a peerless employee."

I hope no one asks you to deliver her eulogy.

"Yes, she was. Dick, I was just wondering, what did the police say to you about Lucy's death? Did they ask you about anybody?"

Dick frowned. "They posited a number of questions about Lucy's work, who were her friends, whether she'd been in any conflicts with a client or anyone else. I'm afraid I wasn't able to help them much. Lucy didn't exactly confide in me."

I decided to try a different method. "Well, I wondered, because they were asking me about Les Banks in particular."

Dick leaned closer, like he was going to tell me a secret. "They also asked me about Les," he whispered. "They want to interrogate him about Lucy. 'Not a suspect at this time,' that's what they said. 'Question him in connection with her death,' they said."

He almost smiled, but controlled himself. Leave it to Dick to become enamored of the vocabulary of homicide inspectors.

"So, did Les come to work today?" I whispered back. Silently I begged for the answer to be yes. I wanted Les to talk to the police and explain everything in such a way that he would be instantly exonerated.

Dick shook his head. "No one has seen him today."

Had Les run away? I must have looked ill, because Dick said, "Angie, why don't you go home? There's no reason for you to be here today. You've had a shock."

I thanked him for his concern and said that work would be the best medicine for me, but that I was going to take a little break and have a coffee. He nodded and let me go. I passed Theresa at her desk in the reception area and she looked up from a pile of tissues, her nose and eyes so red from crying that she looked like a white rabbit with a head cold.

"Oh Angie," she squeaked when she saw me, "you poor thing!"

"Thanks, Theresa. I'm all right. It's going to take a while, for all of us."

Theresa blew her nose into another tissue. "Lucy was always so professional with me. She never asked for things at the last minute." She looked pointedly at the row of offices in front of her, "unlike some other people around here."

I gave Theresa what I hoped was a sympathetic smile, then told her I was going to be out of the office for an hour or so.

With its multifaceted, gleaming red façade, the Bank of America Building is one of the main landmarks in the Financial District. In front of this building is a sculpture. Like many works of art, this one had consequences the artist never intended. It is a glossy black rock, about twenty feet high, more or less in the shape of a closed fist. Almost as soon as it was installed some wag dubbed it "The Banker's Heart," and the name stuck. I touched it as I passed and its coldness stung my hand. Black hearts, hearts of stone, all the images it brought to mind seemed like bad omens. I almost hoped this wasn't his office.

I checked the location of Harbinger, International on the directory next to the elevators. It was on the fourteenth floor. The elevator opened into a foyer with walnut paneling and thick carpets that muted every sound. A small waiting area contained a Japanese tansu, three upholstered wing chairs, and a coffee table with an array of magazines arranged in a neat fan. The ones I could see were *Architectural Digest, Art and Antiquities, Kiplingers,* and *Fortune,* arranged alphabetically.

A receptionist was sitting at a curved desk that was empty of everything except a glass vase of bamboo and black stones. She was the epitome of professionalism, dressed in a tan suit with a silk blouse, brown hair in a bun, light makeup. She was in her mid-forties, neither beautiful nor unattractive, just competent-looking. She wore a headset, into which she was speaking German. Harbinger, International was living up to its name.

"May I help you?" Her smile came quickly and faded just as fast.

"Yes, I'd like to see Eric Taylor." I tried to sound assertive.

"I'm very sorry, but he's not in at the moment. Did you have an appointment?"

Last night I did. That was my rationalization for lying. "Yes, we did."

The receptionist looked confused. She peered at an invisible calendar under the overhang of the desk. "And your name is?"

"Angela McCaffrey." Now I wished I hadn't succumbed to Casual Friday. I pulled my coat more tightly around myself.

"I don't see it on the schedule. May I ask the nature of your business?"

"We're discussing a real estate opportunity, and time is of the essence. I really need to talk to Mr. Taylor today. Can you give me a number for him?"

She shook her head sadly. "I really am sorry. There's no way for me to reach him at the moment. If you'd like to leave your card, I'll have him call you as soon as possible."

There's nothing like unerring politeness to take the wind out of your sails.

Back at the office, I tried to focus on work by writing a To Do list, but the first piece of paper my eyes lit upon was a Post-it telling me to call my mother, so I guiltily put that at the top of my list. I hadn't found the Plump n' Tasty Chicken art, the ostensible reason for my visit to Lucy's house, and I was sure I wouldn't be allowed back to search for them even if I wanted to, so the next item was to get Creative to generate some new copies. But it was Les who had drawn the pictures, and I was sure I wasn't going to see him at work today. I wondered if the police had arrested him. I hoped not, because I believed him when he said he didn't do it, although I had only a gut feeling to go on.

The desire to establish Les's innocence brought out the detective in me. Before I knew it I was thinking about the messages on Lucy's voicemail, and wondering whether there were any clues to her murder in them. Flipping to a fresh page on my notepad, I started a new list, titled: "Lucy's Voicemail."

I wrote, "Moravia, Thursday night."

Moravia had called on Thursday, telling Lucy not to come to the club the next day. Why would Moravia tell Lucy not to come on Friday, then turn around and invite Kimberley and me on Wednesday? Maybe she was really fed up with Lucy and was already planning to give the account to someone else. Or was it something more personal than that?

Then I wrote: "Les, Saturday morning."

Les had told me that the last time he saw Lucy was when they fought on Friday night. If this were true, then it made sense that he would call her the next morning, trying to make up. If he *had* killed her, the message was a cover-up that he knew the police would hear.

But if Les killed Lucy on Friday night, then Sansome was wrong about her being dead only for a day or two. I had a feeling why Sansome thought that, and why he didn't want to tell me his reason. Lucy's body had an odor, but not a terribly strong one. That's why Sansome asked me how long I'd been in the apartment. If she'd been dead for almost a week, I'd have smelled her as soon as I opened the door.

I remembered two coffee cups on the Sunday paper. Someone had been there with Lucy on Sunday morning. Not Les, if his story was to be believed. Maybe the new boyfriend. Lucy went somewhere else, perhaps with him, for the beginning of the week, then ended up back at home, dead, on Wednesday or Thursday.

One thing I could do was check to see where Lucy was on Friday night. Did she go to the House of Usher or was she with Les?

I called the Macabre Factor office, a cavernous former sewing factory south of Market Street. The desks and computers hugged the walls while the center of the room was filled with boxes of Macabre Factor cosmetics waiting to be shipped. Whenever I visited there I wondered anew where the capital was coming from for their advertising campaign. Suleiman had mumbled something about "angel investors" the last time we discussed the budget.

I immediately recognized Moravia's husky voice reciting the name of the company.

"Hi, it's Angie at HFB."

Moravia's voice turned warm. "*Hello*, Angie. Did you have a good time at Usher? We never got to say good-bye to you."

"Oh yes, I'm sorry about that. I started feeling a little ill, so I left early."

"Eric just couldn't stop talking about you."

I felt the blood rush to my cheeks, and suddenly I was off-task. Why hadn't I thought of asking Suleiman and Moravia for Eric's number?

"I'd love to get in touch with Eric. Do you happen to have his number?"

"I don't have any numbers for him. He's elusive,

that one. But if I see him I'll tell him you want to talk to him."

"You don't have to do that," I rushed to say. "Anyway, the reason I called is . . . you know Lucy has been missing the last few days?"

"No, no one told us that. We were just told she was unavailable."

That was the party line, wasn't it? If Moravia knew otherwise, she wasn't going to tell me.

"Well, she was found, I found her, she's dead."

I heard Moravia suck in her breath. "Oh my God, really! That's awful. How did she die?"

"I don't know really. The police are going to do an autopsy."

"Well, I'm so sorry. Please don't worry about our deadlines, we know it will take some time to get things sorted out."

Under the guise of taking over the account I could ask about Lucy and Moravia's interactions over the past few days without looking like I was just being nosy. One could even argue that it was a valid reason for me to have been listening to Lucy's voicemail.

"I think it's better for all of us if we keep things normal and just go on working." I took a deep, silent breath. "So I was wondering, when you saw Lucy on Friday night at Usher, did you all come to any conclusions about the creative strategy that I should know about? Was Lucy on board for the 'normal people embracing the vampire lifestyle' approach?"

There was some static on the line, as if Moravia was moving from one place to another. "That was a social visit, Angie. We've known Lucy since before we became clients at HFB. She had been coming to a private party that we have at Usher on Friday nights. Lately she'd been bringing Les Banks."

"A private party? Isn't the whole club private?" I asked, remembering the guest list.

"This is just a little more private. Anyway, she wasn't there last Friday because the party was canceled."

"Oh, why was that?"

"I can't really remember. It happens sometimes."

After we hung up I thought back over Moravia's message on Lucy's machine. I remembered the words distinctly.

"I know you were planning to come to the club tomorrow, but I think it might be better if you didn't . . ."

That didn't sound like the party had been canceled, that sounded like Lucy had been uninvited.

Moravia had said that both Les and Lucy had been attending the Friday parties. Les had said he wasn't "into the vampire stuff," so one of them was lying. I needed to talk to Les, but of course I didn't know where to find him.

Theresa opened the door without knocking. Still sniffling a little, she dropped my mail on my desk. I was rifling through it before the door closed behind her. Before Eric I would let my mail pile up unopened for days at a time, since any-thing important came by fax, phone, text, or email. But now my mail was precious, because it might contain a message from him.

Today's precious mail consisted of a copy of *Adweek*, a circular advertising a half-off shoe sale at Nordstrom, and a brochure for a conference on "Making the Perfect Pitch" in Maui. As I was toss-ing *Adweek* onto a pile of other unread magazines, a manila envelope fell out. It looked like a normal piece of direct marketing mail, with my name printed on a label, but its lack of return address or postage indicated otherwise. I swooped on it and ripped it open.

Chapter 10

The envelope contained a three-color, trifold brochure. The photo on the front was of a palm-fringed beach lapped by turquoise water. A man lay on his stomach in the sand, being massaged by two beautiful Asian women wearing bikinis. The caption read: "Experience beautiful and exotic Thailand."

Inside were more pictures of women and men. Women serving food to tables of only men in a bamboo-walled restaurant. Women wearing silk dresses in jewel colors, doing what looked like traditional Thai dances. Another man getting a massage. The inside copy read:

Feel the warmth of Southeast Asia. Our tour operators are trained to offer complete satisfaction. You will experience your heart's desire if you travel with us. Discreet, imaginative and professional. Special complete package tours from Germany, Japan, Canada and the United States.

The back of the brochure had an address:

> *Jad Paan Travel Agency*
> *Charoen Rat Road*
> *Bangkok, Thailand*
> *66 (2) 5870541*
> *www.jadpaan.com*

I read through the brochure several times, but found no reason why it should have been sent to me. The website had the exact same information as the brochure, only with more pictures of happy people and a soundtrack of tinkling music. I smelled the manila envelope, hoping to find a tell-tale trace of Eric's scent, but it just smelled vaguely of cigarettes. Why would Eric send me a travel brochure for Bangkok, anyway? Because he was going to take me away to exotic places, my hopeful heart suggested. He did work in *international* real estate, my optimism added. But logic had the last word. Nice try, it said. It's a brochure, not a secret message.

My office door was open, and Kimberley walked in while I was pondering. I hadn't seen her since the Big Meeting yesterday, when Dick had put me in charge of Tangento. I had been meaning to talk to her about it, but in the chaos it had slipped my mind.

"Angie, you're here. Are you all right? I heard from Dick that you found Lucy yesterday. That must have been so terrible for you. I'm sorry I wasn't home to talk to you about it last night." Her brow was attractively furrowed with concern.

"Thanks, Kimberley. I'm fine, I guess. I went out last night with some friends. To take my mind off things. I couldn't sleep anyway."

"I'll be home tonight, though, if you want some support. Mummy and Daddy are coming home today."

Support from Kimberley? I thought about what Lakshmi had said, and wondered whether Kimberley might actually be happy to have Lucy dead.

"Thanks again, but really, I'm fine."

"Well, you don't look fine. I think this has been really hard on you. You should go home and rest."

Now that she mentioned it, I was developing a mother of a headache over my right eye. There seemed to be an unusual glare this morning. I got up to pull the blinds down, then turned to face my roommate, coworker, and adversary.

"Kimberley, look, we should talk about yesterday, about the meeting and Tangento. I want you to know I had no idea Dick was going to do that."

Kimberley held up her hand. "Don't worry, Angie, please, you don't have to say anything. Especially after what has happened with Lucy, this is no time for animosity. We're all going to have to help each other to get through this difficult time."

That would have been a pretty speech if it hadn't sounded so rehearsed. But I didn't have the energy to worry about where Kimberley's magnanimity was coming from.

"I'm glad to know you're okay with it. And of course we'll be working together every step of the way."

Kimberley laid a fluorescent orange file folder on my desk. Only Lucy used fluorescent file folders. "Don't worry about looking at this right now if you don't want to, Angie. But this will help you get up to speed on what we've been doing with Tangento."

"Thanks. I appreciate that." I opened the folder and recognized Lucy's handwriting. She was the only woman I knew who wrote in block capitals, a very time intensive method, as I'd learned from watching her. I knew a few men who wrote that way, and I had thought it was because they were messing around in third grade and missed cursive class. Lucy probably did it because it made everything she wrote look important. I heard a sniffle, and I looked up with surprise to see Kimberley looking at the same piece of paper, but with wet eyes. Immediately I felt guilty.

"Oh gosh, I'm sorry, Kimberley. Here you're offering me support and I didn't even ask about you. I mean, you and I probably spent the most time with Lucy of anybody."

Except Les.

Kimberley smiled through her tears, the very picture of bravery in adversity.

"I think I'm in shock, like everybody else. It'll hit us later. A couple of days from now there'll probably be a line of people at Employee Assistance trying to get counseling. But for now, it's business as usual. At least we don't have to deal with telling all the clients."

This would have been a good time to mention that I'd already spoken to Moravia, but I didn't.

"I think Dick is calling everyone today, with some help from Human Resources. He'll get everyone informed, so we won't have to deal with that part of it when we start getting in touch with clients," Kimberley continued, her tears forgotten for the moment. "Apparently there's a whole protocol to be followed when there's a death in the company. HR has a chapter on it in the handbook." She took a breath. "Angie, if it's not too upsetting for you, I just have to ask, do the police have any idea what happened?"

"No, they wouldn't tell me. I didn't see anything on her, like gunshots, or . . ."

Holes in the neck?

". . . or wounds."

Kimberley shuddered and waved her hands as if shooing away flies.

I picked up the Tangento file. "Well, I guess we should get back to work, huh?" Except that my head was hurting so badly now I thought I would have to go home.

"What's that?" Kimberley pointed at the Thai

brochure, which had been uncovered when I picked up the file. "Are you thinking about going to Thailand?"

"Not me. I must have got on somebody's mailing list."

She headed for the door. "Do go home if you want to. You should take care of yourself."

After she left I opened the Tangento file again. There were reports from several focus groups conducted by the research department. Most people had no opinions of Tangento, either positive or negative. This was fairly common with large corporations, especially ones that owned many subsidiaries. It was a matter of not seeing the forest for the trees. They had heard of the companies that Tangento owned, according to the report, and held positive opinions of them.

Proteus was a name everyone in the focus group was familiar with, and not surprisingly, since a pair of sneakers displaying their trademark trident probably sat in half the closets in America. Proteus Titans were in a niche market, competing with sneakers made by hip-hop moguls Clay Russell and Big Head Eddy, bought by teenagers solely for their brand cachet. Most of the men in the focus groups did not admit to knowing the Venus lingerie brand name, but I was willing to bet a lot of them had sneaked a peek at the mail order catalogue. Tangento had a wealth of strong brands under its umbrella, including clothing, food, and personal care products.

Even after two years at HFB, it was still strange to me that a company like Tangento could own so many different subsidiaries. The kings of industry were no longer men who excelled at making or selling things, like Mr. Ford or Mr. Woolworth. No, the CEO of Tangento knew nothing about what made a comfortable bra or solid pair of sneakers, I'd be willing to bet. But he probably knew plenty about the business of business, of keeping the stockholders flush and happy.

No questions had been asked of the focus group regarding environmental or labor problems in other countries. The report concluded that the time was ripe for Tangento to begin a mass marketing campaign to sell a favorable image of the parent company and raise public awareness of the company name. And boost the stock price while you're at it, read the invisible footnote.

Lucy had written a memo stating that the client was amenable to the idea of a public awareness campaign and was eagerly awaiting our ideas for a tag line. The task had been sent to the creatives for preliminary brainstorming. We were to report back to Tangento next week.

At the end of the file were copies of faxes back and forth between Kimberley, Lucy, and Barry Warner, Tangento's VP of Marketing. He was based in Houston, but had been working in Tangento's San Francisco office and had a local number. He picked up after three rings.

"This is Barry Warner." He had the strongest

southern accent I'd heard since George W. Bush left office. His name had three syllables the way he pronounced it.

"Hello, Mr. Warner, this is Angie McCaffrey, from HFB."

"What can I do for you, Angie? And please, call me Barry."

My name also had three syllables. Barry's voice was as warm and sweet as caramel sauce, and I immediately liked him. I wondered if this was just a prejudice, as in all Southerners are gentlemen, people with BBC British accents are intelligent, and anyone with a Jamaican accent smokes pot and listens to reggae.

"Barry, may I ask, has Dick Partridge been in contact with you today?"

"Nope, haven't had the pleasure."

"Well, I'm afraid I have to be the first to tell you that Lucy Weston, your account executive . . ." I wished I'd thought this out before impetuously picking up the phone, ". . . she passed away."

Silence on the other end of the line.

I tried again. "It happened very unexpectedly, as you can imagine. We're trying to pick up the pieces as best we can."

"Forgive me, Angie, I was just shocked at the news. Lucy was such a sweet girl, we all just loved her over here."

Sweet girl, I never thought I'd hear *that* description.

"Thank you, I appreciate that, Barry. I'm calling

to let you know that I've been assigned to take over for Lucy for the time being. We're going to do our best to keep things moving smoothly. I know you're on the verge of a big promo, and it's an important time for Tangento."

"Well, Angie, you sound like a doll, and I look forward to having you on the team." Doll? Sweet girl? The warm feelings Barry's honey-dripped accent had induced were completely wiped away by his 1960s era word choices.

"I believe I have a meeting with y'all a week from today, is that right?" There was a pause while he presumably checked his calendar. "I know a great little sushi bar right near you that serves the damndest unagi you ever tasted."

Eating fish with a male chauvinist pig was not my idea of heaven, but it was part of the job description. I still had one question to ask, however, and I'd been thinking about the most delicate way to approach it throughout our conversation.

"That sounds great, Barry, I look forward to it, and to meeting you in person. There's just one other little thing . . . A colleague brought up the issue of some negative publicity that might be circulating around Europe, something in the *Economist*, maybe? Is this something y'all are aware of?"

Listen to me, y'alling him. I sounded like Steve, working the neurolinguistic programming.

Barry sighed into the phone. "I'm not aware of that one in particular, sweetheart, but a company as big as ours, we get a story a week like that. It's like that folk tale, what was the lion's name, Andrew? Anyway, the lion got a thorn in his paw, right? Well, you just have to ignore that thorn and get on with the business of being the King of the Jungle, you know what I mean?"

Barry and I said our good-byes. I tried rubbing a spot between my thumb and first finger that I'd been told was an acupressure point for headaches, but this pain wasn't budging. The story he was referring to was Androcles and the Lion. The lion gets a thorn in his paw and is incapacitated by it, until he allows Androcles to help him. Then when the Romans toss Androcles and the lion into the stadium, hoping for a little blood and gore, the big lion refuses to hurt his little human friend.

Barry getting that folk tale wrong was an omen, I could feel it like an old man with a bad knee when a storm's coming in. Somewhere in Asia, Tangento the Lion was ripping up Androcles. Whether Barry knew it or not, there *was* a "brouhaha in Asia," and the story was going to explode if we didn't find it and defuse it first.

I googled Tangento and got 1,490,000 hits. The first was a Wikipedia article, remarkably even-handed in tone considering that anyone in cyberspace could have written it. The second was the company's official site. That was followed by a bunch of obscure legal findings related to the merger of Tangento and Billy Olson, a designer clothing company, some news articles about the merger, and an article about the compensation package of the latest Tangento CEO, Edgar Raider.

I had paged through about thirty Google entries and found nothing about Tangento trouble in Asia when Steve rushed in. Because it was Friday, he was wearing tweed trousers and a cashmere sweater instead of his customary suit. He still looked ready to jump into a photo shoot—until you noticed his face, which was creased with worry.

"Angie, I'm so sorry, I wanted to come over earlier but I had a meeting I couldn't get out of. What a shock, finding Lucy like that. Are you okay?"

I nodded, but I felt my lower lip tremble. Steve came around to my side of the desk and pulled me into a hug. I pressed my face into his soft sweater, and then gently extricated myself.

"I'm okay," I said. "It doesn't seem real."

Steve sat on the edge of my desk. "The police called me last night, asking a bunch of questions about Lucy. I tried to call you but you weren't home."

"I was asleep. I guess I was in shock from what I saw, and I just, fell asleep."

So you're still lying about Eric to your best friend, are you? That seems like a bad precedent for a relationship.

"Sleep's probably the best thing for you. You sure as hell shouldn't be at work." Steve's gaze took in the darkened office. "Why is it so dark in here? Let me open the blinds."

"No, don't. I have a headache. Hey, Steve, look

at this." I showed him the envelope with my address, then the Thailand brochure. "You used to be a travel agent, do you have some insight into what it's advertising? Something about it seems odd to me."

Steve sat down and read the brochure. "Sex," he said matter-of-factly.

"Not now, I have a headache."

"Sex *tours.*"

"They advertise them?"

"Honey, have you been awake the last two years? Advertisers use sex to sell everything, including sex."

"But why go all the way to Thailand to see a prostitute? You can get one three blocks from here."

"Some would say you can get them in this office. But to answer your question, Thailand and Southeast Asia have prostitution down to a science. They cater to every proclivity, at bargain basement prices." Steve picked up the envelope again. "But why would they send it to you? You're the wrong gender, wrong moral code, wrong everything. Maybe they were sending it to Andrew McCaffrey."

"At this agency? I don't think so," I replied.

I took the brochure and looked at the address on the back, running over the conversation with Barry in my mind. "Do you think this might have something to do with Tangento?"

Steve looked confused.

"Don't you remember what Stan Ruckheiser was saying at lunch about Tangento? A 'brouhaha' in Asia? Maybe someone is trying to tell me something."

"Like what? Someone wants you to go to Thailand, buy a prostitute, then check in on the Proteus shoe factory?"

"Do you still have friends in the travel business?"

"But of course."

"Maybe you can make some discreet inquiries, see if you can figure out who this Jad Paan Travel Agency belongs to, or who their clients are, or something."

"I'll try," Steve answered. "Maybe they have an American affiliate. In the meantime you should call your credit card company and see if someone's using your card to," he read from the brochure, "'feel the warmth of Southeast Asia.' A stolen identity could be the answer to this mystery."

My head throbbed, and I must have winced, because Steve suddenly said, "Angie, seriously, you don't look good. Why don't you go home and rest?"

"I guess you're right. I don't seem to be getting much done around here."

My phone rang and I picked it up. Steve left, pointing first at me, then jerking his thumb toward the door to indicate I should go home.

"Hello, Angie, this is Mary Jordan from Human Resources. Lucy Weston's sister, Morgan, is coming from St. Louis on Monday. We have to pack up Lucy's office, so I thought I'd see if you could help us with that, since you knew her so well."

Knew her so well? I almost laughed, but it was too sad. I knew her better dead than I'd ever known her while she was alive.

"Yes, Mary, I'll be glad to help her sister. Just have her call me on Monday. Right now, though, I'm going home. I'm not feeling too well."

When I got home I took three Ibuprofen tablets, washed down with a handful of water, then I went to my room and pulled down the blinds. It still wasn't dark enough so I went back to the bathroom and dug around in my travel bag for my eyeshade. As soon as I put it on I fell into a deep sleep.

I had a dream in which I was wandering the alleys of some medieval European city, with high, stone walls, cobblestone streets, and courtyards with tinkling fountains. It would have been picturesque except I was the only human being around, but for the shadowy figures flitting around corners in the distance. I was looking for Eric. I could smell his maddening scent in the air. I followed it like a hound chasing a fox, except that the fox could easily kill me when I caught him. I was in great danger, I sensed menace everywhere, but I couldn't stop searching for a glimpse of a chiseled white cheek and flame-colored hair.

The phone rang, but trying to wake up was like crawling out of quicksand. I reached for the phone, banging my head into the nightstand in the dark.

"Angie, it's Les."

Instantly I was awake. "Les, my God, where are you, what happened . . ."

"I'm in big trouble."

"The police just wanted to talk to you, why did you run away?"

"Bullshit, Angie, talk means they want to arrest me. I'm their only suspect; they're not looking for anyone else. You've got to help me catch the killer!" His voice was high-pitched and nearly hysterical.

"Who, Les?"

"The vampire!"

"You mean Suleiman?"

Les laughed, an ugly cackling sound. "Suleiman's a pretty boy poser. I'm talking about the real vampire."

Chapter 11

"Les, there are no real vampires." I spoke consolingly, as if to a child having bad dreams.

Les's ragged breathing filled my ears. "One of them is real, the one Lucy fell in love with. It's hard to believe, I know. I didn't believe it myself until I met him."

"You met him? What did he look like?" It was an odd question, but Les was too distraught to notice.

"I don't know, exactly. He was wearing a hood. They have these rituals at the House of Usher where people volunteer to let him suck their blood. You've got to go and record it, for evidence, so the police will believe what we're telling them!"

So Les couldn't confirm that the man I knew as Eric was the one he identified as the real vampire. I was both relieved and disappointed to know this, but I felt that I couldn't hide from the truth for much longer. I owed it to Lucy, not to mention myself. I also felt increasingly sure that the truth, if there even was such a thing, would not change what I felt about him.

"Is this the same ritual you were going to go to with Lucy last week?" I asked.

"How do you know about that? Who have you been talking to?"

"Answer the question, Les."

"Moravia told Lucy not to come anymore. Lucy said it was because her new boyfriend didn't want to be in competition with me, that he was trying to be chivalrous."

"That's good for you, right? The new boyfriend was bowing out."

"Wrong. Lucy said she wasn't going to let me get in her way, that once the vampire knew it was really over between me and her, he'd come back to her."

"So Lucy didn't go to the ritual that night?" *Maybe because you killed her to keep her from going?*

"I don't know. She kicked me out before midnight. I think she did go, and he killed her there. Maybe he'll kill someone else tonight. If you go and get a video I'll be off the hook."

I grabbed for the edge of the table, feeling dizzy. "Les, I can't do that, especially if what you're saying is true. Tell the police, they can go over and see for themselves."

Les laughed again. "Yeah, right, they'll go right over there when I call them and tell them it wasn't me, that it was a vampire. They'll believe *that*, Angie. No, you go. There's a password, they'll let you in. You'll be safe, there's always an audience you can blend in with. Only the person who volunteers is in danger."

"Oh, that makes me feel better."

Les ignored me. "Go in the back entrance, from the alley near the dumpster. At the bottom of the stairs there'll be a guard. Say the password and they'll let you in. Make a video of what they're doing and take it to the police. Then they'll have to believe you. I could get the death penalty! You owe me, Angie, you handed me to the police on a . . ."

An electronic voice interrupted Les, saying "Please deposit fifty cents for three more minutes."

Les shouted, "Shit, I don't have any more money. Requiem, that's the password . . ."

The connection was severed before I could reply.

After talking to Les I tried to sit up and think but it was like I'd taken a tranquilizer. My head kept slumping lower and lower until I was asleep again. When I woke up my alarm clock read 9:58 P.M. I tried to keep my eyes closed, thinking I ought to try to sleep through the night, but I couldn't keep the lids down. My biorhythms were completely confused. I finally gave up and went to the kitchen.

Kimberley was there, dressed in a fluffy white robe, drinking a glass of milk and flipping through *Vogue*.

"Hey, I'm glad you came home and went to bed. How are you feeling now?"

"Better, I guess."

I opened the refrigerator, trying to remember the last time I'd eaten. There was the Irish coffee I'd had with Eric, was that only last night? It seemed like a lifetime ago. Before that was the salad I'd eaten at the Azure Sea. I should have been starving, but nothing in the refrigerator looked appealing. It was all Kimberley's food: soymilk, eggs, buttermilk bread, yogurt, sliced Swiss cheese. I realized for the first time that all of Kimberley's food products were white. I wondered if there was a category of mental illness in the psychology books for white food eaters.

I poured myself a glass of soymilk and sat down opposite Kimberley. She continued to read, no longer acknowledging my presence. If Kimberley had been a different kind of person I was sure we would have been talking a mile a minute, comforting each other, exchanging theories, examining every minute detail of the past few days. But even if Kimberley hadn't sabotaged me with the Macabre Factor account, we still wouldn't have been best-friending it around the kitchen.

I'd been living there almost a year and I still knew only the facts about Kimberley. She'd never shared any of her feelings with me—assuming she had feelings. We lived together as if we were neighbors on the same hallway, waving hello when we ran into each other. We each had our own bathroom and neither of us used the kitchen much. If I used up the last of something I replaced it, and so did Kimberley. We coexisted. Now there were so many things between us—Lucy's death, Kimberley's treachery, and Dick's favoritism toward me—I wasn't sure we could even go back to coexistence. On top of everything else I was probably going to have to find a new place to live. For a second I imagined that the new place might be with Eric, in whatever chalet or chateau or condo he called home. But only for a second.

"What are you going to do tonight?" I asked.

"I'm going to take a sleeping pill and go to bed. I can't wait to have this day over." She looked at me over the magazine. "What about you?"

I'm going to the House of Usher to film a vampire ritual. Wanna go?

"Nothing much. I might go over to Steve's place to watch a movie."

I left Kimberley in the kitchen and sat in the living room without turning on any lamps. The twinkling lights of the city, giving way to soft inky blackness at the edge of the water, had a soothing effect on me. I noticed that, just like yesterday, I was starting to feel better now that it was full night. My headache was gone and I felt wide-awake.

Kimberley came in. "Do you want me to turn a light on for you?"

"No!" I said a little too sharply. I changed my tone. "I like looking at the view this way."

"Okay, I'm going to bed. I'll see you in the morning."

"Good night."

The light in the kitchen was off and the living

room was in even deeper darkness. But as I gazed across the room at the built-in bookshelves where Kimberley kept her library, the titles leapt out at me like there was a spotlight on them. *Feng Shui Your Crib, How to Meditate in 10 Minutes a Day, The Art of Business, The Business of Advertising.* I'd never been able to read those titles from the couch, even in daylight. Was my eyesight getting better?

I thought about what Les had asked me to do. What he had *really* asked, although he didn't know it, was for me to see whether Lucy's boyfriend and mine were one and the same. I wanted to exonerate Les. I wanted to find Lucy's killer and have it be somebody I'd never seen before, someone I didn't give an expletive about. I wanted to see Eric again, but not at the House of Usher. I went to my room to change clothes.

Steve lived in the Castro District, a neighborhood known throughout the world as a gay mecca, now being taken over by the "stroller pushing crowd," as he liked to call heterosexual parents. But on a Friday night at 11:30 the stroller crowd was snug in their beds and Castro Street had reverted back to its previous owners. Handsome men with handlebar mustaches and bulging pectoral muscles strolled arm in arm. Rainbow flags signifying gay liberation fluttered in the wind. 1970s disco music pulsated from the open doors of the bars.

Steve's apartment was on a hill directly above the busy part of Castro Street. Every spot on the street was taken, so I double-parked in front of the building, turning on my hazard lights. I entered the portico of the graying, 1960s-era shoebox building and pushed the intercom button for apartment four.

Steve's garbled voice sounded like he was still under his covers. "This better be an emergency."

"Steve, listen, I need you to come out with me."

"Angie, I was asleep!"

"I need a wingman." Steve and I had been out together many times, but it never worked for meeting potential mates because we always had so much fun with each other that we scared off everybody else.

Steve's voice was weary. "I thought you were sick, now you want to go party? You better come up here so I can chastise you properly." He buzzed me into the building and I climbed a flight of narrow stairs to his door.

Dressed in boxer shorts decorated with hearts and a red T-shirt, Steve gestured me into the living room of his one-bedroom apartment. He had done wonders with the room, making it look like a tiny Tuscan villa, with terra-cotta walls, antique wooden tables laden with flowers and Italian pottery, and even a miniature replica of Michelangelo's David. He tried to get me to sit on the overstuffed velvet couch, but I chose to pace instead.

"So, what are you doing out by yourself at midnight?"

"Steve, I don't have time to explain, we have to go to the House of Usher. Les thinks it was one of the people there who killed Lucy. He asked me to help him, there's no one left except me, he says he's innocent, the police are going to arrest him unless I get some evidence, he told me where we can sneak in . . ." I stopped, knowing I was going in circles.

"Let me get this straight. You think one of these characters might have killed Lucy, but you want to go straight to the lion's den and offer yourself as a rump roast, and bring yours truly along for dessert. I don't think so. That's what we have the police for, Nancy Drew." Steve sat down on his couch and crossed his arms, case closed.

"I've already thought this through. The police are not going to do anything except keep looking for Les, at least until they have some other suspect. They're not going to get another suspect because they have no cause to look for one. Les is right, I did give him up, and if he didn't do it I have to help him."

I wasn't going to mention my other reason, wanting to make sure Eric was not the person Les thought was Lucy's killer. Then he *really* wouldn't let me go.

"And what if these wackos did kill Lucy, Angie? What about this guy, Eric, who drugged you? What if it was him?"

So much for deception.

Steve looked at me closely, then clapped his

hand to his mouth. "You saw him again, Angie, I see it in your eyes. You've completely lost your mind, and I'm not letting you out of this apartment!"

I sat down on a satiny wing chair. Tears prickled my eyes, threatening to spill over. I scrubbed at them roughly with my hand. "Yes, I saw him again. We went out last night. We rode down Highway One on a motorcycle. It was magical . . ." My voice trailed off.

What would Steve say if I told him everything— if I described my encounters with Eric, the strange symptoms I'd been having since the first time he'd touched me, and the desperate longing for him that was starting to consume my waking hours and my dreams? What if the situation were reversed and Steve was telling me the same things about a man he had just met? I would be doing anything in my power to keep him away from the guy.

"Les needs my help. I hope you will go with me, but if you don't, I'm going anyway."

Steve stared at me for a long moment, and then stood up. He pulled off the red T-shirt as he headed for his bedroom.

"I guess black is the color *du jour*?"

We drove by the House of Usher and checked the front entrance. The usual abnormal crowd was waiting to get in, names being checked by the beefy bouncer. We parked around the corner and walked down the alley behind the nightclub. If I hadn't been feeling so nervous I would have laughed at the sight of Steve, looking like Marcel Marceau without the white face in skintight black pants, turtleneck, and beret, tiptoeing at midnight behind a dumpster filled with rotting Chinese food. The black metal door I had used in my escape two days before was slightly ajar, just as it had been then.

When we entered I heard mind numbingly loud music pounding down on us from upstairs. Mercifully, it was muted by a set of closed doors. Following Les's directions we went down one flight and through a dank room filled with cardboard boxes to a door, where a person undistinguishable as to age or gender, in black shapeless clothes, with black shoulder-length hair, was standing. I could hear sounds through the door, chanting or singing and perhaps drums. When Steve hesitated I shoved him forward. This was not something one should think too hard about.

"Look like you know what you're doing," I hissed at him.

The genderless person stared at us impassively.

"Requiem." My voice was a hoarse whisper.

The person opened the door.

Steve pulled back, forcing me to drag him. His expression said: "What the %#*& are we doing here?" I peeled his fingers off my arm and strode in, swallowing the bile my fear was producing.

About fifty people were standing in front of a stage, watching the show in progress. The only light in the large room came from a row of pillar candles near the front, so I dragged Steve with me into the shadows at the side of the room. I opened up my cell phone, trying to hide it under the black shawl I was wearing. I was sure someone would see me recording and throw us out, or worse, but then I noticed that at least two other people were taping the proceedings, one with a phone, and one with a camera. I nudged Steve and pointed. He shrugged and whispered, "They probably have a website. Crazyvampireshit.com."

At first glance what we were seeing appeared to be the kind of lesbian sex show you can see at certain downtown clubs for the price of three watered-down drinks. Two women dressed in little more than G-strings and leather bracelets were writhing in a theatrical approximation of sex. What was different was the blood. One woman's neck and chest were covered with shallow cuts in the shape of circles and stars, from which blood dripped in rivulets. The other woman licked the blood and rubbed her hands over the wounds until the first woman's skin was covered in a red sheen.

We seemed to have come in at the end of the first act because the two women picked themselves up and went behind a curtain. I wondered what they could possibly follow up with, and whether I could stand to look anymore. It helped to be looking through the camera. It gave some distance to the proceedings.

Moravia and several others arrived on the stage,

each holding a pendant flag emblazoned with an abstract coat of arms. They were chanting words I couldn't understand, but it had the rhythmic intonation of a Mass in Latin. It even sounded like Latin, with a lot of the words ending in *um* or *us*. Suleiman entered, wearing a black robe with red satin lining embroidered with fanciful patterns. I pulled my shawl around my face just in case he or Moravia happened to look my way.

"Hey, aren't they your clients?" Steve asked in a loud whisper. I nodded.

"Didn't they say they wanted you to use people in the club for their campaign?"

"Yeah," I said.

"Great idea. Watching the pig blood scene in *Carrie* always makes *me* want to buy cosmetics."

The music and chanting faded and Suleiman's voice boomed out over the audience. "Sons and daughters of the night. Is there one among you who chooses to offer themselves as a sacrifice to the Lord of Darkness, who wishes to taste immortality and rend the fabric that divides this world from the Beyond?"

A young woman pushed through the crowd and climbed the stairs on the side of the stage. She was thin and delicate, with long blond hair. I zoomed in on her face and saw it was Lilith. Her eyes had a drugged, glazed-over look and she stumbled as she walked.

Lilith stood at the front of the stage and held out her arms. It seemed she'd done this act before.

Suleiman and Moravia unbuttoned her shirt, stroking her arms and shoulders and whispering. Two other men in cloaks stepped forward and just as they did Lilith slumped like she was going to fall down. The men grabbed her arms and held her upright.

A tall man entered, his head covered with a black velvet cloak so that his face was obscured. He was holding a dagger about ten inches long. The chanting started again by the participants on the stage and was taken up by the observers. The man held the knife high above his head, then came forward and raised it over Lilith's chest, as if he were going to stab her in the heart. There was a collective intake of breath, then silence. I felt like I was at a bullfight, waiting for the matador to deliver the *coup de grace.* My head swam and I felt I might faint but my feet were frozen to the floor. Steve silently took hold of my free hand.

Chapter 12

The man didn't stab Lilith. Instead he drew a shallow cut across her chest. The blood bubbled up along the length of it, then slowly dripped down her white skin. Lilith didn't open her eyes but she arched her back and raised her face to the ceiling. Her expression was one of ecstasy, not pain.

He put his arms around Lilith and raised her up. He bent his head to the wound on her chest and licked it from bottom to top. His mouth caressed her chest, just the way Eric's lips had caressed me. He lingered over her neck. A spasm went through Lilith's body, and her expression turned into a grimace, but only for a moment. As quickly as it came, the grimace disappeared and her body went limp in his arms. A rivulet of blood ran down her arm and dripped off her fingers onto the floor. The chanting grew louder and louder.

Before I knew it I had lowered the cell phone and was pushing toward the stage, heedless of

Steve and the other people around me, focused only on the shadowy silhouette of the man's face inside the hood.

Is it you? I think I even said it out loud, but no one answered.

The hooded man raised his arms and beckoned to Suleiman and Moravia and the others on the stage. They approached Lilith while drawing knives from hidden places in their clothes or robes. Several of them made cuts in her body, on her arms or stomach, and put their heads down to drink from her. As this happened the hooded man backed up and slipped behind the curtains on the stage.

I felt Steve's grasp like iron around my arm. "I came, I saw, I got the fuck out of Dodge. Let's go, missy, right now." Steve was now dragging me backward. His hold was like a vise all the way up the stairs and back into the alley. The cold air hit me like a slap in the face. I leaned against the car with my head down while Steve rummaged in my purse for the keys to my car.

While he drove I leaned my face against the cold car window, taking deep breaths. After we had gone a few blocks I felt calm enough to turn to Steve.

"What did we just see, Steve?"

Steve didn't answer me, just stared straight ahead as he drove along the deserted street. His knuckles, as he gripped the steering wheel, were white.

* * *

I'm lying on Lucy's bed, kissing a corpse. The motionless body I'm touching is as smooth, cold, and hard as stone, yet I kiss it as fervently as any lover, stroke it with the palms of my hands. I think I can bring it back to life with my love, with the heat of my desire. I wrap my legs around it, press it to the length of my body. I try putting my mouth on the corpse's lips and blowing air into the silent throat. "Lucy," I whisper, "Come back, you're not dead, only frozen." I feel a twitch, hear a sigh, and increase my efforts. It's going to work, I think, I've brought her back to life!

Suddenly the corpse grabs me and sinks its teeth into my neck. The pain is like a reverse bullet, coming up from my heart and trying to exit through my neck. I cry out, try to push Lucy away, but I have no strength. My cries sound like a dying bird. The vampire lifts its head, and the face has become Eric's, blood dripping down his chin.

I woke up with sweat coating my body, the bedclothes twisted around my legs. I tried to calm down and straighten out the covers, then nearly jumped out of my skin because by God there really was a corpse in my bed. I pulled the sheet down and there was Steve, still dressed in his black turtleneck, sleeping like a rock. After watching the video twice (and coming no closer to identifying the hooded man) we'd each taken a sleeping pill washed down with a shot of whiskey. Steve wasn't going anywhere soon.

With my favorite polar fleece robe tied tight around my waist, I stumbled groggily into the kitchen. Kimberley was perched on the edge of her chair, already dressed in a pale green linen dress and a heavy gold choker. She was having her usual breakfast, an oversized mug of coffee with soymilk and a single hard-boiled egg, which she cut up into six equal slices and doused with salt. She put down the third slice when she saw me come in.

"Well, good morning. Look who's finally getting up!"

Kimberley's unfailing morning cheeriness had always bothered me, but it seemed especially inappropriate this morning.

"Hi Kimberley, where are you off to so early? Isn't it Saturday?" I opened the refrigerator, but it was out of habit rather than hunger. The increasingly familiar headache and nausea were upon me again. I'd have sworn I was pregnant if I'd had sex anytime in the last six months.

"Junior League brunch," Kimberley answered. "Did you and Steve go out last night? I heard you come in about two in the morning."

"Yeah, we went dancing at Moby Dick's."

"Really, Steve brought a girl to a gay bar?"

"It's not a big deal, Kimberley. Lots of women go. It's a good place to dance without getting hit on." Kimberley had made a pot of coffee and I poured myself a cup. Normally I liked Kimberley's coffee, but this batch tasted oily and bitter. Still, I enjoyed the warmth in my mouth and stomach.

"Oh, by the way, Kimberley?" I tried to sound nonchalant.

"Yes?" Kimberley speared another egg slice.

"Do you know if Lucy was dating anyone?" I made the question as open-ended as possible.

Kimberley put her fork down. "Well," she said slowly, "Lucy swore me to secrecy, but I guess since she's dead it doesn't matter anymore, does it? She was dating Les Banks. I saw them kissing one day." Kimberley drew a quick breath, her mouth a surprised O. "Oh my God! Angie, are you saying Les had something to do with this? Is that why he wasn't at work yesterday?"

Something about the way Kimberley was reacting wasn't right, but I couldn't put my finger on it.

"You're jumping to conclusions, aren't you, Kimberley? I don't know anything about Les, I was just curious."

"But it's always the boyfriend, isn't it?"

I sure hope not.

"Did you tell the police about Les and Lucy?" I couldn't say anything about my own knowledge of Les and Lucy's relationship, since Sansome had told me to stay quiet.

"Yes, I told that fat policeman that I had seen them kissing, and that Lucy told me they were dating."

"Why do you think Lucy wanted to keep it a secret?" I took another sip of coffee.

Kimberley wrinkled her nose. "If my boyfriend looked like Les I'd keep it a secret too. He's so . . . dirty."

It was pronouncements like that that kept Kimberley from having a boyfriend in the first place.

She stood up and brushed invisible crumbs from the front of her dress. "So, are you doing anything special tonight?"

I shook my head. "Not really. Why?"

"My parents are having a big party. I had a date but it fell through."

I occasionally attended Bennett functions with Kimberley, because they always had fantastic food and I often ran into clients there, causing them to believe that I was much better connected than I really was. I'd even snagged two clients for HFB at Bennett soirées. But going to a party tonight was the last thing I wanted to do.

"I don't think so, Kimberley. I'm wiped out."

She shrugged her shoulders. "Okay. But I think that guy we met at Usher on Wednesday will be there. It seemed like you liked him."

I clenched my cup so hard coffee splashed over my hand. "You mean Eric Taylor?"

"Yes. Daddy's doing some real estate deals with him."

I put the coffee down so Kimberley wouldn't see that my hands were shaking. "Maybe I'll come for an hour or two."

"Meet me here at eight and I'll drive you." She put her dish in the sink. "Oh, and Angie. It's black tie."

After she left I poured another cup of coffee and carried it to my room. I put my bare foot on Steve's face and wiggled my toes. His eyes opened and he pushed my foot away.

"What time is it? I feel like hell," he grumbled.

"It's ten o'clock. You and me both." It was true. I felt like I hadn't slept in days. All I wanted to do was make a nest of blankets and crawl inside.

Steve sat up. "This is novel. I haven't been in a girl's bed since I was sixteen. Yours has a lot less stuffed animals than hers did."

I adjusted the blinds to make the room as dark as possible and lay back down on the bed. "I've been thinking about last night."

Steve pulled the pillow out from under his head and put it over his face.

"Do you want to know what I was thinking?"

He removed the pillow and sighed. "Yes, Angie, what were you thinking?"

"I was thinking that it was all a performance. Performance art, for the pleasure of performer and audience alike. I've seen shows like that before. Well, not the blood part, but the rest of it. And who knows, maybe even the blood was fake." I lay still, staring at a crack in the ceiling. Steve's face appeared in my peripheral vision, his head propped up on one elbow.

"Angie, maybe you can convince your mother with that shit, but this is Uncle Stevie you're talking to."

"What do you mean?" I asked.

He got up and opened the blinds. I groaned and tried to cover my own face with a pillow, but Steve jumped on top of me. He straddled my legs and threw my pillow on the floor.

"First you are attacked by some guy at a vampire club, then your boss ends up dead, and Les says she was killed by a vampire. Not only do you not tell the police," he paused for emphasis, "but you go see the guy again and you start lying to yours truly."

He didn't wait for an answer. "Then we go see this 'performance,' or whatever you want to call it, which sure looks real to me, and you start telling me that it's all faked."

"Steve, come on. There's no such thing as vampires, you know that!" I squeezed out from under him and sat up.

"What's a vampire?" Steve asked, but again he didn't wait for an answer. "A person who drinks blood. *Ergo*, those people are vampires. I'm not even going to get into any supernatural shit. We're taking your video to the police. And I hope your new boyfriend gets arrested, because I'm afraid it's the only way to keep you away from him."

The San Francisco Homicide Division was located in the optimistically named Hall of Justice, a gray boulder of a building dropped by the side of the freeway, surrounded by bail bondsmen and cheap furniture outlets.

It was Saturday and the place was operating with a skeleton crew. The security guard was sitting with his feet up reading a newspaper. Steve and I passed through the metal detector and headed up to the fourth floor for our appointment with Inspector

Sansome. We found him sitting behind a metal
desk so old it was in style again, eating a sandwich
that smelled like pastrami. Trujillo was nowhere to
be seen, but at other desks an attractive, middle-
aged white woman in a bright red suit typed away
on a computer and an older black man in a nylon
sweat suit talked on the phone and shuffled papers.
The woman took off her jacket, revealing a gun
strapped to her hip and handcuffs over her butt.

Sansome waved us into two metal and vinyl
chairs and finished the bite he was working on
before he spoke. "Hello, Ms. McCaffrey, nice to see
you again. Beautiful weather today, isn't it?" Room
450 in the Hall of Justice had only one window,
with opaque scratched glass. I wondered if he was
being facetious.

"Inspector Sansome, I'd like you to meet my
friend, Steve Blomfelt."

The two shook hands.

"I do have some questions for you, Ms. McCaffrey, but perhaps you should begin, since you
called me." He took another bite.

"Les Banks called me yesterday. I don't know
from where. He told me he was innocent, that he
believed 'the vampires' had killed Lucy."

Sansome coughed and banged his chest with
his fist.

"We've been working on an ad campaign for
some clients who are 'living the vampire lifestyle,'
and sell cosmetic products. Lucy had been to this
club with them, but I hadn't, not before last

Wednesday, anyway. Les told me that she partici-
pated in rituals where they drank blood. He said
he thought they killed her, and wanted me to
record a ritual so that you could see what they do."

"And you complied?"

I nodded, holding up my cell phone as evidence.

"Do you think that was wise?"

"I don't know. It seemed like the thing to do at
the time."

"Well, why don't we take a look at the video?" He
took my cell phone and surprised me by quickly
and competently transferring the video to his computer. I had expected to find him typing with
carbon paper on an Underwood typewriter. We
watched the video in silence, which included a
minute of violent shaking and views of my feet as
Steve and I ran up the stairs and out into the alley.

When it was over I sat looking at the floor, fear
and panic churning my stomach. On the larger
screen of Sansome's computer, I had noticed something I hadn't seen the other times I'd watched the
video. The hooded man had elegant hands, the fingers long and tapered. On the pinkie finger of his
left hand he was wearing a gold signet ring with a
worn red stone in it.

"This was at the House of Usher, on Haight
Street?" Sansome asked.

I couldn't answer. My mind and heart were in
turmoil. Instinctively I looked over at my best
friend, then remembered that I was keeping all of

this a secret. But before I could duck my head I caught Steve's eye. I could tell from his expression that he had seen right through me.

"Yes, that's right," Steve answered.

Sansome leaned back and laced his fingers over his ample tummy. "Ms. McCaffrey, Mr. Blomfelt, people are superstitious. When you say vampire, they get scared and want to get out the pitchforks. But in reality, cult killings are very rare. We are aware of this club and what goes on there. There have never been any complaints or any reports of crimes. Their actions are consensual and legal."

"But what about that woman?" Steve interjected. "She looked like she was being killed!"

"All right, I'll get their names and we'll look into it." Sansome's tone was placating. "But I really wouldn't worry about this club, Mr. Blomfelt. If we ever have a problem with a psycho, it's usually a lone individual. In fact, we had a case last year that the newspapers called 'The Vampire Murderer.' Guy claimed to be a three-thousand-year-old vampire. Stabbed his girlfriend twelve times and drank her blood. Ms. McCaffrey, are you all right?"

I had tipped over a little in my seat and had to grab the chair to right myself. "Yes, thank you, I'm fine. I'm just feeling a little tired."

Sansome took us back over to his desk. He got out his notebook and his pen. "What are the names of the individuals you saw?"

"Suleiman and Moravia, well, their real names are Douglas and Marie Claire Paquin."

"And the woman in the tape who's being cut?"

"Lilith, but I don't know her last name, or even if that's her real name."

"No problem." Sansome smiled. "And the cloaked individual? Were you able to ID him?"

Steve shook his head and I said no. "He never took off the hood," I added.

Sansome asked me again whether I knew where Les was, and if I knew the names of any of his friends. He told me to call him immediately if Les got in touch with me again. Then he escorted us to the hall and shook our hands, thanking us for coming.

On Bryant Street Steve bought us each a soft pretzel from a stand. He handed mine over and said, "I want to watch you eat that. You haven't eaten in days, as far as I can tell."

The pretzel looked about as appetizing as a piece of cardboard. I took a bite and chewed slowly.

"Angie, why did you lie to the policeman?"

The pretzel stuck in my throat. "I didn't lie, Steve . . ."

"You know who the hooded man was. I could tell from your face when you were watching the video. It was him, wasn't it?"

"Steve, you're wrong. I swear, I don't know who it was."

Steve looked at me, his expression hurt and bewildered. Then he turned and poured mustard on his pretzel.

I rubbed my eyes with my napkin, hoping Steve

wouldn't see the tears starting in them. He had every right to worry. Hell, I was worried. I was consciously rejecting the notion of vampires, but I was lying, obfuscating, and covering up to protect a man I hardly knew, who might very well be a murderer. The man had a grip on me that was beyond anything I'd ever experienced. It was as if I were still on the back of his motorcycle, driving into the dark and hanging on for dear life.

Chapter 13

I spent the afternoon according to my new routine, asleep. My eyelids popped open just as the sun was setting. Normally it would have taken me an hour to find something to wear to the Bennett's party, but black tie was actually easier. I only had three dresses that would do for black tie and one of them was a peach bridesmaid's dress I wouldn't be caught dead in. Another was a green velvet dress from the fifties with a bell skirt and sweetheart neckline. That one was too sweet. The third was a red, beaded 1920s silk flapper dress. Red lipstick, dangling crystal earrings, and a black velvet shrug completed the ensemble.

I found Kimberley in the living room wearing a black sleeveless sheath that fit her like the dress that Marilyn Monroe wore to sing "Happy Birthday" to President Kennedy. In other words, she was poured into it. Her pumps had heels so high they would have given me a nosebleed from the altitude. Her pearls were the size of gumballs. Her blond hair was arranged in a French twist. She turned and looked at me like I was a favorite pet who had peed on her carpet, like she loved me but found me quite disgusting.

"Vintage, I presume?"

"Yes. Something wrong with it?"

"Not at all. You look charming." She patted me on the shoulder as she walked out of the room.

The Bennett mansion occupied a huge corner lot at the top of the highest hill in San Francisco. A small army of valets stood in a line to receive the Mercedes and BMWs as they disgorged their elegantly dressed occupants, mostly white couples between the ages of forty and seventy. The men held the elbows of their wives as they passed through the white columns of the portico. There was a remarkable similarity among them, the men with steel gray hair and tans from the golf course, the women rigorously thin, with expertly dyed puffballs of hair and extremely large jewels around the neck.

Kimberley pushed a remote control button on her key chain to open an iron gate at the back entrance of the house. We followed a long curving driveway and parked in front of the separate three-car garage. A courtyard filled with tropical plants and a fountain that looked like it was stolen from a Roman plaza separated us from the back door. We entered a bustle of activity in the kitchen, dozens of caterers piling silver trays high with everything from artichokes to ziti.

In the hallway Kimberley swept past a small pen-and-ink drawing of a man in Renaissance clothing, with a cauliflower nose, but I stopped to pay homage because I knew this little picture was a Rembrandt. We continued past a carved ice sculpture of a mermaid. The crushed ice below her displayed oysters on the half shell and wedges of lemon. Kimberley grabbed one and slurped it down. She offered one to me, forgetting that I hate seafood. I took three crackers and a wedge of cheese, arranging them on a tiny plate, porcelain, of course.

"We'd better go and show ourselves to my parents." Kimberley let out a little sigh. I followed her into a marble-lined foyer larger than most people's living rooms, where waiters plied the guests with trays of caviar on toast triangles and little rolls of puff pastry topped with bright pink salmon roe. Kimberley grabbed a glass of champagne as the tray went by.

The Bennetts were standing at the front door, greeting their guests as they entered. We approached them and hovered, waiting to be noticed. Dr. Bennett, dressed in a double-breasted tuxedo, was the very picture of a rich middle-aged playboy. He had a full head of wavy gray hair worn slightly long, as if he wanted to draw attention to it. Mrs. Bennett looked like she had spent too much time in her husband's plastic surgery office. Her button nose and round blue eyes seemed pulled by invisible strings toward the back of her head. She was wearing a strapless silk dress in a shade of pink that ought to be reserved for newborn baby girls, but her figure was years younger than its owner. Dr. Bennett seemed to be using his wife as a living showcase for his surgical talents.

Mrs. Bennett turned to Kimberley and planted an air kiss near her cheek. "Kimmy, sweetheart, you're finally here. I've been trying to call you. You should have told me you were going to use the guest room this week. Esmerelda was in there for half a day yesterday, getting it ready for the Fitzpatricks. Who did you have stay over, by the way?"

"No one, Mummy. I just felt like staying there myself. It has a better view than my room."

I took a sidelong glance at Kimberley. She had told me she was house-sitting, but her parents hadn't invited her. Was there something about our apartment that made her want to get away? Or maybe she needed a break from me?

"Well, now the party can begin!" Dr. Bennett gave his daughter a real kiss on the cheek, and then pumped my hand vigorously. "Glad you could come, girls. Kimberley, you should have come to Bermuda with us and gotten some sun, you look pale as a ghost."

Mrs. Bennett turned to me. "Angie, you darling girl, how are you?" She took my hand and instantly changed her expression to one of kindly sympathy. "Kimmy told us about your colleague, Lucy, was that her name? A terrible tragedy. Kimmy is just broken up, I know. How are you taking it, my dear?"

I nodded somberly. "Thank you, I'm doing all right. Seems like keeping busy is the best medicine. There's always so much to do at work."

"We hear so many great things about the agency. We're so proud of Kimberley. She's getting some very good accounts, I hear. That Tangento company is very high profile."

I looked over at Kimberley to see if she'd heard what her mother was saying, but she and her father were talking to another couple. If her parents didn't know she'd lost Tangento to me I wasn't going to be the one to tell them.

"Yes, Kimberley is a hard worker, that's for sure!" I said heartily. It was odd to me that the Bennetts were taking such an interest in Kimberley's work at the agency. If you asked my parents about my work they'd be hard pressed to say exactly what it is I do for a living, much less the names of particular clients.

"I think Barry Warner is coming to the party tonight. He works at Tangento. We introduced him to Kimmy a couple of months ago. Such a charming gentleman. He's Southern, you know . . ." She lowered her voice to a conspiratorial tone. "We thought he might be a good match for her, but I guess that didn't work out."

"Really? Well, with affairs of the heart you can never predict," I said, trying to sound worldly. "I haven't actually met Barry Warner yet."

"He's around here somewhere." Trudi waved around the room. "I'd be happy to introduce you. It didn't work out with Kimmy, but he's certainly an eligible gentleman!"

"Thanks, Mrs. Bennett, but I'm not really in the market right now, if you know what I mean."

"Already taken, are you?" Mrs. Bennett winked at me as an image of Eric flashed through my mind, his intense blue gaze, the strength in his arms as he pulled me to him . . . I shook my head to snap out of it.

"Taken, no, unfortunately. Just been too busy at work."

"You're just like our Kimmy then. Are you working on anything we might have heard of?" she asked, probably trying to assess the competition.

"Well, Comet Toothpaste is a client of ours." I answered. "Maybe you've heard of them?" Comet Toothpaste was like Ivory Soap, it had been around so long that everyone knew the name but no one used the product. "We're working on some great new ads for them, to reenergize the brand. 'This is not your grandmother's toothpaste!' type of thing."

Then I learned where Kimberley had inherited the glazed-over expression she got when she was bored. Trudi's face had more glaze than an old-fashioned donut. She had obviously decided that our conversation was not going to advance little Kimmy's career, so I was being dismissed.

"Well, that's very interesting, dear, I'm sure you'll do wonders for them. Now, let me look

around and see who's here that you should meet."
Her head bobbed around like one of those ceramic dogs you see in the back window of cars.

"That's all right, Mrs. Bennett, I'm about to go and get a bite to eat anyway. I think I see some folks I know over there."

"Very well, dear, nice to see you." She turned to greet a white-haired couple that had been waiting for her attention.

I had already ascertained that Eric was not in the foyer with the Bennets, so I moved on to the dining room, a giant room with silk wallpaper and oak paneling on the walls, and a box-beamed ceiling. A server was offering champagne in crystal flutes, so I took one, just for something to do with my hands. When I sipped it I was pleased to find it didn't have a metallic taste. I took several big swallows. Because of my empty stomach I immediately felt dizzy, but not in a bad way. Getting drunk seemed like a nice way to make the time pass. Eric was taller than most people so it should have been easy to spot him. I scanned the room, trying to look casual and a bit bored while the butterflies in my stomach leaped and cavorted with concrete wings. The nerves calmed down when I didn't see him, but were replaced by disappointment.

I was standing next to a small buffet table where a man in a chef's hat was carving thin slices of rare roast beef. I watched the pink juices well up and drip down over the carving knife. I drew closer and stared at the meat. Suddenly I was ravenously hungry. I imagined leaping onto the table and grabbing the whole roast, tearing into it like a hyena.

"Would you care for a slice, Ma'am?" The server smiled at me.

"Yes, please." I took the plate he offered and held it up to my nose, took a deep whiff. No, I had no desire whatsoever to eat the gray and pink mass on my plate. Whatever I was hungry for, it wasn't beef.

"Would you like me to get you a fork, or are you just going to use your teeth?"

I'd know that voice anywhere.

Not to mention the smell. As soon as I put the beef down Eric's subtle but insinuating fragrance wafted over me. I gaped at him for several seconds before I realized he was holding his hand out. I shook his hand, embarrassed to note that my palms were sweating. In his immaculate black tuxedo and sparkling white shirt he fit right into the scene at the Bennetts', but for the long hair. He turned my hand palm down and bowed over it like a Knight of the Round Table.

"Angela, we meet again, so soon. I'm sorry I missed you at my office on Friday." Of course he would be aware of my blatant pursuit of him. I wondered if he knew that I'd come to the party looking for him as well, but at the moment his eyes gave nothing away.

"What are you doing here?" I tried for surprise in my tone, but I wasn't very successful.

"Some of my real estate dealings have brought me

into contact with Dr. Bennett. He owns a number of buildings in the city. But you would know that, wouldn't you, since you live in one?" Eric smiled. "I was hoping to see you here, since you work with Kimberley. That's really why I came."

I felt a warm glow in the pit of my stomach. He came to see me. But why did he make me wait two days? Because he was busy doing things at the House of Usher that he didn't want me to know about?

I don't wish to confuse or frighten you. Ask me what you want to know.

I looked at him sharply. I was distinctly sure I hadn't heard his actual voice.

A waiter conveniently walked by, and I grabbed another glass of champagne. I swallowed it down in one gulp and made my decision. Some questions had to be answered before we could go on.

"I was there last night, at the House of Usher. I want to know what you were doing there and if it had anything to do with what happened to Lucy." My voice was rising to a squeak.

"Perhaps we should find a more quiet spot to discuss this, Angela." He took my elbow gently and steered me out of the room.

When Eric touched me illicit visions appeared in my head, of doing things that didn't involve talking. I was amazed at the power of my lust for Eric. It swept away concerns that before I met him would have paralyzed me. I took a deep breath to clear my head but it didn't work, so I moved a few steps away from him.

"There's a little garden in the back of the house. Through the kitchen," I said. "We can talk out there."

Eric nodded and followed me. We dodged the hurrying waiters in the kitchen and opened the back door. There was a small stone bench near the fountain. We sat down and Eric turned to face me.

"So, what would you care to discuss? I'm at your service."

I took a deep breath, wishing I'd brought more champagne with me. "I was there last night, with Steve, at the House of Usher. I recorded the ceremony."

"What ceremony?"

Anger burned in my chest. Why was he being obtuse when he had just said he would answer my questions? "I know it was you, I saw your ring!" I grabbed his left hand and pulled it up to my face. His pinkie finger was bare.

I let his hand drop to my lap.

"Oh God," I whispered. "I don't know what's real anymore."

Eric started to answer me but he was interrupted by the sound of voices raised in argument, coming from the driveway. One of the voices was Kimberley's.

From where we sat I could see down the driveway to where Kimberley was standing with her back against the hood of her car. Facing away from me was a man with the wide shoulders of a football player. Even with the gurgling sounds of the fountain their raised voices were easily heard.

Kimberley was laughing, a bitter sound. "Oh, please. Don't try to play 'poor me' at this point. It just doesn't become you. I'm not asking for much anyway, you know it could be a lot more. Money, for instance. But obviously, I don't need money, just a little helping hand. So, do this for me and I'll forget everything."

"I can't do it, Kimberley, I don't have that kind of power!" The man had a strong Southern accent. Unless the party was full of Southerners I had a pretty good idea who she was talking to. I stood up and quietly moved closer to them, but still under cover of the ferns and trees.

"Now, now, don't be hard on yourself, I know you can be very persuasive." Kimberley's voice was seductive now. "So do it soon. Monday's good for me. Now, I'd better get back to the party. My parents will be wondering where I've gone."

Without waiting for an answer Kimberley turned around and walked away. I held my breath and crouched behind a big fern. She passed by without noticing me. I glanced over at Eric but the bench was in shadow. The man lit a cigarette and walked down the driveway. I heard the drone of the mechanical gate opening and closing.

I went back and sat on the bench next to Eric, who was staring at the ground as if deep in thought.

"Eric?" I touched him lightly on the sleeve.

"What was that all about?"

"That was my new client, Barry Warner. Kimberley is asking him for something, I don't know what. But I'll probably find out soon. She mentioned Monday."

"Barry Warner works for Tangento, I believe?"

"Yes," I answered, "but how do you know all these things?"

I couldn't read Eric's expression. "I meet many people in my work. Our paths must have crossed at some time or another. Are you ready to go?"

"Where?"

He leaned close and touched my cheekbone. "I'd like to see where you live," he whispered in my ear.

His smell permeated my brain and started an avalanche of endorphins. It wasn't until much later that I realized he hadn't answered any of my questions.

There are a few nights every September or October in San Francisco when the fog doesn't roll in and put a damp chill on skin and spirits. The air stays warm, the smell of flowers lingers in the air, and people stay out in shirtsleeves until midnight. These are also the nights when tempers flare and guns go off, and police sirens are heard until the sun rises. Hot nights make people crazy. Maybe that was my excuse.

From the top of the hill in Pacific Heights we could see the lights of the city shining like a well-adorned Christmas tree. The moon was almost full, creating an eerie doppelgänger of daylight that illuminated the mansions around us in all their glory. Eric was reining in his natural gait to keep pace with me. As we walked he removed his jacket, loosened his tie, and rolled up his sleeves. Just the sight of his sinewy forearms set a rippling thrill through my body.

The Angie that I had been all my life—the serious, responsible, cautious Angie—had been rolled up like a rug and tossed into the attic of my consciousness. I could still hear her talking, but she seemed powerless and far away. She was telling me that going off alone with this man was unwise, that I was ignoring all the signs of danger. She said that he could only be two things: run-of-the-mill evil, a crazy man, but a human one; or something else, something bigger, a kind of evil she couldn't begin to fathom.

But as I watched Eric lope alongside me like a strolling tiger, head turning to sniff the air and take in the sights, I didn't care what he was. The things the old Angie was trying to preserve—my job, friends, the security of understanding the way the world worked, even my very life—they all seemed unimportant. Many people risked life and limb for an experience—skydivers, racecar drivers, everyone who'd ever attempted to climb Mount Everest. Experience expands and priorities shift.

We arrived at my building and Eric held the door for me after I unlocked it. We crossed the lobby and I pushed the elevator button. When Mr. Bennett remodeled our apartment building he kept the old elevator, the kind with a mesh gate instead of a sliding door, because it had Art Deco bronze paneling that could never be replicated. I watched the floor numbers light up in descending order, consciously not looking at Eric because I could feel his gaze burning into my face and I knew if I looked at him I would certainly blush. The gate was heavy and stiff and took both my arms to open, but Eric slid it open with one finger. Then I stared at my feet for eight floors.

We went into the living room and I sat down on the couch, facing the sweeping beam of the lighthouse on Alcatraz Island. Eric tossed his suit jacket over the back of the sofa and a faint smell of *eau de Eric* wafted over me. He walked over to the bar in the corner and examined the bottles. He poured us each some Scotch, then went into the kitchen. I heard him getting ice. He put our drinks on the table, and then he took me by the shoulders and turned me so my back was facing him.

He started to gently comb my hair with his fingers. My neck tingled under his touch.

"Ah, Angela, you beautiful, innocent girl. So young . . ." He sounded sad.

"Why do say that? I'm twenty-eight, hardly a girl. How old are you, anyway?"

"Much older than I look. Too old for you. But I can't seem to resist you, Angela. You have a beauty that transcends time."

If that was a line it was a good one. His lips brushed my neck and his hands slid lightly up and down my arms. A warm glow spread over my body. I leaned against his chest and put my head on his shoulder. With one hand he stroked my face from forehead to chin. I felt his heart beat, a delicate susurration deep in his chest. His breath on my neck was cool and fragrant. A now familiar feeling began to take hold of me. The laws of gravity were repealed and I was lifted, weightless, my body floating, unattached to anything except the hands that were stroking me, the mouth that was sliding down the long tendon in the side of my neck.

It took willpower I didn't know I possessed to pull away from Eric, but I did it, and stood up on unsteady feet. I wanted him on my terms this time. I needed to know if he would still want me if I expressed needs and desires of my own, if I were to take control.

"Is something wrong, Angela?"

He was sprawled on the couch, his long body filling it from end to end. His face, and I found this maddening, was completely calm, even a little amused. Not a hair on his head was mussed. The lights of the city were reflected in his eyes, shimmering like refractions from a prism, so they had no depth, no window into his soul. Did these encounters mean anything to him? Was I a mouse being toyed with by a bored cat?

Frustration drove me to take an antithetical action. I had always felt most vulnerable when I was nude, so I usually hid from the few men I had been with, slipping off my clothes under cover of darkness or under the sheets. Even Andy had only seen me naked a handful of times, usually by accident. But now I peeled off my clothes piece by piece, slowly and unhurriedly, holding Eric's gaze, not allowing his eyes to stray until I stood naked in front of him, hiding nothing, offering everything.

Eric's expression changed. What had seemed to be arrogance turned to gentleness and a sweet yearning. He slid to his knees in front of me and bent his head, as if I was an altar at which he was praying.

"Angela, you are perfection," he whispered.

I closed the distance between us, wrapped my arms around him. He pressed his lips against my stomach, then lifted me as easily as a feather.

"Where's your room?" he asked.

Chapter 14

Kissing Eric was when his scent was at its most overwhelming. Its effect was like laughing gas, beginning with numbness in the extremities and moving toward disorientation and euphoria. I couldn't understand it except that maybe I was in love, and this is what the experts mean by the power of pheromones.

At some point I noticed that Eric hadn't removed his own clothes but it didn't seem to matter. The sensation was of six hands stroking my body, three pairs of lips kissing me. Just the feel of his long hair as it swept along my skin sent sparks of electricity down my spine. I wasn't sure what was happening or to which part of me. My body had become a single organ of pure feeling. I could say I had an orgasm, but that would not begin to describe the feeling. I experienced a climax that encompassed my entire body, from my hair to my toenails. I bit my fist to keep from screaming.

In the midst of this storm of sensation I felt a pain like lightning and a pleasure that was too intense for words. I felt Eric enter me in a way that joined our very souls together. My bones melted, my blood coursed through my veins like a flood tide, rushing to pour into him and join us together at our very molecules. At the apex of this union Eric entered my mind and his thoughts became mine.

Eric sits in a room with walls made of rough stone, writing with a quill pen by the light of a flickering candle. A man dressed in priest's robes comes up behind him, puts his arms around his chest, his lips to Eric's neck.

A flash of red, then another vision.

Eric is sitting with Lucy on her couch. I recognize the abstract painting on the wall behind them. There are two wineglasses on the table. Lucy is laughing, her head thrown back. Eric leans toward her, takes her in an embrace. Her arms wind around his neck.

Behind my eyelids I saw the red licks of flame again, but this time instead of a vision I felt my connection with Eric break. I was falling, tumbling, out of control, into an ocean of darkness. Then, oblivion.

I awoke in my bed, facing the window, alone. From the utter stillness of the city I could tell it was predawn, sometime between three and six. I stretched and rolled over. Eric was sitting in my desk chair, dressed in his white shirt and suit pants.

His shirtsleeves were rolled up to his elbows, his hair tangled around his shoulders. In the moonlight I could see streaks of tears on his cheeks.

"Angela, I don't know how it came to this. I have tried to live virtuously, I have tried to fight against my nature, and now I see I have failed."

I sat up and pulled the sheet around my chest. "You know what's happening to me, don't you?"

Eric nodded, and then dropped his head into his hands.

I realized it was time to ask for the truth. Whatever the answer was, I knew I wasn't going to pull away from him now.

"Eric, are you a vampire?" As soon as the words came out I felt both relieved and completely insane.

Eric came over to sit next to me on the bed. He took my hand and turned it over, as if he was reading my palm. He traced the blue vein that ran from my thumb up my wrist. Finally he looked into my eyes.

"If I tell you, you will not believe me, and that is as it should be. This incredulity has a protective property for humans, so they do not learn truths with which they cannot live."

"Eric, I love . . . I would love to know you. I need to know."

He turned to look out the window. "This is my favorite time of night, when everything is quiet. Let's take a walk."

Eric waited silently while I put on jeans and a sweater, then we descended the Pacific Heights hill. When we reached the water we turned right and walked along Jefferson Street, through the heart of Fisherman's Wharf. So bright and cheesy during the day, filled with tourists buying Alcatraz T-shirts and clam chowder, the wharf at 4:30 A.M. was a time portal to the nineteenth century. Fishermen in yellow slickers hauled nets and buoys, getting ready to go out to sea. Fog shrouded the most egregious of the tourist traps, like Hooters and the Wax Museum, but pools of light cast from the old-fashioned street lamps picked out the red brick of the buildings and the glossy gray cobblestones in the streets.

When we reached the Hyde Street Pier Eric picked up his pace. I could hardly keep up as he rushed down the rough wooden pier, but then he stopped so abruptly I almost ran into him. He was staring at the *Balclutha*, a three-masted sailing ship from the 1800s that San Francisco had turned into a museum.

"What is this?" he asked, his voice low.

"A ship." I couldn't understand what he was finding so fascinating, especially when I wanted him to be finding *me* fascinating.

"Yes, but why is it here, now?"

"Read the placard." I pointed it out. I already knew what the ship was. We'd done a photo shoot there not very long ago, but I was miffed and didn't feel like telling him.

He read the placard, and then he walked back over to me. His face was filled with delight, like a

kid at Christmas, and I instantly felt guilty about
being angry with him. Seeing him happy made me
realize how melancholy he normally was, and I
wished it had been me that put that smile on his
face, and not a creaky old boat.

"It's the *Balclutha*," he said.

"You've seen it before?"

"I've sailed on that ship. I went around Cape
Horn on it, from Scotland to San Francisco. How
wonderful to see it again." He gazed at it again,
like he wanted to run up and hug the mast.

"Eric, that ship's been mothballed for seventy
years."

His eyes moved back to my face. The melancholy look had returned, and it was even deeper
now. I grabbed his hand and pulled him onto a
bench.

"I'd say now's as good a time as any to start
telling me the truth, don't you?"

Eric kept my hand in his, but he looked at the
ship, not at me, as he talked. His voice was low and
even, as if he was reciting a poem.

"My human life began in 1591 in the south of
France. My given name was Cyprien."

"Cyprien," I repeated, trying to pronounce it
the same way Eric did. "That's a more appropriate
name than Eric Taylor, for sure. What was your last
name?"

He shrugged. "It doesn't matter anymore. They
are all long gone."

"I'm sorry." So his line had died out. There

weren't even any distant relatives for him to keep an eye on.

He continued. "I was born the last of four boys. My father was a merchant, and although he was successful, he was not rich enough to set up all of his sons in business. As the youngest, I was chosen to enter the religious life. This was fairly common then when a family had more children than it could support, as it took care of the child while providing spiritual tithe for the family in the afterlife. At the age of sixteen I was sent to join an order of Franciscan friars.

"I didn't know how to feel about this. As a young man, with all the feelings and desires of a young man, I felt trapped. But I was also very pious, and began to believe that this was what God had chosen for me. I undertook my duties with zeal and after several years began to feel at peace with my life and work.

"The monastery was in the country, several hours by horse from our town. It was close to a small village where the townspeople supplied the brothers with the physical necessities of life and we provided them with the spiritual ones. Periodically, a brother would be called to the village to minister to someone who had died suddenly, usually visited in their bed by an unknown plague that took them in the night, leaving them white and contorted in their death throes. Some townspeople whispered of demons, witches, or even of vampires, but this was a time when diseases ran rampant and life was precarious at best, and most people took little notice."

Eric stopped talking for a moment, and in the stillness I could hear the sound of the water lapping against the hull of the ship, and the creaking of the masts and rigging.

"An older friar, Brother Vincent, undertook to help me with my studies. A tall, pale, almost ghostly man, Brother Vincent was said to have a disease of the blood that made him delicate and sensitive to the sun. He kept mostly to his room and was rarely seen before dark. He was also a charismatic figure—handsome, intelligent, and kind. Many of the villagers sought him out especially for confessions or other services. He was compelling to me in a strange way I could not name. I found myself falling in love with him.

"Brother Vincent began coming to my room late at night when the monastery was silent. He would take me in his arms and embrace me. He never removed his robes or mine, and I never knew what was happening to me except that it induced feelings of euphoria that in my long life have never been equaled.

"During this time I began to change physically. I became sensitive to light and began to develop headaches. I lost my appetite and slept for hours on end. I also began to hear whispers all around me, the voices of other friars drifting through the walls even when I knew they weren't speaking out loud. I began to think I was dying of one of the diseases that were cursing the village."

"Did you tell Vincent what was happening, ask him for help?"

"One night I confessed my fears to him. He held me against his chest and talked to me without speaking, entered my mind and filled it with his words. He told me he loved me, that he had looked for years for someone to share his life with, and he had chosen me to be his companion. He was undertaking to change me into a different kind of being, a creature that could live forever.

"He explained to me that tonight would be the night when I would change over. He told me that he was going to kill me. I would feel pain, but then I would wake up in my new body, to my new life. Then he wrapped me in the embrace that he had given me so many times before."

I closed my eyes against a rush of feeling so strong it made me feel physically ill. I wanted not to believe this story, but the parallels with my own experience were too uncanny.

"Only this time he didn't stop. At the edge of the pleasure I felt panic. My limbs became numb, a black sky full of silver stars spun in front of my closed eyes. I felt a crushing pain in my chest, like a huge rock had been dropped on my heart. I tried to push it off, tried to push Vincent off, but he clung to me. For the first time I felt intense pain, searing burns where his teeth bit into me. The agony radiated down my arms and legs until my whole body felt on fire. Then there was nothing."

Eric looked so stricken that I shook his arm gently, trying to break him out of the trance that he seemed to be in. But he didn't even look at me, his haunted eyes stayed fixed on the past.

"Out of the darkness I saw a light, a warm glowing light pulsating with love, and I knew that light was heaven. I started to go toward the light but it retreated, became smaller and smaller and the darkness greater, until it was only a pinprick. Then it disappeared and I was desolate.

"I floated in the blackness, as if in the depths of the ocean where no sun could ever touch, and I cried out, 'My Father, why hast thou forsaken me?' In response I heard only silence, and I knew I was alone.

"Finally I heard a voice, and it was Vincent. I heard him as if over a vast distance, calling my name. I moved toward his voice and finally I woke up, and Vincent was holding me and shaking me, rubbing a wet cloth across my face.

"Enraged, I tried to throw Vincent off me, but I was too weak. I flailed at him with my fists, crying, 'You knew, you knew I would be damned! I saw the gates of heaven close in my face! I will never be saved, never! God has forsaken me!'

"Vincent simply held me and ignored my fists, stroking my hair away from my sweating forehead. He said, 'You have no need of heaven, Cyprien. Not any more.' It wasn't long before I found out the true nature of my new existence. Within days of my conversion I was overcome by feelings of hunger the likes of which I couldn't have imagined. I found myself picturing cutting people with my fingernails or with my teeth, putting my face in the blood and drinking it.

"When I told this to Vincent he just nodded. 'The time has come,' he said. We went to the village after midnight on an evening with no moon. I found I could see as if it were daylight. Vincent went right to a cottage door and opened it, motioned me to go inside. It was the home of a family who had recently lost a child, and Vincent had been there administering the last rites.

"A man, a woman, and a young girl were sleeping in a bed in the one-room cottage. I faltered, and Vincent pushed me forward. His voice in my head said, 'We'll take the girl, she will be sweetest.' Vincent swept up to the bed, making no noise, and lifted the covers off the girl. Her chest rose and fell with the rhythm of her breath. She wore a muslin shift that had lifted up over her legs and hips. I looked at her beautiful skin and felt nothing but the desire for her blood. Vincent leaned over her, lifted her up, looking for all the world like a young lover. He placed his face to her neck and the smell of the blood flowing into his mouth was so strong I stepped back.

"He lifted his head and beckoned me over. I looked at Vincent and saw his face, white and dripping with blood, fangs bared, eyes wild. 'No!' I screamed out loud. 'You are the devil!'

    "The parents heard me and woke up. They struggled out of bed, calling for help. I escaped, leaving Vincent in the house. I ran to the edge of town where I knew there was a cliff, a precipitous drop down to a river. I ran toward it and found that I could very nearly fly, my strength and speed were so great. I arrived at the cliff and before I had a chance to stop myself I ran right over the edge."

Chapter 15

Eric was holding my hand so tightly I thought my bones would break. I put my other hand on his and said gently, "Eric, you're hurting me." When he didn't respond I shouted the same words. He looked at me like he couldn't figure out who I was, but then he smiled distractedly and let go of my hand. "I'm sorry, I didn't realize."

I waited for him to continue and when he didn't I asked, "So what happened then? Obviously you didn't die."

Eric shook his head. "Obviously. I found out quickly that it's not as easy as it looks. I never tried it again, by the way. I've thought of it, many times, especially now that I know how to do it correctly, but I found I never again had the stomach for it. I suppose I'm a coward at heart."

"What happened to Vincent?"

"I went back to him. I had to. I had so much to learn. I never loved him again, though. In fact I despised him, and he knew it. We parted soon after. I left the monastery and entered the world. I changed my name. I change it quite often, as the styles change."

"So, what have you been doing all these years?" I was pleased when he laughed. The trance seemed to be broken.

"I move around the world, never staying in one place too long. I have studied in some of the best universities. I've been an art dealer in Brussels, a diamond merchant in South Africa, a stock trader in New York City. I've even been here in San Francisco, once before, as I told you. I came for the gold rush."

"You were a gold miner?" It was hard to imagine Eric swinging a pick.

"No, no. A financier. I sold people equipment in exchange for a piece of their claim. One thing I've learned about business in the last four hundred years: never be the miner, be the guy who sells him the pick."

I imagined Eric over all those years, changing costumes, changing his name, haunting the periphery of human society, profiting from human commerce, living off human blood. All those years. All those people.

The questions I had wanted to ask Eric retreated from my lips. The image of Lucy and Eric in her house flashed in my mind, but I didn't ask the question. Suddenly I understood why I had shied away from asking questions every time the opportunity arose. I realized what Eric meant by the protective factor of ignorance. Had Eric killed Lucy? Had he killed Lilith? And if he hadn't killed *them*, what about the countless others over the years? The truth, if there was such a thing, was incompatible with my feelings for Eric.

The horizon past the Golden Gate Bridge was beginning to take on the unmistakable pinkish tinge of impending dawn. Eric stood and helped me up.

"As you can imagine, Angela, it is about time for me to leave."

"Just stay for another few minutes?"

Eric smiled and put his arm around me. I leaned into his shoulder and we listened to the yelp of seal lions as they arrived to begin their shifts as tourist attractions at Pier 39. For a moment it felt almost normal, two lovers sitting together, enjoying a tranquil moment. Eric planted a soft kiss on my cheek that caused my heart to lurch, it was so tender.

When the sun burst from the shelter of the East Bay hills and shone a laser beam into Eric's translucent eyes, I felt his whole body cringe. He threw up a hand to block the light. I cursed myself for asking him to stay with me.

"Do you have any sunglasses?" he asked.

I dug in my purse and handed him the only pair I had, oversize Jackie O glasses with pearls in the hinges. I thought they would look silly, but the glasses only emphasized his masculinity, like a kilt on a Scotsman or diamond earrings on a muscle-bound rapper.

"What's going to happen to you now?" I asked, as he pulled his collar closed and buttoned his shirt.

"I'll develop wrinkles that a gallon of Botox couldn't cure," he answered, and I was reassured by his joking. But still, he pulled me to my feet without wasting another second.

"Should we call a taxi?"

He shook his head. "Just close your eyes," he said.

I felt him scoop me up in his arms. Then I sensed that he was running, but only because the air was pressing into my face like I was riding in a convertible at seventy miles an hour. There was no feeling of feet pounding the pavement, no strain whatsoever in his body. It had taken us twenty minutes to walk down the pier and we were back at my door in less than sixty seconds. He put me on the ground and I almost toppled over.

"Careful there," he said, holding my arm.

"I guess traveling at the speed of light can make a person dizzy." I looked up and saw Eric crouched in the shadow of the awning.

"Let's go inside," I said.

"No. I must go home."

I wanted to ask him when I would see him again, but by the time I had cleared my throat he was gone, taking my sunglasses with him.

* * *

I went into the kitchen and poured myself a glass of water, eyeing the bananas in the fruit basket and the box of water crackers Kimberley had left on the counter. How long had it been since I'd eaten anything? I counted on my fingers. Wednesday night was my last meal. I'd had part of a pretzel on Saturday morning and two glasses of champagne last night. The longest I'd ever gone without eating before was twenty-four hours, when my sister and I tried a grapefruit juice diet we'd read about in *Seventeen*. Thea and I had both woken up in the middle of the night feeling dizzy and sick. We sneaked downstairs and ate two peanut butter and jelly sandwiches and an ice cream bar each. So much for the grapefruit diet.

It was now going on four days and I wasn't feeling the slightest desire for food. Sure, I felt nauseated, but it was a different kind of nausea, and it only bothered me during the day.

"What is happening to me?" I asked out loud.

The story Eric had told me last night proved what? That *he* believed he was a vampire. Or was he just trying to make *me* believe it? I thought of the old movie *Gaslight*, which I'd watched six times in a row at college because Ingrid Berg-man was so good in it. In the film Charles Boyer, who plays her husband, plots to convince Ingrid that she is insane. Was Eric trying to gas-light me?

I tried to examine the case rationally. First there were my "symptoms": nausea, lack of appetite, and intolerance of light. Then there were Eric's manifestations: incalculable speed and strength, clairvoyance, remarkable healing ability, intolerance of light, and, how to describe his power over me? Inhuman sexiness?

Yet none of these things were facts. They were impressions, feelings, sensations, chimera of the body and mind. Eric could be inducing my experiences with drugs, perhaps hypnosis, creating an illusory world in which I could believe the impossible. But whether Eric himself was delusional, or was trying to create delusions in me, my reaction should have been the same—to get the hell away from him. And yet that simple response seemed completely inconceivable.

Kimberley, unlike me, went with her parents to church every Sunday morning. She had left the newspaper on the table and I flipped through it automatically. There was an election coming up and the front-page article was about how each candidate was going to solve the homeless problem. The current mayor's solution was to confiscate their shopping carts. Normally this would have gotten me angry enough to forget my own troubles. I tried to muster up some indignation, but it wasn't working; I was still far more concerned about myself. I flipped to the next section, the Bay Area news, and read the first headline.

SF WOMAN IS POSSIBLE 'VAMPIRE' VICTIM

A woman found dead in her Richmond District home is the possible victim of a 'vampire' attacker, sources close to the investigation say. Lucy Weston, age 30, an ad agency executive, was found in her home by friends on Thursday evening. Although autopsy results were not yet available, sources said that the cause of death was most likely massive blood loss. The victim had been wounded in the neck.

"We may be looking for a delusional person," one source said, "someone who believes they are a vampire."

The rest of the words swam as tears pooled in my eyes. This was no chimera, no illusion. Lucy's death, and the way it happened, was a fact. But who did it was still up for speculation. The phone rang. Automatically I checked the wall clock above the table. It was one of those plastic cats with bubble eyes that turn back and forth. I'd put it up and Kimberley had left it there, a fact that surprised me. Mr. Cat said it was ten o'clock. It had to be my mother. Nobody else would call me so early on a Sunday.

"Hello, may I speak to Angie McCaffrey?" It was a man's voice I didn't recognize.

"This is she."

"Ms. McCaffrey, this is Chris Neeley from the *Examiner*. I'd like to ask you a few questions about your colleague, Lucy Weston—"

"I have no comment!" I shouted.

"Please, Ms. McCaffrey, I know this must be a difficult—"

I hung up the phone and it immediately rang again. I let it ring six times, hoping the machine would answer, but it was turned off.

I picked up the phone and yelled, "I have no comment, now don't call me again!"

"Angie? This is your mother."

"Oh God, hi Mom, I'm sorry. I thought you were someone else."

"Well, that hardly matters. I don't think anyone deserves to be spoken to that harshly, do you?"

"No," I muttered.

"Who was it, anyway?"

"Oh, just a reporter, wanting some information about a client. Can you imagine, calling on a Sunday morning?"

"Yes, but I would think you could be a little more polite, Angie. I didn't raise you to yell like that. By the way, speaking of polite, I called you last Thursday and invited you over for tonight. May we look forward to the pleasure of your company at dinner?"

The thought of eating made me queasy, but I told my mother I'd be over that afternoon.

I left the apartment to go to my parents at three. I had taken the phone off the hook and spent the day napping and reading the newspaper, trying to keep from worrying—about Eric, Les, Kimberley, and even Barry Warner. It didn't work, of course. Even as I slept my dreams worried.

My Mini was parked in front of a fire hydrant, the only place I could find when I returned from the Hall of Justice the day before. A police car drove by, so I rushed to the car and jumped in, breathing a sigh of relief when the cruiser turned the corner. Blocking a fire hydrant cost two hundred and fifty bucks, a fact I knew from experience.

Ever since I left my house I had been squinting. I rifled through my purse for my sunglasses, only to remember that I'd given them to Eric. I reached into the back seat to see if I'd left a baseball cap that I wear on the rare occasions when I go running. Instead of the cap, my hand touched human flesh. I screamed at the top of my lungs.

Chapter 16

It was Les. He hadn't shaved in days and was wearing the same clothes he'd had on the day we went to Lucy's house. His short hair was matted on one side.

"Oh my God, Les, I almost peed in my pants! What are you doing in my car?"

Les rubbed his eyes. "I needed a place to sleep, and also I wanted to talk to you. Where are you headed, by the way?"

"My parents' house in Noe Valley."

"Okay. Drop me off at the BART station at Sixteenth and Mission."

"How did you get in the car?"

Les reached around and produced a short, flat piece of metal. "Slim Jim."

"Slim Jim," I repeated, imitating his matter-of-fact voice. "Have you overdosed on *Cops*? You can't just go breaking into people's cars!"

"I knew you wouldn't mind."

"You knew I wouldn't mind? This car is six months old. If you broke the lock I'd have to kill you."

"No, you wouldn't." He grinned and a semblance of his old cockiness returned. He was still cute, even in dire straits.

"You're right, I wouldn't." I faced forward and turned on the engine. "How are you, anyway? Are you all right?"

"Oh, I'm fucking great, Angie, just great. The police are watching my apartment, I'm sleeping in cars, they're questioning all my friends, what could be better?"

"I'm sorry, Les, but I told you not to run away," I said, thinking I was sounding a lot like my mother.

"Did you make the videotape like I told you? Did you get anything?"

"I'm not sure. But I took the video to the police, like you wanted."

Les lurched toward me, banging the back of my seat. "What did they say, are they going to arrest anyone?"

"The inspector wasn't convinced. He said they've been watching these people for a while and they don't do anything illegal. He took a copy of the video, but I think he was doing it just to humor me."

I glanced in the mirror and saw Les rubbing his stubbly chin.

"You've got to go deeper, Angie. There must be another place, or get them to take you to their home, something . . ."

"I am deeper, Les. Deeper than you think."

We reached the corner of Sixteenth Street and Mission. The street was busy with loiterers, Sunday shoppers, and people moving in and out of the BART station, San Francisco's subway. I pulled into the bus lane.

"Look at me, Angie," Les said. When I did he stared intently into my face.

"You met the guy too, didn't you?"

I didn't answer, but he didn't wait for a response. "Angie, he could be your way in. Get him to talk to you, get him to tell you what happened with Lucy. I'm sure he's the one . . ." Les was trembling with excitement, leaning over me.

"Stop!" I yelled. "You don't know him. How do I know it's not you, Les, and I'm helping you cover your ass by finding a fall guy?"

Les exhaled slowly through pursed lips. "He's got to you, Angie, hasn't he? You sound just like Lucy. You look like her too, come to think of it. Pale and kind of sick. Wild in the eyes." He looked at me sadly. Then he reached out and put his hand on my shoulder.

"Angie, there's a guy, his name is Nicolai Blaloc, he studies vampires. He might be able to help you break the spell. I found him when I was looking for someone to help me get Lucy away from the coven."

"And did he help you?" *And do I want to get away from Eric?*

"No. Lucy wouldn't talk to him."

"Where is this Nicolai?"

"I don't know, I only talked to him on the phone. He's got a website called vampirehunter.com." He reached for the door handle.

"Les, how can I find you?"

"You can't. I'll get in touch when I can. Be careful, Angie. Sounds like maybe you need more help than me."

In a moment he disappeared into the crowd around the train station.

To get to my parents' house I took Dolores Street, a broad boulevard with green center islands planted with palm trees. I passed Mission Dolores, the street's namesake, and for reasons unknown I found myself parking. The old Mission Dolores, a whitewashed adobe building with broad squat columns and a red tile roof, was built in 1790, making it the oldest building in the city. I'd seen pictures of it taken in the 1800s, looking almost as it did now, but surrounded by nothing but mud and farm animals. The grand cathedral that was built next to it overshadowed the small adobe, but when tourists came for a tour it was the old mission they went to first.

The neighborhood I grew up in was only a few blocks away over the next hill, and we used to go to services fairly regularly at St. Philip's Church. On very special occasions like Christmas Eve or Easter we would come to Mission Dolores Cathedral to hear Mass.

I climbed the wide concrete stairway into the church. It was empty, but the smell of incense from morning services still hung in the air. The statue of Jesus on the cross glowed as if it had just been painted. The blood from his hands, feet, chest and forehead was clearly visible from the back of the room. His heavy-lidded eyes gazed up to the sky, presumably waiting for deliverance from his earthly trials. I sat on the farthest pew and stared at the statue. Images from the story Eric had told me flooded my mind. Eric had been religious at one time, so much so that he was ready to dedicate his life to God. I wondered what he thought of Him now. I was suddenly reminded of something my father used to say, "There are no atheists in fox-holes." Since I was there, I decided to pray.

"Dear God," I said silently, "Please watch over me. I feel I'm in over my head here and I don't know who else to ask for help. You know a thing or two about evil, and protecting people from it, so maybe you'll send me a sign."

I wasn't sure what to say about Eric, but then I realized that if there really was a God He knew all about Eric and my feelings for him. "Guide me in the right direction with Eric. And please watch over Lucy, and I hope she's up there with you now." I crossed myself for good measure.

When I left the church the weather was glorious, or what I would have called glorious before I began detesting the sun. It was a perfect October day, bright and clear and about seventy-five degrees, with a salty breeze blowing in off the bay. I enjoyed the warmth, but the light was oppressive. I found the baseball cap in the back seat and pulled it low over my eyes before I pointed the car up the hill toward my parents' house. Hopefully I could get in, have dinner, and get out without revealing too much about what had been happening. It would be difficult. Normally my parents pumped me like an oil derrick for information about my life.

My parents live on a quiet street in Noe Valley, in the house my grandparents bought in 1955. My grandfather was a firefighter, like my own father. Grandpa died in a warehouse fire when I was a baby, and from then on we all lived together, my parents, my grandmother, my brother and sister and me, all sharing one bathroom. I'd always been able to shower faster than anyone I knew.

My father was trimming a hedge in the postage stamp-sized front yard. Lean and wiry, Frank Mc-Caffrey looked more like my brother than my father, which was understandable, since he'd had me when he was only eighteen. The only indications that he was middle-aged were the wrinkles around his eyes when he laughed, which was often.

Dad put down the shears when I pulled into the driveway. "Ma'am, you can't park here, this is private property." He scowled menacingly.

I held up both hands in surrender. "Get your licks in now," I said.

Dad came over and enveloped me in a bear hug. He smelled of fresh cut grass and sweat. "Glad you came, honey. We read about Lucy Weston in the newspaper this morning."

I squeezed my dad back, knowing that this was all he would say on the subject. He'd experienced deaths a few times as a firefighter, and it seemed he handled it with beer and silence.

"Go in and see your mom, she's been worried about you."

I opened the door and stepped into our front hall. The house I grew up in was what the real estate agents call a "storybook cottage," meaning it was really small. The living room was on the left, with stairs on the right leading to three tiny bedrooms and the bath. Down the hall were a dining room and a recently remodeled kitchen with a deck over-looking the back yard. Everything but the kitchen and bathroom was circa 1895.

The sounds of a gamelan orchestra filled the house, sounding to me like a hundred pots being banged rhythmically. My mother's taste in music was eclectic.

Mom was right in the middle of making spanako-pita when I walked in, spreading cheese and spinach onto thin sheets of filo dough, surrounded by an ex-plosion of dishes and pans. She refused to wash a pot or even put anything away while she was cook-ing for fear of interrupting the creative process. I had learned a lot about cooking from my mother, but I feared the knowledge was getting rusty from disuse.

"Hi Mom, I thought we were having meatloaf . . ."

My mother held up a hand, requesting silence. She lifted a delicate package of filo dough and spinach and deftly folded the rectangle into a triangle, over and over, like two soldiers folding the flag. When she was done she did one more while I watched in silence. She added the last two to a baking pan already holding a dozen others and popped it into the oven. She wiped her hands on a dishtowel and only then did she come over and give me a hug.

Her ample bosom pressed into my chest. That was one thing I hadn't inherited from my mom. Nor the silky blond hair she wore clipped back from her face with two barrettes.

"If you want meatloaf, you have to make your reservations early." She held me at arm's length. "So, how are you doing, sweetie?"

I just couldn't say "fine," like I had with everyone else. Tears started in the corners of my eyes and I pulled away so she wouldn't see them. "Are Frankie and Thea coming?" I asked.

"Frankie will be home anytime now. He's at the library studying. Thea's doing a cocktail party tonight so she won't be coming."

Thea was twenty-five and, having inherited my mother's culinary talents, she had opened her own catering business. Frankie was nineteen, going to San Francisco State University, majoring in creative writing and living at home to save money. Creative writing was a waste of time, according to my father. He had said the same thing about my degree in theater, but still he came to my graduation from Cal Arts and cried. Neither he nor my mother attended college, since they were married and changing my diapers when they should have been rushing frats and sororities.

I sat on a stool at the kitchen bar and watched my mother chop vegetables at the speed of light. There was an open bag of Fig Newtons on the counter and I absentmindedly took one. When I bit into it I almost spit it out, so cloyingly sweet and gritty it was, but I kept chewing, since my mother would surely notice me upchucking one of my formerly favorite comestibles.

"You met a man, didn't you?" Mom asked, without looking up from her flying knife.

"Why do you ask that?" I choked out.

"I remember you sitting there eating Fig Newtons with the same spacey look on your face the summer you met Joey Malone."

Ah, Joey Malone. Too young to drive, we had necked for hours behind a bush at Dolores Park, until my lips were so bruised I couldn't drink from a straw for a week. Strange she should mention that. Of all the experiences I'd had in life, this one felt most like that—dangerous, exciting, tempting beyond any ability to refuse.

"Don't bother denying it. Just tell me whether I get to hear about it or not," she said.

I crushed the rest of the cookie into a crumbly ball. "It's probably not worth talking about, Mom. He may not be around for much longer."

"Why, is he a criminal? Is he on the lam?"

"On the lam, Mom? No, he's not a criminal. He's just, um, a lot older than me."

That's an understatement.

"Well, older men can be good. They have more wisdom. And more money, usually." Mom wiped her forehead with a dishtowel. "It's hot today. I should have ordered Chinese."

She came to sit next to me and brushed against me with her bare arm. When her flesh touched mine a light flared in my vision, so bright that I closed my eyes against it. Suddenly I saw a vision of my mother and father in a doctor's office. My father pacing the floor nervously. My mother sitting like a stone. With her right hand, she was holding her left breast like a sick infant. I opened my eyes and the vision, and the flare, were gone.

"Mom, are you ill?"

She twisted on her stool and slapped one hand into the other. "I told your father I didn't want to tell you children yet, not until I had something definitive to say! Damn the Irish, they can't keep their mouths shut!"

"It wasn't Dad. I just had a feeling." I pressed my head into my hands, overwhelmed by a welter of emotions—fear about my mother's illness mixed with shock that I'd just looked into her mind as clearly as looking through a window.

"No, no, it can't be," I muttered.

Mom took my hands off my face and held them. Her skin felt dry and paper-thin. "It's nothing to freak about, honey. I found a lump in my breast a couple of weeks ago and I had it biopsied. We're still waiting for the results. The doctor says it's probably benign, we don't have any history of breast cancer in our family, but he wants to be sure. I wasn't going to worry you if the tests turned up negative."

I searched her face. "You shouldn't keep things like that to yourself. I always want to know, you know that."

"Well, you've been so preoccupied and busy at work the last few weeks."

She patted my hand almost absentmindedly. I had never been in a position to comfort my mother rather than vice versa, and I knew now should be the time. I was searching for the proper words when we were interrupted by a huge backpack slamming into the chair next to me.

Since he was fourteen my brother Frankie had reminded me of a big, loud horse, with his braying voice and galumphing feet. And usually a strong smell of sweat, since he played on more sports teams than I could count. Whenever he came into the house he headed right for the refrigerator, usually to grab the half-gallon of milk and drain it out of the carton. I could see Frankie had matured because today he took out a glass and filled it with milk before sitting down with us.

"Hey Frankie, take off your hat at the table." I flicked his baseball cap's brim with my thumb and middle finger. So much for Angie the adult.

Frankie turned the cap around so the bill was at the back. "Is that better, Miss Manners?"

"All right. I probably don't want to see your hair, anyway." Frankie had the same wiry red hair as I, while my lucky sister Thea had inherited my mom's blond waves. "How's school going, bro?"

"Good, once I finally managed to get some classes. There were twenty people on the waiting list for 'The Victorian Novel.' It's going to take me five years to graduate just because I can't sign up for any of the classes I need."

"I can't see you taking a class called 'The Victorian Novel,' anyway, Frankie. You seem more the Jack Kerouac type to me. Henry Miller, maybe."

"Don't stereotype me with your bourgeois mentality, man. Henry James wrote some sick shit."

My mom shot him a disapproving look.

"Sorry, Ma. I mean he wrote some sick *literature*." He threw the backpack over his shoulder. "I gotta study. When's dinner?"

"The usual time, Frank Junior. Although if you wanted to come down early to help set the table I wouldn't say no."

Frankie grunted an unintelligible answer as he stomped up to his room.

"Did you tell him?" I asked.

"There's nothing to tell yet. And I want you to forget about it too, Angie. That's an order. Now help me get this dinner on the table."

My knife chopped celery and jicama on autopilot as I thought about the visions I'd had when

Eric and I were touching each other. They had seemed so vivid, as if they were my memories replaying in my head, but I had dismissed them as fevered imaginings. Now I had a different thought about them. Had I tapped into Eric's mind when I touched him? Had he tapped into mine? Did he know how I felt about him?

After I left my parents' house that night I found myself driving around aimlessly, worries circling in my head like goldfish in a bowl. Finally I pulled out my cell phone and dialed directory assistance. They gave me the number for Nicolai Blaloc. It was as simple as that.

"Hello?" The soft, cultured voice was wary, as if he was expecting a telemarketer.

"Is this Mr. Blaloc?"

"Who is this?"

If I had to make a guess as to the origin of his accent I would have said Eastern European, maybe Russian, but I was no expert.

"My name is Angie McCaffrey. I was given your name by Les Banks. He said that you were an expert in, uh, people living the vampire lifestyle."

"What do you want?" This guy was not exactly making things easy for me. If he didn't want people calling him why have a website called vampirehunter.com?

"I need help, Mr. Blaloc. Certain things have

happened to me over the past week. I believe I might have met a vampire."

"Ha ha, very funny. Go and tell your sorority sisters you called the vampire hunter. I'm sure they'll be very impressed." Then he hung up.

I cast around in my mind for something that would make Nicolai believe that what I had to tell him was the farthest thing from a joke. I redialed his number.

"Listen, this person, he has a strange smell," I blurted out.

"Please, call me Nicolai." Suddenly the voice was polite. With his accent, the first syllable of his name was pronounced knee.

"I am intrigued, Ms. McCaffrey. When can you come and see me? I live in the Mission District."

"Actually, that's where I am right now."

Chapter 17

Nicolai's apartment was only four blocks away from where I'd left Les earlier that day. This part of the Mission had been recently identified by the *Chronicle* as the "hippest" neighborhood in the city, but it seemed like only a small portion of the residents could afford to partake of the hipness. Tapas bars and book-lined coffee houses sat cheek by jowl with pool halls, Mexican grocery stores, and tiny travel agencies advertising cheap flights to every city in South America.

The address Nicolai had given me was a large apartment building on the corner of Sixteenth and Guerrero, a gray three-story citadel with security gates on all the entryways and first-floor windows. I rang the bell on the middle door and while the buzzer sounded I pushed open the metal gate. There were three flights of creaky wooden stairs before I reached number twelve.

A tall thin man, whose most distinguishing

characteristic was the high contrast of black and white in his appearance, answered my knock. A snarl of shoulder-length black hair framed a white face marked by black eyebrows and a black goatee. He wore black leather pants, black boots, and a frilly white pirate shirt. He looked to be in his mid-forties.

He shook my hand with a cold, moist palm. "I am Nicolai Blaloc, you must be Angela." He squinted at me as if his eyesight was bad. "Please come into the parlor."

I couldn't suppress a gasp when I entered his "parlor." Normally Victorian apartments bear only the most vague resemblance to what they looked like when Queen V was alive, but Nicolai's made me feel like I'd walked into a time machine. Every inch of wall and ceiling was draped or painted or covered in ornate floral patterns, one laid upon the other in dizzying profusion. A mansion's worth of silk and gilt furniture packed the little room. He even had a baby grand piano with a piece of silky fabric tossed over it. Every table held a collection—crystal figurines, snuffboxes, and tiny pictures in silver frames. He also had an assortment of stuffed birds, some of them under glass bell jars, others mounted on the wall, a few in bamboo cages. The birds gave me the creeps; they all seemed to be staring at me with their glassy eyes. To complete the effect the room was lit with flickering gas lamps. After giving me a few moments to take in the scenery, Nicolai directed me to sit in one of the high-backed chairs.

"Angela, you look somewhat ill at ease. May I offer you a drink? A glass of wine, perhaps?"

His calling me Angela made me uncomfortable, because it reminded me of Eric. "I'll have a glass of wine, sure."

He passed through a curtain-draped archway and returned a few minutes later with two glasses of red wine in tulip-shaped glasses. Nicolai arranged himself on the couch opposite from me and took a sip of wine. Somewhere in the apartment several grandfather clocks chimed.

Nicolai leaned back and stroked his goatee, as candlelight flickered on his face. He looked like Sigmund Freud in hell. "Tell me what you have been experiencing."

Where to begin, how much to tell, how much to trust? I had to tell him some of the truth if he was going to be any help to me. "My boss, Lucy Weston, is dead. It looks like she was killed by a vampire, or someone who wanted to make it look like a vampire's work. The police are after Les Banks, her boyfriend. He's the one who gave me your name. Les says he didn't do it, that Lucy was killed by a 'real vampire.' The man he was referring to is someone I've been, uh, seeing."

I rubbed my eyes. This explanation was bringing on a headache. "This man I've met, he has told me some things that are hard to believe."

"But things have been happening to you that you cannot explain by natural causes."

Startled, I pitched forward to get a better look at Nicolai. "Yes, that's right."

"You are experiencing unusual symptoms. Nausea, headaches, a desire for darkness. Loss of appetite. You hear voices."

"Yes, that's right." My voice was a whisper.

Nicolai continued to stroke his beard. He spoke in a soothing monotone, as if he were hypnotizing me. "This man, he visits you at night. You have, shall we say, encounters, with him that are both frightening and . . ."

He paused. I gulped loudly.

". . . exciting." He put out one finger and stroked the tail of a stuffed black bird perched on a branch-shaped pedestal. "Yet I'll warrant you could not describe the exact nature of these encounters, am I correct?"

I nodded, not trusting my voice to work properly.

"You are powerfully attracted to him, yes, Angela?"

"Who are you?" I was gripping my wineglass so hard I thought I might crack it.

He leaned back, smoothing the ruffles on the collar of his shirt. "I am nobody, simply an observer. I am a scholar, a historian, a researcher. I follow groups such as the one that convenes at the House of Usher because that is where you usually find them."

My mouth felt dry. "Find who?"

Nicolai went to a bookshelf in a corner of the room and took down a large book bound in flaky brown leather with gold embossed text. He put it on the table in front of me and opened it to the front page, which had the spiky and not quite even type of a very old book. The title read: *The Vampire in Legend, Fact and Art*, by Mme. de Laszowska, with a publication date of May 1785. There was a bookmark in the first third of the book so I opened to that page.

It was a print of what had originally been a woodcut, of a man's profile, with a sharp nose, small eyes, and a pointed beard. He wore a simple crown on his head and a fur collar. His eyes glared at some distant enemy. The caption read: "Fourteenth century Transylvanian count Vlad Tepisch, believed by many to be the first vampire."

Nicolai's words floated over the picture, the soothing, cultured voice of a professor giving a lecture. "The history of the vampire begins in fact, but the fabric of truth is frayed with time, interwoven with myth and make-believe to produce a patchwork quilt of legend."

I looked up from the book, pulling my coat around me as if it could offer some protection from the discomfort I was feeling.

Nicolai was looking at me with the professional smile of a therapist, but his eyes glittered in the gaslight. "The term 'vampire' is one of the most misunderstood in human culture. The word has many connotations that are not strictly accurate. For example, vampires are neither immortal nor supernatural."

"So you're saying they don't actually kill people?"

"On the contrary, they do kill people and many of them. One could certainly have killed your friend."

I was shocked. "You mean all the people at the House of Usher are murderers?"

A deep sigh. "No, no, no. Those people are human, engaging in behaviors that are fulfilling to them psychologically. Many of them were abused as children and are drawn to the vampire myth as a means of achieving power, or being close to power, in their own lives. They drink blood when someone consents to give it to them, but they are not vampires. No, the true vampire is something far beyond them, something they will never comprehend."

Nicolai stroked the leather of the book. His fingernails were long and filed to sharp points at the tips, each one a tiny blade.

"The vampire, while not immortal, lives much longer than a mortal life span, perhaps as long as two thousand years. Think of the redwood tree, the Komodo dragon. They breathe but their breath is cold; their hearts beat, but slowly. Like lizards, their body temperature adjusts to the ambient temperature. Naturally cold, they are warmed by blood, human contact, and warm environments."

I thought of Eric's cold hands, warming when he touched my skin.

"They require blood to survive, but the amount can vary, depending on the particular vampire. Some go for long periods of time without killing, while others, particularly in earlier centuries when it was easier to hide, vanquished entire cities."

"Nicolai, the things I've been experiencing . . ."

"Yes, you're wondering if you are becoming a vampire."

"No! That's not what I was going to ask. I don't believe in vampires. He could be doing this with drugs, with hypnosis . . ."

Nicolai turned to stare at me, tiny fires reflected in each of his eyes. "Angela, let's not waste each other's time. Why have you sought me out, instead of the police, or a psychiatrist, or, what are they called, a cult deprogrammer? I'll tell you why. Because you already know the truth, that only I can help you."

Unless you have experienced a religious epiphany yourself, any description of what I felt at that moment would be inadequate. What I had been denying over the last few days finally stood in front of me and blocked every other exit. Eric had been telling me *the truth*.

Nicolai's lips twitched into a smile, and he nodded slowly. "I see that you are coming into acknowledgment. This is good, for I have much more to tell you. The vampire is inducing a conversion in you."

"Conversion?"

Before answering he pulled out another book. It was a decrepit, leather-bound version of *Dracula*, by Bram Stoker.

"You have read this, I presume?"

"Does seeing the movie count?"

He sniffed in disgust.

"I mean the one by Francis Ford Coppola. It was a very good movie. Keanu Reeves sucked, but still." I was babbling to cover my nervousness.

Nicolai flipped through the dusty pages and began reading out loud, squinting even more. "She was initially bitten by the vampire when she was in a trance, sleep-walking . . . and in trance could he best come to take more blood. In trance she died, and in trance she is UnDead, too."

He closed the book and a piece of its leather binding fell to the floor.

"Bram Stoker was close to correct in his portrayal of Mina. An older vampire must induce the conversion over an extended period of time, during which he 'visits' the subject and induces what Stoker called a trance state. I would call it a euphoric state. What would you call it, Angela?"

"Just go on, Nicolai, please." I took a gulp of wine.

"Very well. The body fluids of vampires contain a virus that causes the biochemical changes that produce another vampire. However, to become a vampire the person must have certain genetic characteristics that predispose him or her to vampirism, that is, the gene to which the virus attaches itself."

"I can see I should have stayed awake in chemistry class."

Nicolai continued, ignoring my attempts to lighten the atmosphere. "The gene, like all genes, runs in families. Famous powerful families, such as the Medicis in Italy and the British royal family, would make vampires within the family and discourage any 'outbreeding.' This also helped to limit the number of vampires in the world, which was important for its survival as a species. And the human species too, of course."

"So you're saying I have a vampire gene?"

"Yes. And it must be very strong in you if you are able to see your vampire's thoughts. Are you able to read anyone else's thoughts?"

"Yes, my mother's."

Nicolai nodded. "Of course. You would have inherited it from her."

My finger traced the outline of the face of Vlad Tepisch. "What, uh, other powers, might someone acquire if they became a vampire?"

Nicolai clapped his hands together like an excited child. "An excellent question, Angela, and so very timely! In addition to the already mentioned longevity and clairvoyance with other genetically related individuals, there is superhuman strength and agility."

I closed my eyes and remembered Eric lifting me in his arms and moving me from the Hyde Street Pier to my apartment in Pacific Heights in the blink of an eye.

I ran to the edge of town where I knew there was a cliff, a precipitous drop down to a river. I ran toward it and found that I could very nearly fly, my strength and speed were so great.

Nicolai was still speaking. ". . . scholars say that there is also superhuman intelligence, but my research indicates that this is probably simply the result of judicious use of the other powers, such as clairvoyance. Although if you believe the adage that with age comes wisdom, well, what vampire wouldn't have an advantage over us there?"

I remembered Eric's nose, squashed in the parking lot and miraculously healing. From there it wasn't that far a leap to my mother and her possible cancer. "Could a person, I mean a vampire, cure someone of an illness?"

Nicolai nodded. "The vampire venom does have curative powers, for both the vampire and those he feeds on. As long as he doesn't kill them, of course."

It was time to ask the most important question. "So," I was so nervous I had to strain to make my voice work, "how does one actually become a vampire?"

"The human being walks around in a semi-vampiric state for a period of several days or weeks, while the vampire visits them and feeds on them, injecting small amounts of venom each time. They may experience symptoms—headaches, nausea, sensitivity to light—which are hints of what is to come. If the fluid transfer stops during this period, the human most likely reverts back."

"And if they don't revert back?" I asked.

Nicolai pressed closer to me and I saw beads of sweat on his forehead. He was no longer smiling.

"At the climax of the blood exchange the vampire-to-be must die. This is always a dangerous proposition because there is no way to know whether the vampire virus has 'taken' until you die. So if you wake up it was successful, and if you don't . . ." Nicolai shrugged and held up his hands. "It's a risk well worth taking."

"How do you die, Nicolai?" I whispered.

"The vampire ends your mortal life, of course, by draining your blood." Nicolai inched even closer and touched me on the arm. I felt his nails through my coat.

"Angela, if you are being visited by a vampire and you are not dead, then you are a very special person. You have been chosen, don't you see?"

One of the sweat beads rolled from his forehead down his cheek. "The vampire only does this for one reason that I've been able to discern. To find a partner. I've been waiting for years to find someone like you, Angela. A vampire has chosen you, and now you are hovering on the precipice between life and conversion. For you, dying would be an opportunity of the highest magnitude."

"But I'd have to kill people in order to live . . ." The room seemed to have no air. The wine I had drunk threatened to make a return appearance.

"How would I stop it?" I choked out the words.

Nicolai leapt to his feet and slashed the air with his hand. "Stop it? Impossible! The only way would be to kill the vampire, and I'm sure you don't want to do that, do you, Angela? Think of the possibilities you're being offered . . ."

"Nicolai, I have to get some fresh air . . ." I stood up.

"Please don't go, Angela, there's so much more to say—"

Nicolai clutched at me, but I brushed him off and left the apartment. In the street I leaned over a garbage can and threw up.

I forced myself to go to bed when I got home, to at least pretend I was normal, but it was like trying to sleep while on speed (which I've only tried once, for the record). My mind raced, my hands and feet twitched, I felt jitters all over my body. Finally I gave up and sat in the living room with the TV on and the sound off. As infomercials for thigh machines and acne creams flickered across the screen, I stared out the window, wondering where in the darkness Eric was and whether he was thinking about me. Part of my jitters was caused by an acute desire to go out into the city and look for him, starting at his office and working my way through every inch of San Francisco's forty-seven square miles until I found him and checked us into the nearest hotel where I could unbutton his shirt and run my tongue along the cleft of his collarbone, fill my nose with his aroma. The desire for him was a physical pain, like I'd swallowed hot rocks and they had burned their way down my throat and through my body.

But still my rational mind, the famous McCaffrey cool head that had saved many a citizen from burning alive when my father and grandfather applied it to fighting a fire, told me to step back from my feelings and analyze the situation. Thanks to Nicolai, even my rational mind had accepted that Eric was something else, something not human. I didn't want to use the V word, but he had powers far beyond those of a human, powers he paid for in all-too-human guilt and loneliness. Wasn't loving him like loving the sun, so beautiful and warm, essential to life but deadly if you got too close?

As I watched the light break over the horizon, a torpor came over my body that I could only compare to going under general anesthesia. The doctor says count backward from ten and by the time you get to eight you have as much consciousness as a log. But it couldn't have been as bad as that, because I did hear my alarm clock, albeit two hours after it started ringing at seven.

In the shower I washed my hair several times, forgetting after each time whether I'd done it. Getting dressed, a task I had always considered easy, became an agonizing chore because I couldn't figure out which tops went with which bottoms. Outside it was cool and foggy, but the sunlight still hit my eyes so strongly I felt like I was getting a migraine. I stopped at a street vendor outside my office and bought three pairs of the cheapest, darkest sunglasses I could find.

I stopped in at Steve's office and found him

with his head in a file drawer. As soon as he sat up I could tell something was wrong. His blue silk tie was loosened and the top button of his starched white shirt was undone. For someone else this would mean they were relaxing, but Steve was not a relaxed guy.

"Angie, someone was in my office last night."

Chapter 18

I looked around. Everything looked exactly as it always did. Steve's San Francisco Museum of Modern Art mug was still sitting on his desk, filled with pens, his stapler and staple remover right next to it. His papers were neatly stacked in three metal trays labeled In, Out, and Pending.

Steve said, "They weren't trying to make a mess. They were trying to find something, unobtrusively."

"And did they?" I asked.

Steve nodded, his face ominous.

"That brochure you gave me is gone."

I shook my head in disbelief. "Why would anybody want that?"

"Good question. By the way, I still have a copy. I had faxed it to a couple of my friends, so one of them just faxed it right back." He waved some fuzzy copies at me. "One of my travel agent buddies called this place up and pretended to have a client interested in these, uh, recreational activities. When you talk to the agents in Asia they use a very practiced script that leaves out anything that might be construed as illegal, but you can get the gist of things. This agency specializes in very young girls, ten-, twelve-year-olds, purportedly virgins. Virgins are big business in the sex industry."

I shuddered at the grotesque image. "Did you find out any connections we might have with this company?"

"I was limited in my ability to search, since I couldn't get a customer list without a police search warrant."

"But maybe it's not the clients that are the issue for us, maybe it's the owners."

"Exactly. I started looking into the ownership of the agency. And I came up with something very interesting." Steve raised his eyebrows at me, then pushed the blurred photocopy over. He pointed to the address on the back: Jad Paan Travel Agency, Charoen Rat Road, Bangkok, Thailand.

"This little company is owned by a larger Thai company, translated as the Royal Orchid Company. They own a number of businesses in the travel industry, such as hotels and tour companies. This took some digging to find out, but the Royal Orchid Company is owned by Tangento Corporation."

Steve leaned back in his chair and smiled, proud of himself for finding the answer I was hoping he wouldn't find. Brouhaha in Asia, indeed.

"What can we do about this, Steve? Whoever

sent me this brochure must have wanted me to do something."

"Well, this is a problem. Prostitution is illegal, even in those countries, so Tangento owns a company that owns a company that is engaged in illegal activities. The connection is awfully far down the line, though, and far away. We'd be hard pressed to get someone in Asia to break down doors and start arresting people for something that is well known and widely tolerated."

"Well the least we could do is fire Tangento as a client, right? Or expose them here in the United States?"

Steve shook his head. "I don't know if anyone here would even care, Angie. The public already knows that Proteus shoes are made by six-year-olds in Pakistan, don't they? That doesn't stop them from paying $150 a pair for them. Why would they care about this?"

"Oh, Steve, that is so depressing. We've got to do something."

"I'm with you, Sojourner Truth. Let's free those slaves. Just tell me the game plan."

I picked up the photocopied brochure and Steve's handwritten notes. "Let me think about this for a while. I'll get back to you."

When I got to my office I saw a Post-it note stuck to the face of my computer, which read:

10:30 A.M. Please come to my office as soon as you get in.

—Dick

I checked my watch. It was already 10:50. I scurried over to Dick's office and looked in the window. Seated next to Dick at the conference table was Kimberley, wearing a white skirt and a pink sweater with a collar that appeared to be made of cotton candy. A man was sitting next to her. His face was turned away from me, but from the size of his shoulders and the wave of his dark hair, I recognized him as the man Kimberley had been talking to the night of the Bennetts' party.

I knocked, but opened the door without waiting for an answer. The stranger stood up, an act of chivalry virtually unheard of in the egalitarian halls of HFB. Dick seemed perturbed, half stood, then sat back down again. Kimberley smiled and patted her collar. The man looked like a model from the classic Arrow shirt advertisements, or the father on a 1950s TV show. He had blue eyes under thick straight brows, a square jaw with a cleft chin. His thick brown hair waved expertly back over his head with no part in sight. He was dressed in a starched Oxford shirt with an open neck tucked into beige Dockers. A slight thickening around the middle was his only concession to having left his college days behind. He held out a hand twice the size of mine.

"Hello, Angie, I'm Barry Warner. Let me say again how terribly sorry we were to hear about

Lucy. All of us at Tangento were shocked when we heard the news." When he smiled he displayed two rows of gleaming white teeth. He could have eaten an elephant with those teeth.

"Please sit down, Angie." Dick sounded pained, but that was nothing new. I wondered if this meeting was scheduled and I had just forgotten it in the chaos of the last few days.

"I'm so sorry to be late," I said quickly. My mind was spinning. Kimberley had been threatening Barry at her parents' party on Saturday night, asking him to give her a "helping hand" in exchange for her forgetting about something. I was about to find out what Kimberley had asked for.

"Barry called me this morning," Dick began, "and asked to convene the team working on the Tangento account. He has an announcement he'd like to make, so, uh, Barry, now that we're all here, why don't you commence?"

Barry beamed his huge smile at each of us. "I'm afraid I made y'all jump through hoops this morning to get together and meet with me. When I got the news about Lucy, well, you know the higher ups got a little antsy, and they wanted me to get on in here and find out what the game plan was going to be. We've all been very pleased with Kimberley and Lucy's work . . ." He paused, and had the decency to look chagrined at having to talk business at such a time.

"We need to be sure we got a team over here that's gonna run our ball into the end zone, if you know what I mean." Barry pointed his open palm at Dick in a "now it's your turn" gesture.

Dick cleared his throat and straightened some papers that were already straight. "Angie, after some discussion with Barry this morning, we've decided that Kimberley is going to manage the Tangento account, with your assistance. We've just been discussing some of the particulars."

On Thursday Dick had told me that Kimberley couldn't handle Tangento. Now it seemed Kimberley had blackmailed Barry into making her the manager of his account. But was Dick in on it too?

"Well, that seems logical," I said, deciding to play along. "After all, Kimberley is the one most familiar with the account at this point. I'll be happy to assist her."

Dick nodded, drumming his fingers on the table. "Kimberley brought some of the materials. She was just going to bring us all up to speed. Kimberley?"

Kimberley passed me a folder embossed with the HFB logo, a duplicate of the ones everyone else already had in front of them. I opened it and saw it contained graphs and pie charts assembled from the focus group information that I had seen in Lucy's Tangento file.

Kimberley spoke in a high, clear voice. "The last time we met with Barry, we presented the findings from our focus groups, namely that 65% of the people are not familiar with the Tangento name. On the other hand, 78% were familiar with Mercury sports apparel and 28% had purchased a pair of

Proteus athletic shoes in the past three years. While only 15% had purchased an item from the Venus line of ladies undergarments, 60% of women were familiar with the brand and had a positive opinion."

Barry nodded and winked at me.

"In our preliminary meetings we discussed Tangento's desire for an umbrella campaign such as the ones currently being run by Pacific Electric, Apex Industries, and many drug companies. The goal of the advertising would not be to sell a particular product line, but to increase familiarity with Tangento's range of products and to develop positive associations with the Tangento brand in the mind of the consumer."

Kimberley pursed her lips. "You may be aware, Angie, that there has been some negative press associated with Tangento in Southeast Asia."

I looked over at Barry, trying to read his expression. When I asked him on Friday he had claimed to know nothing.

"We all know these are gross misrepresentations of the facts, perpetrated by muckraking journalists who hate big companies." Barry said this calmly and we all nodded like we knew it was the truth.

Kimberley shuffled her stack of charts. "The story had already broken in several newspapers when we were doing the last of our focus groups, so we were able to assess the impact."

That hadn't been in the folder Kimberley gave me. She must have been withholding the information until now.

"It never appeared on the front page of any American newspaper; it was always relegated to the World news section, which it appears no one reads." Kimberley smiled brightly to show what a lucky break this was. "Only 12% of our focus group members were aware of the articles."

Barry said, "So as long as none of these rabble-rousing groups get their hands on the story we'll be all right. Our PR department has advised us to deal directly with the stories if they get enough ink, such as issuing press releases rebutting the accusations, but otherwise to continue as if nothing had happened. Let a sleepin' dog lay, my mama always said."

"Excuse me," I said, "since I just came on to the team, I hope you'll forgive me if I have to ask you to bring me up to speed on what exactly the negative publicity is about." Even though I thought I knew, I wanted to hear it from one of them. I looked at Kimberley as the most likely one to answer the question. She fidgeted and stole a look at Barry.

Barry coughed into his hand. "Angie, Tangento is a big company. Sometimes the right hand don't know what the left one is doing. It seems that there were some of our contractors in Southeast Asia were using labor that wasn't exactly voluntary. I stress the word 'contractor.' We're moving to disassociate ourselves from those plants, in fact it's probably already been done." He brushed his hands together to indicate a *fait accompli*.

Steve had told me once from his neurolinguistic programming training that people will often look up when they are lying, as if trying to find the source of their inventions in the sky. I hoped Barry would do something obvious to show me that he knew more than he was telling, but his gaze was steady and his hands didn't fidget. Either he was telling the truth and this was all he knew about Tangento's troubles, or he was a practiced liar.

"So that means we're going to move on developing the ads for the campaign." Kimberley was back in presentation mode. "The only difference is that instead of trying to identify Tangento with the names of all of its subsidiaries, we'll conduct a campaign aimed at raising the general positive association with the Tangento brand."

Barry leaned forward eagerly. "You know this song?" In a strong tenor he sang a jingle about a certain chemical company that had been flooding the airwaves. I knew every word, as I was sure everyone at the table did. The song was like a dental filling, once they'd drilled it into your head it wasn't going anywhere.

"That's what we want. A catchy ditty that people will sing in the shower." Barry looked at his watch, a gold Rolex with a face the size of a hamburger. "I'm afraid I've got to be leaving soon. Do we have all our ducks in a row?"

Kimberley looked momentarily annoyed, but regained her composure quickly. "Yes, I think so, Barry. Our next meeting will be to deliver some options for you in terms of slogans and songs."

Barry patted me on the back. "Glad to have you

on the team, Angie. I think this is going to work out great for us all." He stood up and shook hands all around. After he left the room seemed twice as large.

Dick stood up. "It looks like you've got this well under control. The next step is to reconnoiter with Creative and begin work on those slogans. Put Web Northrup on it today, will you, Kimberley?"

Kimberley smiled. "Already in the works, Dick. Angie, are you coming?"

"You go ahead, Kimberley," I answered. "I'd like to talk to Dick about the Unicorn account. Something's come up."

"Fine. I'll catch up with you later, Angie. Maybe we can do lunch."

I closed the door after Kimberley left, then sat down.

"Is there a problem with Unicorn?" Dick asked.

"No, Dick, I just wanted to ask what was going on here this morning. Quite an about-face from last week, when you were begging me to take Tangento."

Dick rubbed his face, making it even redder. "Tangento is a high-profile company for us, and we want to keep the client satisfied. Barry was simply relaying the desires of his higher-ups at Tangento that, in order to maintain continuity, Kimberley must manage the account."

Dick wasn't about to let any cats out of the bag, so I expressed hopefully convincing delight about the direction everything was going in, and said good-bye.

* * *

Between my office and Dick's I was surprised to find Barry, leaning with one arm against the wall, taking up half the hallway. I walked around to see who he was talking to and saw Lakshmi Roy, practically hidden under his arm, laughing uproariously at some joke he had just told.

"Hi Barry," I said. "I thought you were in a hurry to get somewhere."

"Well, I was, Angie," Barry answered without looking at me, "but then I ran into this exotic flower in the hall and plumb forgot where I was going."

Lakshmi giggled, a sound I'd never heard from her before.

"Well, don't let me interrupt you," I said.

After returning to my office I turned off the overhead lights, gulped four Tylenol straight and put my head down on my desk. I was massaging my temples when Theresa called from the reception area.

"Hello Angie, I just wanted to let you know that Lucy's sister is here. Mary from HR brought her over to meet you."

"Thanks, I'll be right out."

As I turned the corner I was stopped in my tracks by a vision of Lucy come back from the dead. Even though I knew it was Lucy's sister, I still felt a wave of shock from seeing her standing there with Theresa just as I'd seen Lucy almost every day for the past two years.

Up close it was obvious that Morgan Weston was not Lucy's twin. They had the same tall, reed thin body and heart-shaped face. They both had straight brown hair, but Lucy's had been cut in a chin-length bob and highlighted with blond while Morgan's was cut short. Lucy had worn stylish black-rimmed glasses. Morgan wore no glasses, no makeup, no adornments whatsoever. She looked reliable, honest, and very midwestern.

"It's a pleasure to meet you, Morgan." I found her handshake firm and warm. "I'm sorry it had to be under these circumstances and I'm very sorry for your loss."

I wished there were better words to use than these old chestnuts, but I don't suppose it really matters what you say. All the words in the dictionary won't bring back a loved one.

Morgan said, "Thank you, Angie. God has her now, and she's in a better place."

Mary from HR, a heavyset, middle-aged woman with the stern face of a middle school teacher, nodded sagely. "Are you ready to go to her office now?"

A few minutes later Morgan and I were alone in Lucy's office, Mary having been called away on some HR emergency. I was relieved when Morgan started talking.

"Lucy and I hadn't seen very much of each other since she moved away from St. Louis. She was so busy she often didn't come back for holidays. Our mom has MS and has lived in a nursing home since my father died. She's really broken up about this, of course, she wanted to come herself but she just couldn't make it onto the airplane. I'm going to bring Lucy home so that we can have a funeral for her there. I guess I'm going to have to wait for a while until they release the body." Her lips pressed together and tears welled up in her eyes.

I responded, "Well, there are keys to Lucy's house. I'll be happy to tell you where they are, or go over there with you and help you pack things up, if that's what you want to do."

Morgan's glance took in all of Lucy's office. "The police tell me they're looking for someone who works here. Les Banks, I think his name was. They say he and Lucy were dating. I guess it was some kind of lover's quarrel."

So the police hadn't told her anything about the vampire angle, and she hadn't read the newspapers, which made sense since she'd just come into town.

"Yeah, I guess that's what they say." I caught myself fidgeting and picking my fingernails. I wanted to get out of Lucy's office ASAP. "Would you like to start packing things up?" Mary had sent some boxes, which were stacked in the middle of the room.

"That's a good idea," Morgan sighed.

But when it came to actually packing Morgan sat like a lump watching me as I put things into boxes. Three coffee cups with logos from various conferences. A makeup bag filled with cosmetics. Several bottles of vitamins and aspirin. Morgan pointed to a framed collage of pictures of Lucy with various members of her family at a ski resort. As I handed it over my hand brushed Morgan's.

Suddenly there was a flash of light, and I heard Morgan's voice in my head.

Chapter 19

Oh God, this is so like Lucy. She was always a trouble-maker, always making Mom suffer. It's like she planned this to make it as difficult as possible for us!

I looked up at Morgan, who was blowing her nose into a tissue. "Uh, Morgan, did you say something to me?"

"No, I was just blowing my nose."

The situation was too close to what had happened with my mother to be coincidence. I picked up a small glass vase and asked Morgan if she could read the inscription on it. As I handed it to her I made sure that my hand touched hers.

I wonder how soon they'll let me close out her checking account?

I swept a carved granite paperweight and a Dilbert desk calendar into the box. I wanted to touch Morgan again and test my theory and I also wanted to run out of the room and never come back. The concept that I might be able to read people's minds

was both intriguing and repulsive. It was like the
Midas touch, where everything Midas touched
turned to gold. At first it seemed like a lucky break,
until he turned his beloved wife into a golden
statue.

Then my confusion was magnified by a faint perfume that I began to notice in the air. Like a blood-
hound chasing prey, I sniffed around the room
without a care as to whether Morgan was noticing.
The odor was coming from a green wool cardigan
that Lucy often wore, now lying over the back of
her chair. I put the sweater to my face. Faint as it
was, it was unmistakable. The smell was Eric. Both
my knees and brain turned to jelly as I sank into a
reverie of longing, tempered only slightly by the
fact that this odor meant that the vision I'd received from Eric was a fact, that he had embraced
Lucy at some point in the not-so-distant past.

Morgan coughed loudly. When I looked up she
was staring at me, obviously wondering why I was
caressing her sister's sweater. I quickly thought up
a lie. "Morgan, this is my sweater. Lucy borrowed it
from me. I'm going to take it back, if that's all
right with you?"

"Sure, no problem," Morgan said, still eyeing
me warily.

As if she'd decided she wanted to get away from
me as soon as possible, Morgan began helping
to pack Lucy's things. We finished quickly and I
avoided touching her while we were doing it. As we
said good-bye in the front lobby, she held out her

hand to shake. I took a deep breath and grabbed
her hand.

*I heard San Francisco was full of weirdos but you take
the cake.*

When I was back in my office I closed the door
behind me, wishing I could lock it. I sat down and
put my face into Lucy's sweater. The vision of Eric
and Lucy in an embrace floated back into my
head. I pushed it out in order to think about what
had just happened with Morgan.

If I used Nicolai's information to analyze the situation, it was the vampire gene that was causing
me to read minds. But why just my mom and
Morgan? Why hadn't I known about Lakshmi getting married, or Kimberley's nefarious plot to take
over Tangento? It had to be because Morgan had
the vampire gene, as did my mother. That probably meant Lucy also had the vampire gene. Eric
had been converting Lucy, the same way he was
now converting me. She had broken up with Les
to be with Eric. But she had died before she had
a chance, and Eric had moved on to Bachelorette
Number Two.

It now made sense why Suleiman and Moravia
had said they didn't like Lucy's concepts for their
campaign. They were working for Eric (and that
was probably where the money for their ad campaign was coming from). They had deliberately
said those things in order to get me to come to the

club so that Eric could get his hooks (or more accurately, fangs) into me.

But what did he want me for? Oh, I wanted to believe that it was love, but the clinch with Lucy cast an awful lot of doubt on that theory. Could he have been in love with Lucy? One possible scenario was that Lucy had been Eric's first choice to be his companion for life, but she had accidentally died in the conversion, as Nicolai warned might happen. An unfortunate event, no harm intended. The other one was that Eric had meant to kill Lucy, and been successful. Neither of these scenarios boded well for me.

There were only a few possible outcomes to the journey I was on now. I could allow myself to be converted and become Eric's companion for however long our lifespans ran, if Nicolai was right and that was what he wanted. In doing that I could be with the man to whom I was becoming increasingly (alarmingly) attached. I tried not to think about the other, more selfish perks, such as reading my client's minds and giving them the ad campaigns they'd always hoped for, thereby becoming HFB's star employee, or even starting acting again, reading the casting director's mind for the exact kind of performance they wanted. But if I chose this I would have to live as a vampire, not the nicest choice of lifestyle for a perennial Girl Scout like myself. I couldn't imagine spending years on end hugging the fringes of human society, a parasite and a pariah, slinking around in the dark . . .

Or I could just die, like Lucy.

There was, however, one other choice. It was the one Nicolai the vampire hunter had begged me not to contemplate. I could kill the vampire before he killed me.

I walked through the office like a zombie, not noticing if I passed anyone on my way. I was already at the parking lot before I remembered I hadn't brought my car. I went around the corner to the Fairmont Hotel. Under an ornate porte cochere, a bellman dressed as an English Beefeater was holding a cab for a fat couple wearing sweatshirts that read: "I got locked up in Alcatraz."

I pushed in front of them and said to the bellman, "I need this cab. I'm pregnant and I think I'm having a miscarriage."

The couple backed away in horror and the bellman held my arm as he put me into the cab. I gave the taxi driver, who happened to be a middle-aged woman with a crew cut and a cigarette dangling out of her mouth, the address of Nicolai's apartment. Through the haze of smoke she looked at me in the rearview mirror.

"Don't you want to go to the hospital?" she asked.

I smiled apologetically. "I lied."

The driver shrugged her shoulders. "It's all right. I don't like tourists anyway. Are you going to score? Can you get me something?"

I was about to be offended by her assumption

that I was on my way to buy drugs, but then I thought about it. I looked like death warmed over, I was pushing in front of people to get a cab, and then wanted to be taken to an address in the Mission District that was on the corner of Heroin Street and Meth Avenue. All right, she had her reasons.

"I don't think you want any of what I'm going to get," I replied.

"Be that way." We drove in silence the rest of the way. When we arrived at Nicolai's apartment I gave her a ten-dollar bill.

"Good luck," she said, deadpan.

As soon as she drove off I regretted not asking the cab to wait, since I had no idea whether Nicolai would be at home. At 3 o'clock in the afternoon most people are at work. I pushed the buzzer.

There was no answer. After trying it again I walked around to the back of the apartment building where there was a small parking alley. An old Chevy Impala sat with its hood up, two men bent over the engine. I figured the one in the pirate shirt and black leather pants was probably Nicolai.

I approached and heard Nicolai say, "*Lo siento. Necesitas una nueva transmisión.*"

"Hey Nicolai," I said, and he backed out abruptly. The young Hispanic man with him looked at me with no curiosity.

"I didn't know you could fix cars," I said stupidly. *But don't all Eastern European vampire hunters speak Spanish?*

Nicolai reached for a greasy towel and rubbed his

hands. "We all have to make money somehow. I'm glad to see you again, Angela. There's still so much more to be said."

He turned to his companion and said, "*Espérame.*" We left the man peering into the engine, perhaps hoping for a miracle.

We climbed the stairs to his apartment. Nicolai directed me to sit in the same wing chair as before. He sat opposite me on the couch and placed his hands on his thighs, waiting expectantly. Last time I'd been there I'd thought about Sigmund Freud in hell, but now this just felt like hell.

"I need to know how to get away from him." The sentence popped unexpectedly, like a burp, out of my mouth.

Nicolai just sat, waiting for the whole story to come out.

"He killed Lucy while trying to convert her, and now he's working on me. I don't have much time." I licked my lips, my mouth dry and cottony. "I can only talk to you now because it's been two days since I've seen him. If it happens again I'm sure I won't have the strength to protect myself."

If I saw him again I wouldn't care what he was or who he had killed. I wouldn't care if he killed me, as long as I could be embracing him when it happened.

"Why would you want to get away?"

I took a moment to decide how to answer that question. The most obvious answer seemed the best. "I don't want to die."

"Aren't there some things worth dying for?" Nicolai picked up one of his stuffed birds, a pure white little puffball that might have been a dove. He stroked its neck and then looked up at me, his dark eyes glittering like obsidian. "Angela, I am descended from a line of vampires. The first one on record is Vladimir Blaloc, born 1437 in the Carpathian mountains of Romania." He nodded when I raised my eyebrows. "Yes, Transylvania."

He looked at his hands, stained with black grease from the car engine. One of his long fingernails had broken off. "I have traced a family tree that reaches all the way back to that ancestor. The power was lost somewhere in the eighteenth century, along with the money. I have been unable to find any evidence of true vampiric abilities in the last six generations, including my own. The gene appears to have been dissipated."

He pulled his chair closer to me. "Angela, take my hand." I hesitated, but took his cold hand, trying not to recoil from the touch of his dirty, pointed fingernails.

"I know you have the clairvoyance. Try to read my mind, I beg you."

I closed my eyes. At first there was nothing, then a soft buzzing sound, like static on a telephone line, followed by a flash of light. Grainy images appeared in my mind: a tiny kitchen in a dilapidated postwar apartment building. The view from the grimy window was of a row of similar buildings stretching off into infinity. A woman with lank gray hair was sitting in a plastic chair, smoking. A young boy, about four years old, wearing only a grayish undershirt and dirty shorts, sat on the floor, aimlessly pushing a tin truck with three wheels. I could feel his hunger, his exhaustion, his desperation.

I pulled my hand away from Nicolai.

"Tell me, Angela, did you see or hear anything, anything at all?"

I couldn't meet his eager eyes. "No, Nicolai, nothing. I'm sorry."

He pushed his chair away from me, his face sagging with disappointment.

"You don't know what you're wishing for," I said quietly.

"And you don't know what you're giving up!" Nicolai shouted, jumping up with such violence he knocked over one of his bell jars. "You're trying to put the genie back in the bottle!"

He collapsed onto his knees in front of me. "Angela, after the vampire is finished with you, you could convert me, I know it must be possible." His voice was low and beseeching. "I could show you how to escape from Eric. We could work together. We could use our abilities to create such immense wealth and power that any goal would be within our grasp. Think about it, Angela! Anything you want. Forever and forever!"

I sat quietly, squeezing my hands together, waiting for Nicolai to calm down. I felt like I had fallen into quicksand and if I didn't pull myself out soon, it would be too late.

"Your life may not seem like much to you, Nicolai, but at least you have one."

"But you may not die!"

I leaned forward so that our faces were only inches apart. "You do die, Nicolai, even if you're converted. You die, and you go to hell, where you spend the rest of eternity. I can't help you. I *can't* give you back what you lost. Eric *won't* give you what your family lost. But you can help me."

"No, I can't."

"You have to. We can't let him keep killing people!" At this point I lost it. Crying hysterically, I fell onto the couch and curled into a fetal position, clutching hanks of my own hair in each hand. Nicolai sat on the floor next to me and patted my back. He began singing what had to be a Romanian lullaby. The song was sweet and gentle, but sad and full of loss, like "Rockabye Baby," like all the old Irish tunes my mother used to sing to me, passed down from the times when many babies didn't live through their first year.

After I had been calm for a little while, Nicolai got up. Moving stiffly, like a man much older than he was, he left the room. He returned carrying a rectangular wooden box, cracked with age, carved with designs of hunters and dogs. Holding the box on his arm like a fancy bottle of wine, he opened it. Lying on a bed of disintegrating velvet was a dagger.

Chapter 20

It was about a foot long, with a handle set with red stones and a blade curved like an elongated *S*. Nicolai ran his finger along the edge of the blade, and a necklace of blood beads appeared. He put his finger in his mouth and dreamily sucked the blood.

"This knife has been passed down in my family for generations. According to legend it was used to kill one of my ancestors, a local pest who had been preying on the villagers of Sieghesa for years. It is pure silver, and he was stabbed in the heart with it while he slept. My ancestor's wife pulled it out of his body and kept it so that it couldn't be used again."

He held the knife up and the blade seemed to catch fire in the reflected candlelight. I wondered about the physics of getting a knife of that shape into a person. Then I shuddered at my own thought.

Nicolai presented the knife to me with an air of resignation, like an actor who thinks he's going to win an Academy Award, only to be asked to present it to someone else.

I whispered, "You stab them while they're asleep? In the heart? Like in the stories?"

"You can stab them anytime but when they're asleep is the only time they won't see you and kill you first. My grandfather had this lovely case made for it. By then, nobody believed the stories and the knife had become just an attractive family heirloom."

Squinting in the sunlight outside Nicolai's apartment, I fumbled for my sunglasses as passersby jostled for space, nearly knocking me into the street. With no car, my parents' house was a half-hour climb uphill. With the knife box tucked under my arm I started walking. I imagined sitting in my mother's lap and having her tell me that it was all a bad dream.

I opened the front door using the key that was always under the mat. Immediately I thought my mother must not be home, because there was no music playing. I went in anyway and headed up the stairs to my old room. It was now a guest room, but my bed was still there, covered with a pink and green quilt my mother had made for me when I was three. I wanted nothing more than to lie down under that quilt and sleep until my problems disappeared. Then I heard a sound from my parents' bedroom.

My mother was sitting in the rocking chair that she used to rock us to sleep when we were babies, facing the window over the street. She rubbed her face, but not quickly enough to hide the evidence of tears. I abandoned the idea of climbing into her lap.

"Mom?" My voice came out as a whisper.

"I got the results of the biopsy back. It's positive, and there's metastasis to the lymph nodes."

I could see she was struggling to speak calmly.

"Have you told Dad?" I asked.

She shook her head. "I keep meaning to pick up the phone, and then I think, 'Oh, why not wait another hour, another day?' I sort of wish the doctor had waited to call me. Such a beautiful day, why ruin it." We both looked out the window at our little front yard, at my father's rose bushes. A crimson pool of petals surrounded each bush, the last blossoms of the long California season.

I kneeled in front of my mother and put my arms around her, my face against her neck. I could feel her heart beating against my lips. How much would I be willing to give to save my mother's life?

Her voice broke into my desperate reverie. "By the way, Angie, it's 3 o'clock on a Monday. What are you doing here?"

"I just wanted to talk to you."

"What about?"

"It doesn't matter."

She lifted my face and smoothed back my hair. "Go ahead, honey. I want to hear it."

I sat back on my haunches and looked out the window. "What's the hardest decision you ever had to make in your life?"

She let out a deep sigh. "Okay, here goes. I fell in love with another man."

"What? Really? When?"

"About twenty years ago, when you all were small."

"Who was it?"

"I don't want to say. You know him."

"Did you . . ." I couldn't bring myself to ask my mother if she'd slept with someone else.

"No. But we talked. He felt the same way I did." She ran her fingers through her beautiful blond hair. "You see, Angie, your father and I married too young. We were kids. How can kids know what they'll want for the rest of their lives?"

"Why didn't you get a divorce? A lot of people were doing it. Are doing it."

"Other people were involved, other people's hearts. I had to do what was right, Angie, and I don't regret it. I've had a wonderful life with your father and you kids . . ."

Her voice caught in her throat and she started to cry.

"It's not over, Mom."

"No, it's not over." She gently disengaged my arms so she could look into my face. "Angie, I think what you're asking me is about choosing between what is right and what you want. Is that right?"

I nodded.

"Listen to your heart, it will tell you what to do. Usually when you do what's right you find out it was what you wanted all along."

I stayed with my mom for another hour, until I had convinced her to call my father. As I knew he would, he found someone to take over his shift at the firehouse and came straight home.

I decided to take the streetcar back to the office and see if Steve could give me a ride home. I sat next to an old man snoring with his head thrown back and put the box Nicolai had given me on my lap. I felt it without looking at it, watching the commuters instead as they read newspapers or stared with bored expressions into the darkness of the tunnel under Market Street. I imagined nudging the old guy next to me. "Hey, mister! Guess what I've got in this box?"

Steve wasn't in his office when I arrived, so I left him a note and went to my office. There was another manila envelope, with my name printed on a clear label, no postage stamp and no return address. At first the envelope appeared empty, but when I shook it a clipping dropped out. It was from the *International Herald Tribune*, dated October 1.

Bangkok—*Authorities in Taiwan have discovered three female stowaways packed into a container on the freighter* Orient Express, *bound for San Francisco. The girls, all Thai nationals, ranged in age from twelve to seventeen. They had been nailed into one of the freight containers with a supply of food and water.*

The girls stated that their parents in Thailand had been given a sum of money and in exchange the girls were to be sent to the United States to work in garment factories until the debt was repaid. They admitted in interviews that they had been made to work as prostitutes in Bangkok while they waited for their ship.

It is assumed by police that the girls had been sold as prostitutes or slave labor to a connection in the United States, but no arrests have been made in the case. The freighter contained a shipment of athletic shoes and apparel bound for U.S. markets.

I ran to Theresa's desk and dangled the envelope in front of her. "Where did this come from?"

"What is it?" Theresa was typing and she didn't stop to look up.

"Yes, that's what I'm asking you, Theresa. Will you look at it, please?"

She glanced at the envelope. "Oh yeah, this was delivered. I had to sign for it."

Now we were getting somewhere. "Delivered by whom?" I asked.

Theresa pursed her lips, thinking. "A bike messenger. He was wearing those fingerless gloves."

"Which company? Do you remember?"

"No, sorry."

I walked straight to Steve's office and dropped the article on top of the work he was doing. As he read it his tanned face turned pale.

When he looked up I said, "It's time to get rid of Tangento."

"I agree," Steve said, "but there's no evidence here that directly connects to Tangento."

"I don't think we're the only ones at HFB who know about this. Let's go talk to Dick. You can use your neurolinguistic programming stuff to figure out if he's lying."

Steve and I sat in Dick's office while he examined the photocopies we had made of the newspaper article and the brochure. When he was finished Dick looked up and said politely, "Yes?"

"What are we going to do about this?" I asked indignantly.

"About what?"

"About Tangento owning a prostitution ring!" I was yelling, I couldn't help it.

Dick stroked his chin. "Now Angie, I don't know where you came to that conclusion. These girls on the ship, they had no connection to Tangento that I can discern. As for this other situation in Thailand," he held the brochure with two fingers like it was a smelly sock, "Steve says that Tangento owns this little company, and he *alleges* that they're doing illegal things. Tangento is a huge corporation; they probably have no knowledge of what this travel agency is up to, if indeed it is up to anything."

"Surely we should inform them, Dick? And perhaps stop doing business with them until the situation is corrected?" Steve said calmly.

Dick smiled at us like an indulgent parent. "Angie, Steve, Tangento is one of our biggest clients. The onus of responsibility does not lie on us to investigate these allegations. Enough said?"

Steve and I just stared at him.

"Our job is not to interrogate or prosecute. Our job is to *sell product*. Now, I know both of you have had a difficult time the last few days. I think you should take the rest of the week off, with pay, of course."

"Can we have those papers back?" I asked, trying to sound nonchalant.

Dick whisked the papers into his desk drawer. "I'll keep them, if you don't mind."

"That guy was lying like a Turkish carpet," Steve announced as we walked toward our offices.

"Let's wait to talk until we're in my office," I said quietly. "I don't know who to trust around here anymore."

We went to my office and closed the door, then

sat on the floor behind my desk so no one walking by would be able to see us through the window.

"I heard Kimberley talking to Barry at the Bennetts' party on Saturday night, telling him she'd 'forget everything' if he'd do something for her, she didn't say what. This morning Barry appeared here and announced that the bigwigs at Tangento wanted Kimberley to manage the account. Dick went along with this as if it were his idea, even though he'd given Tangento to me last week. He's Barry's puppet."

"Well, smack me with the reality stick." Steve scratched his head, a gesture he avoided unless he was really upset, because it put his hair out of alignment.

"And now he's giving us both the week off, when we're already short-staffed. Dick might be doing this just because Barry threatened to take Tangento away, or he may know something more, but it really doesn't matter, because he wouldn't do anything different whether he knew about the Thai girls or didn't."

Steve scratched his head again. His hair was starting to look like birds were nesting in it. "I think we need a drink," he announced.

"And I need to get out of here. This office is starting to stink. I'll meet you at the End Up in ten minutes. I'm going to finish up a few things."

Steve left and I rummaged under my desk until I found an old shopping bag. I stuck the photocopies of what I was now calling the "Tangento Dirt" into

Lucy's fluorescent Tangento file and put it in the bag along with the wooden knife box wrapped in Lucy's Eric-scented sweater. With all my problems now mingled together, I left the office.

The Financial District is full of yuppie bars where brash young titans convene after work to drink away the stress of trading dollar amounts their grandfathers wouldn't have known how to write. Thankfully, in the midst of it all is the End Up, a bar populated by old-school businessmen and serious alcoholics. No wine and no cosmopolitans are served at the End Up. The women, what few there are, can order manhattans, but the men have to stick to martinis or straight up shots of various lighter fluids chased with beer. Anybody who looks like they're going to order a mai tai or slap a high five with a comrade is told by Sam, the granite-faced owner, that the place is full, even if there are ten bar stools open. Steve and I had been there so often that Sam was now willing to pour me glasses of the Italian Chianti he kept for his "ladies."

I sat on a stool next to Steve and placed the bag on the floor under my feet.

"A martini and a wine, Sam." Steve waved at the bartender and he nodded curtly. Sam never greeted anyone by name, no matter how long they'd been coming in. We waited in silence until our drinks came, listening to the liquid breathing of the old alkie next to us. It sounded like he was slurping out of a straw.

"So, what's next?" Steve asked, after we'd each taken a big slug of booze. Oddly enough, alcohol was the only thing that still tasted good to me.

"Can you do a Southern accent?" I asked.

"Frankly, Scahlett, ah don't give ah dahm!" Steve replied.

"Hopefully the people in Thailand don't know too many Southerners," I said. "What's the time difference over there?"

"Eleven hours ahead. But what do you have in mind?"

"So business hours in Thailand begin at," I looked at my watch, "eleven P.M. My pen pal thinks there's a connection between the Jad Paan Travel Agency and that shipment of girls. And Tangento generally, or maybe Barry Warner specifically. The way to find out is to call them, pretending to be Barry Warner. Try to arrange another shipment."

Chapter 21

Steve threw up his hands. "Wait, wait, wait. When did we become the FBI?"

"We've been looking into things, right? So now we're just looking into them a little deeper."

"I don't want any trouble, Angie." Steve took another big swallow of martini.

Steve had no idea what trouble was. Trouble was Eric and the knife in the wooden box. "They're the ones committing the crimes. What's the worst that can happen to us?"

Steve pursed his lips as he considered my question. "We could definitely get fired."

"You're right. That's something I'm willing to risk." I put my hand on his arm. "Steve, these are little girls. You have two sisters, think about it. Isn't this more important than what we've been doing at HFB?"

Steve gave a dramatic sigh and polished off his

drink. "And what are you going to do while I'm running up huge long distance phone bills?"

I pushed the balls of my feet down, feeling the wooden box beneath my shoe soles. "I just have a few loose ends to tie up."

The House of Usher looked just as it had last Wednesday night, before my life had been turned upside down and vigorously shaken until all my pre-conceptions fell out. I checked the back door and found it locked, so I went around the front. The same beefy guy in a bowler hat was checking IDs, the same line of nocturnal denizens was waiting to get inside and have their eardrums shattered. I was nervous, wondering whether the bouncer would search me. If he did, he would certainly find the knife. I had taken it out of its wooden box and wrapped it in paper towels in my purse. I held the bag carefully against my side, not wanting to bump into anyone. The crowd around me chatted about decidedly ungothic topics, like sky-high rents and where to get the best bagels in the city.

When I arrived at the head of the line I froze. I had forgotten about the guest list.

"Name?"

"Angie McCaffrey."

"Not on the list." Biggie was already looking at the next person in line.

"You mean Suleiman and Moravia forgot to put me on the list?" I feigned indignation. "Look, I'm a good friend of theirs, and of Eric Taylor. I'm supposed to meet them here tonight. Are they here yet? I'm late." *At least it was worth a try.*

He squinted at me. "Yeah, they're here. But they didn't mention you. Hold on a minute." He reached behind him and pulled out a phone receiver. He shouted a few words into it and hung up.

"Stand over there, I'll let you know if they okay it." He went back to checking IDs and I stood behind him in the foyer. After a minute or two the phone rang. Biggie barked a few more words, then jerked his thumb to indicate I was to go. So much for the element of surprise, but at least I was in.

Suleiman and Moravia were sitting at their usual table in the bar area. Someone else was with them, a woman, but she was sitting with her back to me. Moravia saw me and waved.

When I got to the table I almost fell over. It was Lilith, looking none the worse for wear since her evening of playing sacrificial lamb. She was smoking a cigarette like it was oxygen and she was deep sea diving.

"Lilith, you're all right!"

Moravia and Suleiman exchanged a look. Moravia pointed to the seat next to hers. When I sat down she gave me a sly, conspiratorial smile.

"So, been sneaking around, have you, Angie?"

"What do you mean?" I asked, but the guilt crept into my voice.

"The police came and talked to us after you gave them the tape, of course. They said you were all freaked out by your little experience. Luckily, they know nobody gets hurt, right, Lilith?"

Lilith shrugged and sucked nicotine.

"So who told you to do it?" Moravia continued. "Someone must have given you the password."

"Les Banks. He's wanted by the police for Lucy's murder, but he told me it wasn't him, that it was a vampire. He wanted me to go and videotape the ritual. He said there would be enough evidence to exonerate him."

I waited for a moment, then added, "He also said that Lucy had a new boyfriend. Was she going out with anyone in your group?"

"Not that I know of." Moravia dipped her black nails into her martini and pulled out an olive.

"I found some evidence that she and Eric knew each other. Is it possible Eric was the new boyfriend?" I almost choked on the question.

Moravia looked over at Suleiman, who had been listening silently. He answered, "We told you that Lucy used to come to the club. Eric had met her, of course, several times. Whether he saw her outside of the club we don't know."

"What was Lucy's connection with the group?" The waitress walked up, but I waved her away.

"Coven, Angie," said Moravia. "You can call it a coven. When you say group you make us sound like insurance salesmen. Lucy had been a 'donor.' That's what we call the people who give blood, like Lilith. All perfectly consensual, of course. Lucy swore us to secrecy. She didn't want people at work to find out. That's why you didn't know anything about it, and why you hadn't come to the club."

"But you invited Kimberley!"

"No, she wormed her way in. I think she bribed the bouncer."

"Why did you tell Lucy not to come last week? Did Eric tell you to say that?"

"No, of course not. I told you, it was canceled that night."

"So, if you weren't trying to cut Lucy out of the group, why did you invite Kimberley and me the other night and tell us not to tell Lucy?"

Moravia shrugged. "When we got to know you a little better at the meeting you seemed cool. We didn't see why Lucy should dictate who we could or couldn't invite. After all, we didn't invite you to the ritual. You invited yourself to that."

"But what about Lucy's death?" I asked, trying to sound just curious, not desperate. "Surely these rituals involve a certain amount of danger. Couldn't someone have gone overboard, so to speak? Maybe not even here at the club, but at her house, in private?"

Moravia leaned closer and put her lips to my ear. Her hair smelled like sandalwood, nice, but nothing like Eric's odor. Even so, she was so gorgeous her proximity made me a little nervous.

"Angie," she whispered, "when you take another person's blood you draw their power into you, their life force. It makes you feel invincible."

"And what does the donor get out of it?" My

nervous whisper sounded like Marilyn Monroe on helium.

Moravia touched my ear with her finger. "*You* don't have to ask me that, now do you, Angie? The blood ritual is a fulfillment of the wishes of both donor and vampire. However it ends"—she paused to let me imagine Lucy—"that is also desire fulfilled. Who are we to question it? By the way, he's in the back room."

The Members Only Room was almost empty, just a few figures haunting the shadows. Eric glowed in the darkness like he was sitting in a shaft of moonlight. My heart leaped at the sight of him, despite the desperate resolution I'd made. I closed my eyes, praying for strength.

Before I'd taken another step I felt his cool lips brush my cheek. The smell followed, flowing like incense from his skin and hair, enveloping me. I breathed deeply, and right away felt calmer. The scent was like a drug, not just because of the attraction it created toward Eric, but because it induced a sense of calm and well-being. I'd heard that spider venom had the same effect, right before it killed you.

"Angela, please come and sit down. I had been hoping to see you tonight." He led me to the couch, gently brushing my arms and shoulders with his fingertips.

I tried to remember everything I'd learned about Eric and Lucy, tried to remember my fear of being next. But entering into Eric's periphery was like walking into an opium den. All I wanted was a fix. I sat on the couch, but I pulled my purse containing the knife close to my thigh.

Eric leaned over me, stroked my hair back from my forehead. The room seemed to pitch, like the couch had become a boat. I heard Eric's voice in my mind, his tone low and caressing.

I know what you have, Angela, don't forget I can read your thoughts. I'm not angry, no, in fact I welcome it. I have been trying to throw myself off that cliff ever since Vincent dragged me into this cursed life.

I felt him press the purse into my hands, the knife's sharp edge digging into my fingers through the cloth.

"Do it, Angela! I beg you!" Before I saw his hand move he had grabbed the purse and pulled the knife out. He wrapped my hands around the hilt and pressed it against the left side of his chest. "This is as close as anyone has ever come."

As I stared into Eric's sea blue gaze I knew I couldn't do it. It would be as impossible as killing my own child. I loved him, no matter where it led me, even into death. The realization made me angrier than I'd ever been in my life. I felt trapped, frenzied, like a wild animal who's just been caged.

"I can't do it!" I choked on the words. "I wish I could!"

We struggled. I tried to put down the knife but he held onto my hands, pushing the blade against his chest. I felt the immense strength of his hands. If he wanted to he could break my fingers like toothpicks as he forced the knife into his own heart, but he was restraining himself. He didn't want to hurt me; he wanted it the other way around.

"I—won't—do—it," I grunted.

I put all my effort into pulling the blade away. Suddenly he let go. I would have fallen on the floor, but he caught me, pulling me into a tight embrace. His lips joined with mine, even as I felt the knife slice through the fabric of his shirt. Eric grunted with pain, and I smelled the pungent, strangely sweet odor of burning flesh.

"No!"

I slipped out of his embrace and threw the knife. I heard it clattering to the floor as I ripped the buttons off Eric's shirt to see the wound. I cringed when I saw that the fabric was adhering to his burned flesh. Eric groaned as a patch of his skin lifted along with the shirt. For the first time I saw pain in his expression, pure human suffering. Nicolai had been correct. The knife worked, although in a way probably not even the vampire scholar could explain.

"Eric, you're hurt. What are we going to do?" I began to cry, feeling helpless and overwhelmed with guilt for bringing this weapon into Eric's presence.

Gently, almost absentmindedly, he patted me on the back. "Calm down, Angela, I'm fine."

"You mean it's going to heal?"

He smiled slightly, although his face was still clenched with pain. "I don't believe so. I have read about these knives, but I had never seen one until now. They are quite efficacious, I believe. But the wound is not life-threatening, you were successful in that regard."

I put my hand on his chest, just above the wound, felt his calmly beating heart. I laid my face against his neck, clutching his left shoulder with one hand while I pounded his other shoulder with my fist.

"I love you, I love you," I sobbed, punching him as hard as I could.

I love you too.

I stopped struggling and just lay against him. Finally I asked the question, even while my heart begged to remain ignorant.

"Did you kill Lucy?"

Would you believe me if I said no? Does it matter? You fixate on Lucy because you knew her, but you are aware there were others, countless others, and there will be countless more. You know what I am, Angela. That's why you brought the knife.

I slowly untangled myself from him and stood up. Shaking, but feeling strangely calm, I picked up the knife and wiped it on the tablecloth before placing it back in my purse. He said nothing as I walked out of the club.

There are times when a sound you hear at night is familiar, even comforting, like a partner rolling over in bed and sighing in their sleep. Sometimes a sound is annoying, such as your drunken neighbors arguing in the hallway. But the sound I'm talking

278 Clare Willis

about is the "someone in the house" sound. The sound that paralyzes your extremities while your heart races and your stomach acidifies. When you realize that it's actually a branch scratching against your windowpane or your cat getting a late night snack, you laugh and think, "Well, if that really was someone, I'd be dead now, because I sure as hell wasn't getting up to do anything about it."

Like a sleepwalker waking up in the middle of the street, I had no idea how I got home. The knife went into its wooden box, then back in the shopping bag. I showered, put on a big T-shirt of my dad's, and then lay down on the bed and literally cried myself to sleep.

Only to be awakened by a *sound*.

It was coming from Kimberley's room: first a muffled crash, like a lamp falling on a carpeted floor, then a bang against our common wall and a muffled, grunting shriek. My underarms and palms leaked sweat. Saliva filled my mouth, but I was so frozen I couldn't swallow. My body was trying to press itself into the sheets, to disappear into the mattress. There was another muffled bang, the sound of something else hitting the floor.

I would love to say I jumped up to save Kimberley, or that I at least picked up the phone and dialed 911, but if I said that I would be lying. Instead I lay there and fervently prayed that the intruder would leave without coming into my room. But my prayer was not to be answered. After a moment of silence, the footsteps appeared again in the hallway.

"Please God, let him leave now," I begged silently. My eyes, the only part of my body that could still move, were darting around the dark room. I could see perfectly, but nothing looked like a weapon. Then I remembered the knife. I was inching toward it when the door opened.

Adrenaline flooded my body. I sat up and with all my body weight lunged at my bedside table, thrusting it forward with both arms. There was a great crash as phone, lamp, and books tumbled to the ground. Under the cover of the noise I leaped out of bed and tried to run for the door, hoping that somehow I would get past the intruder.

Instead I ran right into him. An arm encased in leather circled my neck, while the other arm pulled something over my head. It was silky soft and smelled of roses, a pillowcase from Kimberley's bed. I was shoved back and the entire weight of the man's body came down on me. The man was actually kneeling on my chest. Only the softness of the mattress kept him from breaking every one of my ribs.

The slice of the knife was too quick for me to feel cold steel. Instead I felt heat, a searing burn as my skin separated and rushing warmth as the blood started pumping out of my neck. I could feel it gush with each beat of my heart. Inside the pillowcase I could hear my blood, like holding a shell up to your ear and knowing that the sounds of the ocean are really the waves inside your own body.

Then the man's mouth was on my neck. What was he doing? His pathetic lapping was like a cat trying to lick up a gallon of milk dropped on the floor. I pictured him drowning in the waves of blood pulsing out of my body.

The intruder tried to get closer. As he did this he moved his knees. This was my chance. I pulled free and grabbed at his face, feeling for the soft eye sockets. Then I pushed with all the strength I had left.

"Fuck!"

He screamed and fell off the side of the bed, onto the pile of books. I sat up, fumbling for the pillowcase. But before I could get it off the knife came again, this time in my chest. Under the pillowcase, under my closed eyelids, I saw a floodtide of red. As my lungs filled with blood I felt like a hooked fish tossed onto the shore to slowly suffocate. The man fumbled around my room. Drawers opened and slammed shut. Then came the sound of footsteps in the hall.

Suddenly all was quiet. I was listening to my body again, hearing the waves receding. It seemed my heart was slowing down. Slowly, I reached my hand up toward my neck. I found the wound and my fingers slipped inside my own flesh up to the first knuckle.

"Uh-oh, that's not good," I thought.

Oddly, I felt calm, even tranquil. Breathing came easily, or maybe I just wasn't doing it anymore. The liquid red behind my eyes was giving way to inky blackness. In my mind I crawled into my mother's lap and went to sleep.

Chapter 22

I awoke to a soft sound, a moan that was almost a sigh, coming from Kimberley's room. I pulled the pillowcase off my head. It took both hands to push myself out of bed. My legs moved like crowbars across the hall. I heard little whimpers in a voice I didn't recognize. They were coming out of my own mouth.

Kimberley was lying on her bed like a tossed rag doll, her legs splayed out and one arm above her head. The bedside lamp was on, casting a circle of yellow light onto her head and shoulders. She was wearing a lavender nightgown I'd seen many times before, but now parts of it were stained deep purple with blood. Her face, neck and chest were smeared with it, as was her white duvet cover. Her eyes were closed.

"Oh my God, Kimberley," I gasped, rushing over.

Her neck was drenched in blood, running from a wound that ran from just below her right ear to the hollow between her collarbones. What had been a rush of blood was now a trickle. I laid my head on her chest to feel for a heartbeat. There was none.

Another thing I'm sorry for is that I never learned CPR. I lurched to the phone on her bedside table and dialed 911.

"San Francisco Emergency." The female voice was brisk and efficient.

"Someone broke into the apartment. My roommate is hurt."

I heard the clicking of computer keys, the sound of the operator tracing my address.

"Is the intruder still in the apartment? Are you safe at this moment?"

"Yes, he's gone."

"Your roommate, is she conscious?"

"No, I think she's dead." The last word came out a whisper.

"Are you all right, Ma'am? Were you hurt?"

"Oh my God." I was feeling my neck, looking for the wound that I remembered. I touched my left breast and felt that my T-shirt was soaked in blood.

"Why didn't I die?" I whispered.

"Ma'am, please hold the line. Someone should be there any minute."

Thinking I was about to be sick, I ignored the operator's orders and dropped the telephone on the floor, then staggered to the bathroom and kneeled over the toilet bowl. I was nauseated, like you feel after a car accident when adrenaline has left you shaken and quivering, but I didn't feel any pain. I stood up warily and looked in the bathroom mirror. My hair was scraggly and my T-shirt hung off me like I had jumped into a swimming pool. It was sodden with my own blood. A rich, salty, mineral smell filled my nostrils.

But the wound, it was gone. I leaned closer, not believing my eyes. I tried to put my finger into the fissure, but now it was just a flesh wound, a thin little scratch that a cat's claw could have made. I pulled up the wet shirt and looked at my chest. I almost gagged at the sight of my own breasts coated in blood, but I could see no wound.

Sirens blared from the street. How was I going to explain the blood? I knew I ought to be dead, in fact I had expected it. I could just imagine the conversation.

"Well, you see, Officer, it's this vampire venom. I just heal up quicker than most folks." Uh-huh, that would go over really well.

I grabbed a washcloth and scrubbed at my face and neck. Back in my room I pulled off my shirt and grabbed another one out of the drawer. I shoved the wet shirt in the back of my closet and pulled the comforter over the blood-soaked sheets before the doorbell rang.

An hour later Kimberley's room looked like a pharmacy after a riot. The bed and floor were littered with IV bottles, syringes, tubes, and pieces of torn paper. The paramedics had made a valiant attempt to bring Kimberley back to life. After all the shouting and beeping from the machines the apartment was now silent as a grave.

The paramedics checked me out, then left me in the living room with Inspectors Sansome and Trujillo, my friends from Lucy's house, while various other personnel tramped in and out of Kimberley's room.

"Would you like us to call anybody for you, Angie?" This latest event had put me on a first name basis with Inspector Sansome. I thought about calling my parents and decided against it. What could they do now except worry?

"Yes, I'd like to call my friend Steve."

"We need to ask you some questions, Ms. McCaffrey." Inspector Trujillo was getting bored with waiting.

"Let's wait until her friend gets here, Ernesto." Sansome's voice was faintly admonishing. "Why don't you sit down, Angie?"

He pointed to the sofa. My immediate thought was Kimberley would go ballistic if any blood got on her white sofa, but then I remembered she wasn't going to be getting angry about anything. Still, I couldn't bring myself to sit there.

"Why don't we go in the kitchen?" I offered.

Inspector Sansome offered to let me use his cell phone and a minute later Steve was on his way. Sansome and I sat across from each other in the two kitchen chairs. Trujillo leaned over to examine the outside of the kitchen window without touching the sill.

"He came into the apartment while we were asleep," I blurted out.

"It was just one person, a man?" asked Sansome.

I nodded. "That's all I saw. Actually I didn't really see him. He put a pillowcase over my head, one from Kimberley's room. I just heard and felt him."

"So you can't give us any description?" Trujillo was determined to ask his questions.

I shook my head, but then I thought about it.

"He was tall. He was wearing a leather jacket."

"Do you have any idea how he might have gotten in? You have to buzz people into your building, right?" Trujillo spoke with his back to me, still checking out the window. He pulled rubber gloves out of his pocket and put them on before trying the lock.

"Yes, but he might have come in the window you're looking at. There's a fire escape that goes all the way down. Well, to the second floor, anyway." I couldn't imagine anyone would have the guts to use it, old and rusty as it was. "We always leave that window open a little bit."

"What happened next?" Sansome had his note pad out.

"He came into Kimberley's room first. I heard noises in there, bangs and crashes, then a scream. I didn't go in. I was being quiet, hoping he would just go away."

I picked at my fingernails, feeling dangerously

close to crying. Sansome put down his pen and touched me lightly on the arm. "Don't feel bad that you didn't go in there, Angie. No one would expect you to."

I thought of my own wound, the slick warm feeling of blood exiting my body. If I'd known he couldn't kill me, would I have acted differently, would I have saved Kimberley's life?

Trujillo was hovering over me now, having finished with the window. I smelled cologne, something spicy and subtle, coming from his overcoat. "What happened next?" Trujillo asked briskly.

Sansome shrugged at me conspiratorially from behind Trujillo's back.

"Then he came into my room. He grabbed me and pushed me on the bed. He had a knife, he was trying to cut me, but I pushed him off."

I couldn't keep myself from fingering the scratch on my neck. Sansome leaned forward a little. "Looks like he got you, Angie."

"I guess he was going to cut me, or he did cut me, but I pushed my fingers into his eyes, and he fell over the side of the bed."

I heard a sharp intake of breath from Trujillo. He looked eagerly at my right hand, resting on the kitchen table.

"We should sample under her fingernails, Andy." Trujillo hovered over me like he was going to put my hands in an evidence bag and cart them away.

Sansome smiled at me, ignoring Trujillo. "You

washed your hands already, didn't you, Angie?
Face too?"

Instantly I felt guilty. "Yes, I was feeling sick. I
thought some cold water . . . I'm sorry."

Trujillo backed away, his face red with indignation. Sansome just nodded.

"Of course, you did. That's perfectly natural.
What happened after he fell down?"

"He ran away, out the front door."

"Did you hear the bolt, by any chance? Like he
was unlocking the door?" Sansome scratched away
in his notebook, not looking at me.

"I don't know if I heard the bolt or not."

"Don't worry, we can check on that." Sansome
looked up at the ceiling as if he was trying to remember something. "Do you mind if Inspector
Trujillo takes a look at the front door, Angie?"
Trujillo took the cue and left the room.

Sansome was flipping pages in his notebook.
"Then you went into Kimberley's room, is that
right?"

"I went in and she was, well, like you saw her. I
couldn't feel any heartbeat. I called 911."

"Is there anything else you can remember about
the man? Any smells?"

Instantly I thought about Eric, his sweet, haunting fragrance. "Like what?" I asked.

"Sometimes people smell something, even when
they can't see. Like pipe smoke, or a particular after-
shave. Caught one perp after the lady told me she

smelled pepperoni after her place had been broken into. Turned out to be the pizza delivery guy."

I followed Sansome's gaze to Kimberley's $700 Illy espresso machine.

"Do you want some coffee?"

He laughed and patted my hand. "No, thank you, but aren't you sweet? Smells, Angie?"

"Only Kimberley's perfume, from the pillowcase. It smells like roses."

"Did he say anything?"

"He said 'Fuck' when I poked him in the eyes."

"Anything distinguishing about his voice?"

"Not that I can remember. He was kind of grunting. His voice was low."

"Angie, after your assailant cut you, did he do anything else to you, anything at all?"

I remembered the man's tongue lapping at my neck, his teeth probing the wound. At that moment Trujillo reappeared.

"No sign of forced entry here or at the lobby. Ms. McCaffrey, did anyone else have a key to this apartment besides you and Kimberley?"

"Just Kimberley's parents, the Bennetts, as far as I know. They own the building."

Sansome waved at Trujillo, as if swatting a fly. It was the first time I'd seen any discomposure on his part. "Ernesto, could you go and see if Angie's friend has arrived yet?"

Trujillo walked away, looking chastised. Sansome pulled on a loose thread holding the first button on his jacket. The button came off in his hand.

"I can't sew worth a damn. My wife, she used to take care of all those things." He sighed and put the button in his pocket, then looked up.

"So Angie, was there anything else you wanted to add?"

He knew I had been thinking of something. I remained silent, staring at the swirling pattern in the linoleum under my bare left foot.

"All right," said Sansome. "I think it would be better if you stayed somewhere else for a few days. The crime scene team might be returning."

"That's all right, I can stay at Steve's place. Can I go in my room and get some clothes?"

"Yes, but I'd like to accompany you, if you don't mind."

We walked slowly, like an elderly couple, back to my room. I went to my closet and grabbed a bag. Moving the door so Sansome couldn't see what I was doing, I shoved the bloody T-shirt to the bottom, and then put some clean underwear, shirts, and pants on top. When I came out Sansome was waiting silently.

He was still waiting for me to tell him the information that we both knew I had withheld. My mind was in turmoil. Who was I protecting? I was sure the pathetic monster that had attacked me bore no relation to Eric, except perhaps in his own imagination. No, the problem was that if I mentioned that the man had tried to drink my blood, the trail might lead back to Eric, even though I knew he had nothing to do with the murder. This one, anyway.

* * *

When Sansome and I left the elevator I saw
Steve and Inspector Trujillo talking near the fountain in the lobby, their gelled, dark heads close together. Steve's hair was perfectly arranged, but I
could see the checked pattern of a pajama top
sticking up from his sweater collar.

Steve saw me and ran over. He didn't hug me
but instead touched me all over, as if taking inven-
tory. He touched my cheeks, my shoulders, my
arms, as tenderly as if he were stroking a butterfly
wing. I started crying uncontrollably for the first
time that night. Steve put his arm around my
shoulders, supporting my now wobbly legs.

Back at his apartment, Steve gave me the royal
treatment, or what would have been the royal treatment if the queen had pneumonia. After a long
shower, he put me in his bed with a heating pad on
my back, a hot water bottle on my feet, a cup of echi-
nacea tea in my right hand and the TV remote in
my left. I had already filled him in on the basic story
on the way over, minus the miraculous healing, so I
lay quietly and allowed him to minister to me. I felt
completely exhausted but also wide-awake.

Finally Steve yawned. "I'm going to go and sleep
on the couch. We can talk in the morning."

"Aren't you going to give me a dose of castor
oil?" I asked.

Steve just gave me a look and fluffed up my
pillow.

The last thing I wanted was to be left alone. "The bed's plenty big for both of us, Steve."

"I can't tell you how many times I've heard that line before. First time from a woman, though." Steve lifted the comforter and slid in to the other side of the bed. I flipped through the TV channels with the mute on, just for something to do. There was no way I was going to sleep that night.

Steve watched the images flitting across the screen. The silence was like a blanket wrapped around the two of us, so I was startled when Steve spoke.

"Angie, we have to talk. I know you've been holding out on me about this Eric. But I have to know, was he the one who did this?"

I contrasted the erotic, hallucinatory effect of whatever Eric had been doing to me with the pitiful, desperate, all too human actions of my attacker. "No, this wasn't Eric. This was just a man."

"What do you mean *just?*"

I had been withholding so much information from Steve about Eric that now was hardly the time to begin telling the truth. Steve already thought I was losing my grip on reality.

"I think the attacker was trying to make me think that he was one of the House of Usher blood drinkers, but I know it wasn't Eric."

"So who was it then?"

"I don't know, Steve. Maybe it was Les."

"No, it wasn't Les," Steve spoke with surprising conviction.

"How do you know?"

"He was here, Angie, earlier tonight. I was letting him sleep on the couch."

"You were what?"

"I felt sorry for him. But listen to what I'm saying. He was here with me when you and Kimberley were attacked."

"That doesn't prove he's not Lucy's killer."

Steve flipped onto his side and narrowed his eyes. "Angie, do you really believe that?"

I paused for a moment. "No, I really don't. If he'd asked to stay with me I'd have let him too. Where is he now?"

"I dropped him off at another friend's house when I came to get you. He said you had too many cops following you."

He picked up the remote and turned the TV off. "I think we should try to get some sleep."

"Sure."

Steve turned off the light and I stared at the ceiling. For a long time we lay in the dark, tossing and turning, knowing that the other one was awake. Finally Steve's breathing became slow and deep. I continued to go over the night's events in my mind, trying to make sense of them. There was another thing I hadn't told anyone. When I went to my room with Inspector Sansome to get some clothes, I had also been planning to retrieve the bag I'd brought from the office, the one containing the Tangento file and the knife. But the bag was gone.

Chapter 23

I woke up completely disoriented and clueless as to where I was. The curtains at the window were so thick they let in just the barest sliver of light, from which I could ascertain it was daytime. The sun illuminated a Victorian dresser topped with a vase of white flowers whose name I didn't know, which reminded me I was at Steve's. I looked over to his side of the bed, but he was gone, the pillow fluffed and his side of the comforter neatly pulled up.

The digital clock on the bedside table read 10:30. I had finally drifted off to sleep about 4:00 A.M., listening to Bing Crosby sing "White Christmas" in the movie *Holiday Inn*. It was the most cheerful thing I could find on TV, but it didn't help me a bit.

I reluctantly left Steve's soft bed to go to the bathroom. When I looked at my neck in the mirror I thought I could detect a faint pink line, but when I leaned closer I couldn't see anything. Last night Inspector Sansome had taken a long, hard look at me, and I'd thought that maybe I'd missed some blood when I washed up. I knew that it would be helpful to his investigation to know that I'd been slashed as well as Kimberley, but I couldn't bear to give him any information that might lead him, even erroneously, to Eric.

After putting on the clothes I'd brought from home I went to the kitchen and poured a bowl of Raisin Bran with milk. I chewed, but it tasted so much like sawdust that I spat it out. I pushed the bowl away and laid my arms on the table, then my head. Sadness overwhelmed me and I cried onto the wooden table.

The sound of Steve singing dried up my tears. Through the window I saw him weeding in his garden, knees on a rubber gardening cushion, iPod speakers in his ears. The day was bright, the sky was blue and his flowers brilliant red. It was a beautiful, sunlit moment, one Eric would never get to experience for the rest of his long life. To never see the sun again, what would that be like?

It seemed like I was on the way to finding out, as the light was stinging my eyes, even from indoors. Steve had left the *Chronicle* on the table and I scanned the front page. A wooly mammoth had been hacked out of the ice in Antarctica and scientists were hoping to clone it. I turned to the local news. A venerable printing press was being evicted because a brand new blog-hosting company had bought the building. The press employees were desperately trying to finish printing six hundred

copies of an illuminated Bible before they ceased
to exist.

Below the picture of a man laying tiny metal letters into a plate was the next story's headline: "Autopsy Report on 'Vampire' Victim: Blood Loss
Cause of Death." At first I thought the article was
about Kimberley, then realized that it had to be
about Lucy. There was no way they could have
done an autopsy on Kimberley so quickly.

The autopsy report on Lucy's body stated the
cause of death as massive blood loss from two
wounds in the carotid artery, made by a weapon
similar to an ice pick. Toxicology had found traces
of Rohypnol, the "date rape" drug, in her system.
Time of death was estimated to have been between
nine P.M. and midnight on Tuesday. I wondered
whether the police were still looking for Les.

The feeling I had then would have been giddy
relief if I hadn't been reading about a dead colleague, but I was still relieved. Lucy had been
drugged with Rohypnol. As I could attest, Eric
didn't ply anyone with drugs. He didn't need to,
since his own scent was a drug to humans. Lucy's
murder had been staged to look like a vampire's
handiwork, or more accurately, a fake vampire's handiwork. So now Eric was exonerated, at
least in my mind, of both murders.

I went back to the bedroom and rooted around
in Steve's closet for a hat. He had a shelf of brand
new baseball caps, acquired while squiring clients
to Giants games. I took one, found my sunglasses

in my purse, and headed downstairs to the garden. I handed Steve the newspaper, folded over to the Lucy article. He sat down on his weeding cushion and began reading.

I couldn't wait for him to finish. "Eric didn't kill Lucy!" I shouted.

Steve looked up. "The article says that?"

"No, but it says that Lucy was . . ." I stopped myself. Unless I was going to tell a long and unbelievable story I'd better keep my mouth shut.

Steve sighed. "I wish you felt you could trust me, Angie."

Instantly I was filled with remorse. "Oh, Steve, of course I trust you."

His baleful expression told me he didn't believe me, and why should he?

He looked back down at the newspaper. "So he didn't kill Lucy. But what about Kimberley?"

"Oh, no, he definitely didn't kill her."

"Don't worry, I'm not going to ask you how you know that. So your vampire boyfriend is as harmless as a kitten, huh? No wonder you're happy."

Was Eric harmless? I paused to think that through. He may not have killed Lucy or Kimberley, but that didn't change what Nicolai had been telling me: "If you die in the conversion you're out of luck . . ." Eric could still kill me in the conversion process, if he decided to continue it. And then there was the person who had killed Lucy and Kimberley, and attempted to kill me. That person was still at large.

"I'm not happy," I answered, and by then it was true.

Steve got back on his knees and pulled some yellow flowers out of the ground.

"How can you do that at a time like this?" I asked.

"It calms the mind. You should try it. Actually, never mind. You don't know an oxalis from a delphinium."

"Steve, did you try calling Bangkok yesterday?"

He moved his knee cushion farther down the flowerbed. He was wearing a leather gardening belt, the slots filled with pruning shears, weed diggers, a ball of twine, and other tools. Steve was nothing if not prepared.

"Yes, they know Barry Warner over there, that's a fact."

"Really?" I leaned forward eagerly. Maybe the theory that I'd been formulating about Tangento might turn out to be true.

"But I didn't get anything. The woman who answered said, 'You not Barry!' and hung up. I guess my accent wasn't convincing."

I picked a flower and put it to my nose. I used to think fresh flowers were the prettiest scent in the world, but now I knew better. "Steve, there's something I need to tell you. The man who attacked me, he took the Tangento file, with all my information in it."

Steve stopped weeding, his trowel in midair. "Huh? Did you tell the police?"

"No, not yet."

"Why not?" he asked.

I couldn't tell him it was because I had a vampire-killing knife in the bag that was also stolen, so I just shrugged.

"I have a theory," I said.

"Go ahead."

"I think last night's attack was about Tangento. Kimberley must have been using information about Tangento to blackmail Barry Warner. And then I got a hold of the same information. Someone was trying to shut us both up."

"And what about Lucy?" asked Steve. "Did she know about Tangento too?"

"I don't know, that's what we need to find out. We need to know what Lucy knew."

"And who sent you those envelopes," Steve added. He sighed heavily and stood up, brushing off his knees. "I guess it's time to get to work."

At the front entrance of HFB Steve and I almost collided with a skinny delivery boy hidden behind a basket of extremely tall flowers. When we followed him into the lobby he announced to the front desk receptionist, "I have a delivery for Angela McCaffrey."

The receptionist was new and didn't know me on sight. She was flipping through the directory when I answered, "I'm Angie McCaffrey."

The boy looked relieved to relinquish his burden. I signed for the flowers, then peered around them to find my way to the elevator. The flowers had a strong, sweet yet somehow depressing smell. I remembered my grandmother's funeral, six months before, in St. Philip's Cathedral. It had been a cold day and the old radiators had heated the chapel like a sauna, cooking the flowers and making the smell almost unbearable. That had been my first experience of death. Now I could write a book on the subject.

When I put the bouquet down on my desk I found an envelope tucked into the blossoms. It was heavy ivory card stock with nothing written on it. Inside I felt something small, with sharp edges. I ripped open the envelope and a necklace fell into my hand: a red stone carved in the shape of a teardrop, placed at its narrow end into a delicate gold setting studded with tiny diamonds. I'm no connoisseur, but I'd been to enough vintage clothing and jewelry shows to know this was Victorian.

I touched the stone. It really was beautiful. About an inch long, it had such clarity I could see the table right through it. But a red teardrop? What was the meaning of that? I checked the envelope again and found a card inside it.

My dear Angela,
   You are astute, so I imagine you're wondering why I would choose a symbol of sadness as a gift. It represents my regret at having to withdraw from your life. However, I know what happened at your apartment last night. How sorry I am I cannot begin to tell you.

How I wish that you had been able to accomplish your task when you came to the House of Usher, wielding that ancient blade. But since I am still alive, if I can call this existence living, I must leave this place. I implore you not to try to find me, simply trust that I know what I am doing, and that the difficulties you have been experiencing will begin to dissipate as soon as I am safely at a distance.

> *Even from afar, I remain,*
> *Your humble servant, Cyprien*

Eric knew about the attack on Kimberley and me, and he blamed himself. He knew who Barry Warner was. In fact, it seemed he had known everything about Tangento before I knew it. As I looked into the red stone I suddenly saw everything with a clarity that I'd never had before. The threads of information I'd been gathering, that I'd thought had been separate, braided together into one cohesive story. Eric had sent me the information about Tangento's misdeeds; he had wanted me to do something about it. Perhaps he had given the information to Lucy first, but whoever wanted to keep the information secret had silenced her permanently, just as they'd silenced Kimberley and tried to silence me.

Eric had put me in mortal danger—and not from his own vampiric nature, but from someone pretending to be what Eric was. The only solution he saw was to leave and hopefully take the murderer with him. I understood why he was doing it but the thought of never seeing Eric again was unbearable. If I let him go now he would leave the city, change his name, and disappear as completely as if he'd never existed.

A half-hour later I was charging into the walnut-paneled lobby of Harbinger, International.

"May I help you?" The same receptionist smiled helpfully, with no recognition on her face.

"Yes, I need to go to Eric Taylor's office."

"I'm very sorry, but he's not in at the moment."

This time around, the lies tripped easily off my tongue. "I know that, but we met here last night, and I left some papers. I'll just go and get them."

"I'm sorry, that won't be possible," the receptionist replied.

I had seen a few of my clients get everything they wanted by being pushy as hell. I thought now was the time to give it a try.

"I need those papers right now!" My voice was loud. "And when I tell Mr. Taylor how rude you've been to his best client, you'll never work in this town again!"

I marched down one of the hallways, fervently hoping that it was the correct one. The receptionist trailed after me.

"Oh no, I'm sorry, you can't come in here, it's not allowed, if you'll just . . ."

On the right there were three cubicles containing people talking on telephones. On the left there were two offices, one of which was on the corner. I bet on that one, and without pausing, swept in.

The corner office had windows on two sides, overlooking the Financial District and the Bay Bridge. A huge mahogany JFK-style desk faced the window. It looked like the occupant was in the process of moving out. Packing boxes half filled with books and papers were scattered around the room. I imagined Steve's voice saying, "Nice work, Nancy Drew, what's your next move?"

"Is Mr. Taylor moving?" I asked.

The secretary was touching my sleeve. "I'm not at liberty to say anything about that. Really, Ms. uh, I'm afraid I must ask you to leave now."

I cast one last, desperate look around the room, but there was nothing there to help me.

At midnight I snuck out of Steve's bed, leaving him snoring under his pillow. I went into the living room and sat on the couch, facing his tiny statue of David, holding the red stone necklace in my hand. Not knowing exactly what I was doing, but following an instinct, I closed my eyes and focused all my energy on Eric. He was somewhere in the city, and we were linked—psychically, physically, and emotionally. Somehow I would find him.

I pictured him at the House of Usher in sapphire blue velvet, eyes sparkling with amusement at my attempts to spar with him; his hand at the small of my back, guiding me in a perfect waltz. I felt him wrap me in a blanket on a cold night in Half Moon Bay and tell me I was beautiful. I saw the sadness in his eyes as he told me of his betrayal by the monk; and the pure delight on his face upon discovering the *Balclutha*, a ship he thought existed only in his memories . . .

I grabbed my car keys and headed for the door. "Just stay put, now," I muttered.

Chapter 24

I parked the car in a no parking zone in front of the Maritime Museum, a beautiful Art Deco building in the shape of a ship. Between it and the water was a small beach, which I crossed on my way to the pier. There was a gate across the entrance, with a lone security guard in a kiosk staring at a tiny television set. Keeping to the shadows, I slipped around the gate and walked as quickly as possible down the pier while trying to keep my footsteps light on the old wood.

The *Balclutha* loomed in the darkness, its towering masts outlined against a gauzy purple sky. I stopped in front of the empty bench, filled with disappointment. Somehow I'd thought he would just be there, sitting on the bench, as easy to find as the ship itself. I squinted up at her as she rocked gently in her berth, trying to marshal my new powers of vision to locate a shadowy figure lurking on the deck, remembering a trip around Cape Horn that was lost now to any human memory.

As I stared at the creaking hulk, thinking I'd never realized before that there are so many different shades of black, I felt him at my side. The awareness of his presence was followed by his scent. Its sweet, haunting fragrance overwhelmed the odors of saltwater and tar that blew in on the breeze. I didn't turn, not wanting to see anger or rejection on his face. If I stayed just like that I could imagine that at any moment he would take me in his arms and tell me he felt the same as I did, that he couldn't bear to be without me.

Then I heard his voice, soft in my ear. "I told you not to look for me, but I see you didn't listen."

I spun around to face him, ready to leap to my own defense, but stopped when I saw him. Eric had changed. His long copper hair was cut short, stopping just above the collar of the dark, button-down shirt that he wore, topped with a heavy overcoat. His face was tired, and lines had appeared that I'd never seen before. Even his eyes looked darker, azure instead of cerulean, the color of a cold Northern sea, forbidding and opaque.

"I shouldn't have gone to Nicolai, I shouldn't have taken the knife. I could have prevented Kimberley's death, I could have done so many things if I'd just trusted you, but I was a coward. I was afraid of what might happen to me. But then I realized I didn't care what happened, as long as I could be with you. I'm ready now, Eric."

He was silent, staring out at the ship, his hands in his pockets. He seemed to have forgotten I was there. Finally I reached for his arm.

"Eric, did you hear what I said?"

He shrank from my touch. "Angela, I am the cause of your troubles, not the solution. Please, let me go. Tell me you'll never try to find me again."

"No, that's not going to work. We're connected now, whether you like it or not."

Eric looked at me then, searching my eyes. Finally he sighed, and a slight smile lifted his lips. "Yes, I suppose you're right."

"Why did you send me that information about Tangento?" I asked.

He took my hand and we walked down the pier. Eric showed no concern for the security guard, but why should he? If the guard caught him he would be the unfortunate one, not Eric.

"I've told you that in my human life I was religious. I believed in good and evil, that virtue would be rewarded and evil punished in the afterlife. I've since learned that this is not the case. The afterlife is a convenient myth for those who think life is too short. In this world goodness goes unrewarded and evil exists unchecked. My very existence is proof of this."

There was no sound except the slap of waves against the pier. The vibrant city was dark and silent. "As I have lived these many years among humans, granted with the dubious gift of reading their minds, I found evil lurking unchecked to an extent that surprised even me. At first I despaired, but eventually I realized that perhaps my maker, whomever that might be, had not forsaken me entirely. Perhaps there was a reason for my existence, some great cosmic scale to balance out."

A spark lit up his eyes, lightening his dark countenance. "I was able to dedicate my life to a cause, and to live within certain parameters. This made it all somehow more bearable."

"What cause? What parameters?"

"These are the parameters." He held up his pointer finger. "One: I will only feed on those people who have evil in their hearts." He added his middle finger. "Two: I will stop acts of evil whenever possible, wherever I find them." He lifted his ring finger. "And Three: When One and Two are no longer possible I will kill myself."

"So that balances everything out?" I asked.

Eric shrugged. "Maybe, maybe not. But I already told you I'm too cowardly to just kill myself."

"So where did I fit into this plan?"

Eric looked uncomfortable. "Sometimes I find the need for a human accomplice."

"So you were trying to make me into a vampire, like Nicolai said, so I could be your accomplice?" It was a struggle not to burst into tears in front of him. The thought that he was using me as some part of an elaborate plot, rather than wanting me as his companion for life, was like a knife to the heart. And I knew now, literally, what that felt like.

"No, I was not trying to convert you, although

I'd be lying if I said the thought never crossed my mind, especially after I realized how special you are. But I *was* trying to use you, my dear Angela."

"What does *that* mean?" I was amazed that he had found something even more painful to say.

"In order to avoid arousing suspicion myself, another trick I have learned over the years is that by injecting just enough venom into certain humans, I can insinuate myself into their thoughts, then guide their actions toward my intended goal."

I felt sick. "You were trying to control my mind?"

"In the beginning, yes. In fact, Lucy was my first accomplice. That is why you saw the image of Lucy and me on the couch in her apartment. Lucy was involved with the coven, which made it easy for me to approach her. They were an ideal cover for me."

I rubbed my hands together. It was getting very cold out here. "You don't seem very upset about her death," I said. "More like you lost your best hammer."

"I deeply regret what happened, but please don't expect me to become emotional over the death of one individual. Death is like breathing to me. It's always there."

"So Lucy died, and you took me as second choice?"

"Not exactly. I had already decided Lucy was not suitable, because she, ah, she . . ."

I said it for him. "She fell in love with you. She broke up with Les over you. She told Les she was going to be with you forever."

"Yes. At the time she died I was trying to extricate myself from her. I had Moravia tell her not to come to the club anymore."

"And you also had Moravia and Suleiman invite Kimberley and me to the club?"

"Yes, I wanted to look for some other potentials. But then once again things didn't work out as I had planned."

"I wasn't what you were hoping for?"

He brushed some hair off my cheek, causing the tingle that happened every time he touched me. "You were more than I was hoping for, Angela. I've never told a human being any of this. You are the first."

He slid his hand down my arm and into his pocket, then took a step back.

"That is why I had to break away from you. I decided to let go of the 'project' I had in mind, and you with it, because I realized that these women had died because of their involvement."

"If her death had nothing to do with vampirism, then why was Lucy's body drained of blood?"

He made a derisive noise. "You and I both know it wasn't a real vampire who killed Lucy. But we do make convenient scapegoats. I assumed that it was her boyfriend Les, that it had nothing to do with Tangento and what we were trying to accomplish. It wasn't until you and Kimberley were attacked that I realized how dangerous things had become."

"But Eric, the vampire venom, I can't be hurt, can I? I mean, I'm converting over . . ." My fingers found their way up to my neck, feeling for a scar that wasn't there.

"Once the venom exchange stops, the symptoms fade. How quickly, I don't know, because the gene is obviously very strong in you. But as I have no intention of giving you any more venom, you will become vulnerable again, it's just a matter of time."

"But Eric, I've changed my mind. I want to be converted. We're going to finish what we started. You wanted to take down Tangento, right?"

Eric closed the space he created between us. He grabbed my arms and exerted just enough pressure to make me remember seeing him throw a two-hundred-pound man like a rag doll.

"Did you hear a word I said to you?" Eric hissed. His lips drew back and I saw a hint of the famous fangs Suleiman had mentioned at our first meeting. Cold fear clutched at my stomach, but as quickly as they appeared they were gone. The pressure from his hands eased. "Go back to Steve's, lock yourself in for a few days, and by the time you come out I'll have taken care of everything, in my own way."

"Eric, how can you say that to me, after all you've said about fighting evil? I want to help you, I want to bring these guys down!"

"No!" Eric shouted. My mouth snapped shut and I backed away.

"We *are* going to let this go! Two people have already died because of me. I am not going to let the woman I love die as well! I can't protect you,

Angela. I don't have eyes in the back of my head. You will let this go, Angela. You *will* obey me!"

My fear was swept away. I ran to him and threw my arms around his neck. I closed my eyes and concentrated on projecting my words into his mind. After a moment I felt his arms encircle me. His head fell against my shoulder and I stroked his hair.

Yes, I love you, Angela. And that is why I must leave, don't you see?

"No, I don't see! I don't see at all."

Eric took one step away from me, and then another. His face became a mask, with his true feelings hidden behind it.

"Yes. That was also my failing when I was human."

He took another step back and the shadow of the ship enveloped him. "Good-bye, Angela. We shall not see each other again."

The police took the Caution tape off my door and let me back into my apartment on Friday morning. I went straight to my room and took down my suitcases from the top shelf of the closet. I planned to pack up as much as I could of my clothes and books and take them over to Steve's. I'd stay there until I found a new apartment, unless I decided to move out of the city. Right now I was too wounded and shell-shocked to be able to think long term. I wanted to leave San Francisco, but there was my mom to think about, helping her through whatever might happen with her cancer.

But whatever I did, I knew I wasn't going to live here anymore, and I wasn't going back to HFB.

I had packed about half a suitcase when that now familiar feeling of daytime exhaustion came over me. I pulled the blind and lay down on my bed. As I had done so often in the last few days, I had another long cry. It seemed that every time I slowed down I started to cry.

The phone rang. There was no one I wanted to talk to, so I let the answering machine pick up. It was a telemarketer calling for Kimberley. Obviously the telemarketers didn't know yet that she was dead, although death was probably not a criterion they would recognize for putting a person on the Do Not Call list.

Poor Kimberley. She had been lucky in so many ways, blessed with good looks and wealth and privilege. Yet she had been miserable. Her parents had lavished her with gifts, but they hadn't given her the one thing she really needed—their love and approval. She had been forced to use thievery and deceit to get ahead at work, because she couldn't trust that her own talents could carry her anywhere. Instead of marrying Barry Warner, as her parents hoped she might, she had blackmailed him into getting her a position that she could have earned by hard work if she'd had the self-confidence to attempt it.

Blackmailed him . . .

I sat up in bed, fully awake and alert, my mind racing. I had tried to find Eric after he left me at the *Balclutha*, but the pathways to him were shut down like a mountain road in the winter. Suleiman and Moravia hadn't seen him. His office was locked. The Tangento case, too, had closed up like a clam. When I called Dick at work he said that Barry had put everything on hold and gone back to Texas when he heard about Kimberley.

But for Kimberley to blackmail Barry she must have had evidence. And the evidence had to *be* somewhere. Kimberley hadn't expected to die, she wouldn't have had time to hide or destroy it. Maybe it was somewhere in the apartment. It was a long shot, but worth a try.

I tiptoed into Kimberley's room. All the paramedic paraphernalia was still strewn around the floor, but the mattress was missing, taken as evidence by the police, for which I was grateful. I looked under the bed and saw a stray earring and some dust bunnies. Her nightstand held a vibrator, eyeshade, earplugs, a bottle of Xanax prescribed to her mother, and a little book called *365 Daily Meditations*. I pulled the drawer out and looked behind it at the unfinished wood. I searched her dresser, pawing through panties and bras stacked in Lucite boxes.

Kimberley's closet smelled of roses and cedar, with a rainbow of clothes evenly spaced across the rods. I pushed the clothes aside and there it was: a large envelope with the HFB logo thumbtacked to the back wall. Amazed at how simple it had been to find it, I shook the contents onto the box spring.

Arrayed across Kimberley's dust ruffle were several photographs, a videotape, and some folded sheets of paper.

The first photo I picked up was of a young Asian girl with broad cheekbones and long dark hair, dressed only in a miniskirt, lying sprawled on a bed with a single sheet crumpled underneath her. I'm not a great judge of age in adolescent girls, but from the budding breasts she couldn't have been more than twelve. She wore an expression of sad resignation, her turned-down mouth looked as if it had never smiled. Her eyes were open, the irises milky and clouded. Her neck was encircled with a ring of purple and red bruises. There was a scarf tossed to the side of the bed, partially hidden by the sheet. On the back of the photo someone had written, "Jinda, Thaniya Road, Bangkok," in handwriting I didn't recognize.

There were several more photos, all the same but heartbreakingly unique in that each was of a different girl. All were naked or partly so, all had been strangled, and all were photographed alone in a bed in some godforsaken dump. I went to the window and took some deep breaths to clear my head, but I knew I would never be able to wipe those images away, not if I lived forever.

I picked up the videotape and walked into the living room, my steps heavy, like a witness at an execution. After a few moments of scratchy darkness, an image sprung to life. I watched in silence for five minutes, but it seemed like an hour. The sound was almost worse than the picture, the grunting, pig-like sound of the man and the high thin screams of the girl. It was the first girl, I recognized her big eyes and broad rosy cheeks. The man was Barry Warner.

Chapter 25

I ejected the tape and sat down on the couch, staring at the tape box like it was a rattlesnake. A prostitution ring was running under Tangento's auspices, with Barry as its biggest customer. But Barry's proclivities were so sadistic, so macabre, that only females whose lives were completely expendable could be used. I thought about Eric and Barry. They were both killers, both evil from society's point of view, and both would be dealt with in the same way if they were caught. Yet they were so different. My parents taught me that there was no such thing as circumstantial morality, only right and wrong, but experience had now taught me that it was much more complex than that.

I opened one of the sheets of paper, and then dropped it as if it was a burning match. I ran into my room and pulled out of my purse the letter that Eric had written, telling me he was leaving town. I had known right away it was the same handwriting, but now I had proof. I carried the letter back to the living room. The sheets of paper contained a list of names, all of them Asian, written in Eric's archaic cursive. This was evidence that Eric had given to Lucy, and Kimberley had stolen it from her.

I could see what Eric's plan had been. If he had trusted this to the police, Barry would have found a way to weasel out of it. No bodies would ever be found, and dredging up witnesses in Asia would be impossible. Eric had provided this material to Lucy because of HFB's access to the court of public opinion, hoping she would expose Barry and Tangento and cause a public scandal from which neither would recover. Lucy hadn't been interested in being a vigilante, however, but even so what she knew had gotten her killed. Kimberley had tried to use it to her own advantage, to further her obsessive desire to succeed at HFB, and she too earned a spot in the morgue for her efforts.

Now it was my turn. Perhaps I'd never get to see Eric again, but at least I could finish the job that he had left undone.

I left my building with two suitcases packed with a few clothes, books, and toiletries. I'd pick up the rest of my possessions later, or maybe I wouldn't. These trivial things didn't seem to matter much anymore. I stood for a moment in the portico and looked outside. The day was gray and overcast, with fog thick enough that the houses and apartment buildings across the street seemed wavering and insubstantial, like images on decaying celluloid film.

The lack of direct sunlight meant that I wouldn't need sunglasses, so I simply adjusted the suitcases to make them more comfortable in my hands and walked out the door. Immediately I entered a scene straight out of an old movie: a man in a trench coat and fedora materialized out of the fog, pointing a gun at my chest. The scene was so contrived it took me a moment to get scared.

"Now what kind of a gentleman would I be if I didn't offer to help you with those bags?" The syrupy southern accent was unmistakable. Barry Warner had not gone back to Texas, he was right here.

He gestured with his other hand toward a shiny, silver Mercedes parked in the loading zone. "Are you going to the airport? Let me give you a ride, taxis are so scarce in this town."

"That's okay, my car's just down the street."

Would Barry Warner shoot me on the street in the middle of the day? Was he that crazy?

"If you're thinking about running away, don't try it. I dropped two eight-point bucks last season, and I guarantee they were faster than you are." He smiled, showing his white, elephant-sized teeth.

Okay, so he was that crazy. I'd have to come up with a better plan than wildly running down the street.

Barry opened the trunk of his car with a remote control and gestured that I should put my suitcases in it, so I obeyed.

"Now get in the back seat," he said.

I opened the door but Barry didn't wait for me to sit down. He shoved me roughly into the foot space below the back seat. Then he kneeled on my spine while he blindfolded me with a scarf and tied my hands behind my back with scratchy rope. I lay in a torment of pain from my wrenched arms and crushed back and listened to him climb into the driver's seat and start the car.

"Where are we going, Barry?" I managed to grunt.

"To your friend Eric's house, to bring him a little present."

I didn't think my heart could pound faster than it already was, but it surprised me by doubling its rhythm. He knew who Eric was? And more importantly, he knew *where* he was?

"I don't know what you're talking about," I said, probably not very convincingly.

"You aren't the only one who's been doing their homework. I've been following you for days. Your weirdo friend Nicolai Blaloc was particularly helpful."

I was freezing cold, but droplets of sweat were dripping between my breasts. "Who's Nicolai Blaloc?" I asked, deliberately mispronouncing the name.

Barry snickered like I'd told a dirty joke. "After the incident in your apartment, when you didn't die like a good girl should, I started to get a little suspicious. With a little, um, persuasion, Nicolai explained it all to me. When I realized that I had the very knife he was talking about in my possession, well, y'all can't imagine how happy I was!"

"How do you know where Eric lives?" I was wiggling my hands, trying to loosen the ropes.

"Same way I learned about you. Surveillance! For a vampire, he sure is oblivious. Although I guess he figures ain't nobody gonna hurt him, right?" The more animated Barry become, the more pronounced his accent.

The car droned. I could feel the wheels turning, but of course I had no idea where we were going. The rough rope chafed mercilessly, but it loosened a little as I rotated my wrists.

Barry seemed to be in a garrulous mood. "Yep, I'll tell you, I was more than a little surprised when I saw you again after I left you and Kimberley in your apartment. It was like seein' a ghost."

Hoping to capitalize on the average human's fear of the supernatural, I said, "If you believe Eric is a real vampire, aren't you scared to confront him?"

He chuckled. "Let me tell you a little story. When I was a boy in Mississippi my grandfather used to handle rattlesnakes in church. Every Sunday for twelve years he'd go into a trance and let those damn things crawl all over him like ants at a picnic. One day a snake bit him and he up and died. The question is, does the fact that he handled the snakes for twelve years without being bit mean that miracles exist, or does the fact that he died mean that they don't?"

"And your point is . . . ?" I squeezed my fingers together to make my right hand as narrow as possible and pulled hard. The rope was definitely loosening.

"My point is, *I* stayed well clear of those rattlers, miracle or no. You might be alive now because I nicked a rib instead of getting the knife in properly.

Or this Nicolai fella might be right. Whether Eric is a vampire or just a human nutcase, he's gonna die when I stick the fancy knife in him. So that's what I'm gonna do."

"Did you know about Eric when you killed Lucy? Is that why you drained her blood, to make it look like he did it?"

Barry chuckled again. "I didn't kill Lucy, Angie! That was Kimberley. I didn't know Lucy had a damn thing on me."

"Kimberley?" This time my ignorance was utterly convincing.

"Kimberley is ambitious, in case you didn't notice. She went over to Lucy's house that Sunday, to put a little pressure on her. She had found out that Lucy was planning to fire her and she wanted to, uh, convince her otherwise. She took her to the Bennetts' and kept her there for a few days. Kimberley was dosing Lucy with drugs and Lucy naturally developed loose lips. She told Kimberley about the vampire coven, about dating Les, and unfortunately, about me."

I turned my head so my other cheek could be rubbed raw by the all-weather carpet. "So Kimberley had a scapegoat for murder in the vampire coven and someone else who could help her advance at HFB besides Lucy."

There were clues galore that I hadn't seen: Kimberley's absence from our apartment at the same time that Lucy was missing; her attempts to steal Macabre Factor from me; the comments her parents had made about her at their party; her obvious blackmailing of Barry. Had I been too obsessed with Eric to pay attention to what was going on around me?

I smelled smoke. Barry had lit up a cigarette. "So, Kimberley kills Lucy on Tuesday night and dumps her back home, trying her best to make it look like a vampire killing. Then she comes to me and says, 'Put me in charge of Tangento or you're gonna find your dirty laundry spread all over Market Street.'"

"I heard that, actually, at the Bennetts' party," I said.

"Really, well, you *do* know too much, don't you?" Barry said amiably.

"But why did you decide to kill Kimberley if you'd already given her what she wanted?" At that moment I managed to slip my right wrist out of the rope. I rubbed it quickly against my pants and then put it back inside the loops, so that it looked as if I was still bound.

Barry clicked his tongue, making a tut-tutting sound. "You'da thought she was my ex-wife, the way she expected me to keep paying out, Angie. She planned to start her own firm, and she was going to get me to *persuade*, shall we say, certain men at other companies who had dealings with Tangento's more subterranean commerce to give her their advertising accounts."

"Why me? Was I just in the wrong place at the wrong time?"

"No, Kimberley told me some snitch had been sending you envelopes, leaking little bits of information about my business to you."

"So, two ducks with one bullet, huh, Barry?"

"Do you hunt, Angie?"

"Just for the right words," I answered.

The car screeched to a halt. The door slammed as Barry exited the car. A new wave of fear prickled my skin and clenched my gut. Had Barry brought me to a quiet place in the woods to kill me? But when he climbed into the back seat, pulled me upright and took off my blindfold I saw that we were still in the city. I didn't know the street specifically, but I could tell from the houses—a stately mix of Tudor and Arts and Crafts styles—that we were in Sea Cliff, an upscale neighborhood near the Golden Gate Bridge. It was quiet here, but not the woods by any stretch.

Barry had taken off his trench coat and fedora. In his starched white button-down shirt and Dockers slacks he now epitomized the banality of evil. He pointed out the window.

"That's the Count's castle, right there."

Eric's house was an anomaly in this old-fashioned neighborhood, a stunningly modern building of cement and glass. It looked like two shoeboxes, one standing on its edge and the other emerging from the side of the first, cantilevered over a hill and resting on pilings. Barry opened the door and pushed me to the sidewalk, not noticing that the rope was loose around my wrists. Now would be the moment to run away, as Barry was hefting his linebacker frame out of the back seat, but I didn't consider it. Eric might be asleep inside the house, helpless against Nicolai's ancient knife. I couldn't let Barry reach him.

Instead of turning toward the house, Barry prodded me to walk up the street. He kept the gun against my ribs, hidden under the trench coat that he had placed over his arm. Under his other arm was the ornate box containing Nicolai's knife. Barry peered in the window of each car we passed.

When we came upon a huge blue SUV Barry said, "This one will do."

With the butt of the gun he hit the glass in the passenger window. As the alarm wailed, ear-splittingly loud, Barry rushed me back to Eric's house. He pulled out the gun and shot the door lock, the sound drowned out by the alarm.

"People have no idea that car alarms are a criminal's best friend."

We walked into an expansive living room. Floor to ceiling windows framed a three-sided view of the bay. The two towers of the Golden Gate Bridge peeked out of the fog. Because of the way the house was cantilevered over the hillside I felt like we were on the deck of a ship. The room was bright with sunlight, even on this foggy day, and there were no curtains.

"Guess he doesn't sleep in here," Barry said, echoing my thoughts. He took hold of my arm again and led me into the hallway.

"I figure he doesn't walk around during the day, right?" he asked.

I shook my head. "Yes, he does. And the gun won't do anything to him, and neither will the knife. I know, I tried it already."

Barry just laughed. "Never cheat a cheater, or lie to a liar," he quipped. "Besides, I got a plan for all eventualities. Want to hear it?"

Of course I did, so I nodded.

"Well, Angie," he said. "If he's a normal human freak, I'm going to shoot him. If we find him sleeping in some coffin like a supernatural freak I'm going to stab him, and then shoot him. What do you think?"

I turned to look at his broad, handsome, cartoon-character face, and saw that he was smiling at me like I was his co-conspirator.

"Good idea," I replied.

In front of us was a circular iron staircase spiraling both up and down from the main floor. Barry guided me down the stairs into a long hallway. Recessed lighting highlighted a collection of old photographs of different cities. I recognized Paris and Venice before Barry opened a door and pushed me into a room. The interior was dark but Barry patted the wall until he found a light switch.

It looked like the bedroom of any well-to-do San Francisco bachelor, not that I had been in many for comparison. Tasteful abstract oil paintings decorated the walls. An ancient-looking Oriental rug covered the oak floor. The bedroom set was black and modern, with a tweedy gray coverlet that matched the tweedy gray drapes. A small, oval portrait hanging near the bed caught my attention. It was framed in gilt and dark with age. Fascinated, I moved closer. It was an oil painting of an ethereally lovely woman. With her copper-colored hair and light blue eyes, it had to be Eric's mother. The picture confirmed that it wasn't just his vampire powers that made him attractive: it was in the genes as well. No wonder a vampire had chosen him as a permanent companion.

"This must be his bedroom, but dang, where he is he, Angie?"

"How should I know?" I shrieked. I was trying to stay calm but the tension of walking through this silent house, trying to be ready for whatever battle was around the corner, was almost unbearable. If something was going to happen I needed it to hurry up, because I couldn't hold myself together for much longer.

Barry threw open the two closets and even banged on the walls and felt the floor. I watched him, my mouth dry with fear. I could only hope that if Eric really was asleep in the house that he had hidden himself really well. I had been using all my senses to locate him, not just looking but sniffing the air and sending out mental feelers to sense his presence around a corner or behind a wall. The bedroom held a slight vestige of Eric's scent, enough to tell me that he had been there recently. But even as I searched for him I hoped he was nowhere nearby.

We returned to the hallway. The next room had a reinforced door with a lock on it, but the key was in the lock. Barry pocketed the key and we went inside.

This room was much larger than Eric's bedroom and looked like it was just used for storage. I say just, but it was filled with things that would have amazed me had I not been in such dire circumstances. It was like visiting the basement of the Metropolitan Museum. Standing on a stone column was a marble statue at least eight feet high, of a young naked man with chiseled abs and a tiny penis. Two holes gaped where his jeweled eyes should have been. There was a gleaming black and red vase, its circumference decorated with pictures of men in togas hunting various animals. A richly engraved warrior's shield that looked like it was made of pure gold sat in an open wooden crate filled with Styrofoam peanuts. A stack of oil paintings leaned haphazardly against one wall. The one in front was of ballet dancers in gauzy white tutus pirouetting in a high-ceilinged studio. My sister had a very similar print in her half of our room while we were growing up. It was either a Degas or a mighty good knock-off, and why would Eric own a fake when he could have bought this painting in Paris when it first went on sale?

"Hell's bells, Angie, look at this stash," said Barry, running his hand over a marble bust of some long dead conqueror wearing a wreath of pressed gold leaves. He picked up the wreath and placed it on his own head. "I'm no expert, but this looks like some valuable stuff. And just think, it'll all be mine when you're both dead. What an unexpected bonus."

He wandered through the room, picking things up and putting them down with no reverence whatsoever. Ancient vases and delicate statuary wobbled and teetered under his ham fists.

"Do you know what any of this stuff is?" he asked.

"No, but I know Eric's going to kill you when he finds you here," I replied, with more bravado than I felt.

"Not if I find him first," Barry said.

We finished searching the first storeroom and then crossed the hallway into a second room with a reinforced door. It also had a key that Barry took with him. We moved much more swiftly through this room, as my captor had ceased to be impressed by the treasure trove around him. We were near the back of the room when Barry stopped abruptly.

"Hey, that looks promising."

A massive stone sarcophagus with an ornately carved top and sides stood against the far wall, surrounded by packing crates, Chinese porcelain vases, and a giant wooden statue of the Virgin Mary. My heart sank.

"What do you think, Angie?"

"It's Egyptian, or maybe Roman."

He laughed. "No, I mean, do you think Count Chocula might be sleeping it off in there? It looks pretty sturdy."

To my great dismay, I thought that he might be. The sweet fragrance of vampire was much stronger in this room. I wondered if Barry had noticed it.

"I told you, Barry, he doesn't sleep during the day. That's a myth."

Barry made the tut-tutting sound of disapproval again. "I went to college too, missy. After five years at Ole Miss you think I don't understand reverse psychology?" He pushed at the lid of the sarcophagus. "Jesus, that's heavy. Could you help me?" He looked up. "No, of course you can't, your hands are tied, aren't they?"

He stuck the gun in the waistband of his pants and placed the knife box on a nearby table, and then he crouched so that he could apply all of his considerable strength to the task at hand. Now was my chance. Slipping my hands out of the rope, I grabbed the nearest thing, a large porcelain vase, and raised it over his head. But Barry's football instincts were still intact. He swung around and rushed me with his shoulder, sending me flying into the statue of the Virgin. Mary and I hit the ground amid shards of the probably priceless vase. My head bounced like a tennis ball on the concrete floor. I tried desperately to stay conscious, but a galaxy of stars whirled in front of my eyes and an inky blackness crept in on both sides until it finally engulfed me.

Chapter 26

When I woke up I was propped against the wall with the Virgin Mary in my lap. My hands were tied again, in front this time, and much more tightly. My head throbbed and my eyes didn't seem to be working. Everything I looked at had a shadowy doppelgänger attached to it, wavering in and out of focus.

"Hey, are you awake? I want you to see this."

The statue was lifted and Barry's smirking face appeared, a double image attached to the side of his head like some monstrous conjoined twin. He grabbed my arm and pulled me upright. Jolts of pain like electric shocks ran through my trussed wrists. He was holding the wavy knife, and it was stained red.

"I found him, look!"

Barry had managed to shift the heavy cover, and it lay tilted against the bottom half of the sarcophagus. The coffin was deep, at least four feet, and I couldn't see inside until I walked right up to it. I approached on tottering feet. The heavenly fragrance grew more and more powerful in my nostrils, but it was mixed with another smell, bitter and awful. When I looked inside bile rose in my throat and I almost threw up.

Eric lay naked in his marble bed, with no blanket or mattress as protection from the cold. This pained me, although I knew he couldn't feel anything. His expression was calm and his arms lay at his sides, his long fingers curled slightly inward. My eyes flicked over the angry, puckered burn scar that lay over his left nipple, and rested on the fresh knife wound, a diagonal slash from collarbone to the bottom of his rib cage. It was this wound that had made me gag. The two edges of his pale skin curled like black, waxy parchment away from the wet, red muscles in the center. Acrid smoke was rising from the wound, as if his flesh had been dipped in acid and was still actively burning.

"What did you do?" I cried out.

The wound was horrible, deep and vicious, but it wasn't bleeding. Understanding neither vampire anatomy nor the effects of magic swords on the undead, I had no idea whether such an injury was life-threatening. For all I knew Eric could already be dead. I put my fingers under his nose and was relieved beyond words to feel his cool, dry breath. I moved my hands lower and felt his heart beating, the rhythm slow but steady. Clenching his cold, hard shoulder between my bound hands, I shook him, all the while knowing that if the pain of his injury hadn't roused him I wouldn't be able to. I still had double vision, and a shadowy second Eric moved under my hands as well, and failed to wake up.

I heard Barry's insane titter behind me. "I tested the knife on him, and look what happened! His skin flared up like a tiki torch, and it's still burning. If that ain't magic I don't know what is!"

A tear dripped from my eye onto Eric's cheek. "Why didn't you just kill him?"

"Because I wanted you to watch, of course!" Another hysterical laugh.

Of course he wanted me to watch. Barry was a sadist of the most macabre kind, as evidenced by the trail of misery he'd left behind in Asia. He'd make me watch him kill Eric, and then he'd do the same to me afterward. And more.

I pressed against the coffin, staring at the only man I'd ever truly loved. He was helpless as a pupa, his limbs frozen, awaiting the metamorphosis of night. I had to do something, and do it now. A parade of images marched through my mind of Barry's previous crimes, and those grotesque pictures gave me an idea. It was the only glimmer of hope I'd had since I regained consciousness. I blinked furiously to amass more tears, and manufactured a few sobs as I gazed at Eric. Then I turned around to face Barry. It was a terrible risk I was taking, and I hated to think of the consequences if I failed, but it was my only option.

"Please just kill me now," I begged, as the tears

poured down my face. "Just don't hurt me, like you hurt those other girls."

Barry approached me, the wavy silver blade in his right hand, his left hand empty. The gun was in his waistband. I cried and whimpered, backing away from him with my bound hands held up in supplication. His smiling countenance slowly changed, as he turned from a crazy man into a rabid wolf. His eyes narrowed. His lips drew back and exposed his giant white teeth. It was working. Barry had forgotten about Eric for the moment and turned his attention to his favorite prey, a helpless woman.

His eyes moved up and down my body, resting for a long moment on my breasts. Then he made a guttural sound, low in his throat, and launched himself at me. We both fell onto the hard concrete floor. Any semblance of humanity he had maintained dropped away as he tore blindly at my clothes. His teeth raked my cheek. The knife clattered to the floor but he made no attempt to retrieve it. His entire weight pressed down on me, on my bound hands, and I almost passed out from the pain and lack of oxygen. He lifted himself to fumble with his zipper, giving me a tiny bit of space to maneuver. I could feel the hard contours of the gun pressing into my hip, only inches from my hands. I clasped the crosshatched metal of the handle and worked my finger into the trigger.

"I have your gun, Barry," I yelled. "Get off me."

Barry stopped moving. "It's got the safety on. Bet you don't know how to switch it off."

"Bet you the safety's not on, and all I have to do is twitch my finger and your guts are going to be all over the ceiling."

A shudder passed through his body.

"Now get off me."

He moved his weight onto his elbows and then rolled to one side, holding his hands up next to his head. I pointed the gun at his stunned, terrified face and awkwardly hoisted myself to a standing position. I still had double vision and it took all of my effort to aim the gun at the more substantial of the two Barrys and not get confused by the ghost that hovered next to him.

"Pick up the knife," I ordered. "Don't try anything sneaky."

I could see Barry wrestling to control his emotions. His face turned into a smiling mask.

"Let's not play games, sweetheart. You're not going to shoot me and you certainly . . ."

The blast almost knocked me into the wall. I barely managed to keep hold of the gun. When I looked at Barry he was curled like a pill bug, grabbing his lower left leg. Blood seeped under his hands, staining his khaki pants.

"Ahh, you fucking shot me!"

"That's right. Now do what I say or the next one's going to be aimed higher. Stand up."

"I can't fucking stand up! You shot me in my fucking leg!"

"Okay, then. Crawl into the next room."

"What?"

"You heard me! Crawl." I kicked him just above his broken leg.

"Argh! Stop! All right, I'll do it." He pulled himself to his hands and knees, holding the injured leg up as best he could, and slowly slid, crawled, and dragged himself through the hall to the adjacent storage room.

"You're going to be so fucking sorry, Angie."

When he was over the threshold I shoved him the last few feet with my foot in the seat of his pants.

"I am sorry," I said. "Sorry I'm letting you live."

He rolled onto his back and clutched his injured leg. Tears rolled down his sweaty red face.

"I almost forgot," I added. "Give me the keys."

He didn't argue this time, just reached into his pocket and pulled out the keys, then slid them along the floor. I kicked them into the hallway and walked out, closing the door with difficulty while still clutching the gun between my trussed hands. I had to put the gun down to lock the door, and I accomplished that as quickly as I could, while listening to Barry groan and cry inside the room.

I returned to the room where Eric was and hurried over to the sarcophagus. He was lying as before, silent and still as the coffin itself, but his heart was still beating, so I knew he was alive. The wound on his chest had stopped smoking. It wasn't bleeding, as a human's would, but it was also not spontaneously healing. There was nothing to do but wait for Eric to wake up when night fell. Hopefully he'd be strong enough to deal with Barry. But now I needed to get my hands free. I found the knife on the floor and sat down, then picked it up and positioned it between my feet.

"Just don't slit your wrists, hotshot," I muttered.

I slid the razor sharp blade between my palms. The cold metal didn't burn me, I was happy to note. I sawed my hands up and down two or three times and the ropes were off.

I searched through the mind-boggling contents of the storage room and found a gorgeous silk tapestry, at least ten feet long, stitched with a design of a medieval maiden in a pointed hat lying with a lion in a field of green grass. The colors were still brilliant. Trying not to think about how old and certainly valuable the tapestry was, I wrapped it around myself like a shawl and settled down at the foot of the sarcophagus. I kept the gun in my hand just in case Barry managed to break out of the room where he was trapped.

It was difficult to stay awake, but I knew I had to try. The double vision was probably caused by a concussion, and I'd read somewhere that if you fell asleep with a concussion you might never wake up. So whenever I felt myself nodding off I stood up and walked around the room, admiring the objets d'art and checking on Eric. I had no means of telling time, but every minute seemed like an hour. Occasionally I heard thumps from the other room and I rushed over to point the gun at the door, but then it would grow quiet again.

Finally I heard a rustling sound from inside the sarcophagus. Before I could stand there was a rush of movement. Something flew through the air. But it wasn't Eric, it was a wild creature with flaming eyes and glittering fangs. He leaped on me, and his hands were like metal vises, crushing my arms. He had awakened, threatened and in pain, and he was going to eliminate the source of the threat. His head arched, preparing to sink his teeth into my neck.

"Eric, it's me!"

I was still screaming when he wrapped his arms around me.

"Angela, I'm so sorry. Thank goodness I didn't kill you."

"Yes, thank goodness."

Eric stood up, beautiful in his nakedness. He stared at the wound on his chest, and then at the knife on the floor. In his expression was a mixture of confusion and pain.

"What happened?" he asked.

"Oh, Eric, you don't think I did that, do you?"

He shook his head. "Of course not. Where is he? Did you kill him?"

"No, he's locked in the other room. I did shoot him in the leg, though."

He smiled when he heard that. "Are you hurt, Angela? Your eyes look strange."

"Yeah, well, you look strange yourself. Both of you."

"You have a head injury?"

I nodded very slightly. I had found it was less painful to keep my head stationary.

"Do you have the key? I need to go in and get some clothes."

"What about Barry?"

"I shall take care of him. Then we'll get you to a hospital."

"What about you? You need medical attention too."

Eric delicately probed the wound on his chest with one finger. "Hmm," he said. "Yes, it appears so. I know of a physician who can help me. But first things first."

He took the key from me and disappeared into the hallway.

I woke up in an unfamiliar room, tucked into stiff sheets on a narrow bed. It was dark, and quiet but for the beeps and drones that emanated from somewhere behind my head. There was a tube snaking out of a bandage on top of my left hand. I would have been concerned, but Eric's aroma floated around the bed in a luscious miasma, inducing such feelings of euphoria and well-being that it was impossible to be worried. After a moment I remembered that I had been admitted to California General Hospital for treatment of my concussion.

"Eric?"

He was sitting in the far corner of the room, looking out the window at the winking lights of the city. A neon sign gave a crimson cast to his pale face. He stood up and walked over to the bed. He was dressed in slacks and a dark V-neck sweater. His short hair was neatly combed back from his high forehead. He smiled at me.

"I believe I owe you my thanks. More than that, I owe you my life."

Even in the dim light I could see his smile fade and a deep sadness settle onto his features.

"Would you rather I let you die?" I couldn't keep the anger out of my voice. How dare he look like that when I had risked my life for him?

He sat down, careful not to disturb my IV tube, and stroked my cheek. "No, of course not. I am grateful to you, truly grateful. And also truly ashamed that I could not come to your defense as I should have."

"How's your chest?" I asked.

He lifted his sweater, revealing those chiseled muscles I loved so much. The long red slash of the knife wound was now crisscrossed with dozens of bristly black stitches.

"You had to get stitches?" I ran my finger across the smaller, older scar, remembering the smoke rising from it, and my fear of losing Eric forever.

He laughed ruefully. "There's a first time for everything, I suppose."

"Will these scars ever go away?"

He shook his head. "Not from that knife, no. I shall bear them forever."

"What happened to Barry?"

His eyes drifted to the machines on the wall behind me. "He was, uh, very useful in my healing."

"I see."

"It wasn't the end I planned for him, but he won't be doing any more damage to anyone."

"What about Tangento?"

Eric smiled enigmatically. "The proper documents have been sent to the proper people. I have faith that they will receive their just deserts."

"So what happens now?" I rubbed my wrists, which were bruised and chafed from the ropes, and tried not to look at Eric.

"It's over now, Angela. You can go home, live as a normal person."

I took a deep breath. "What if I don't want to go home? What if I don't want to be normal?"

He shook his head, pushing my words away. "You don't know what you're saying."

I sat up and put my arms around his neck. "But I want to be with you! You said you loved me, did you mean it?"

He stroked my hair, tucking a curl behind my ear. "With all my heart."

"So bring me over. We can be together forever. I could cure my mother of her cancer." Tears welled in my eyes and threatened to spill over.

"Angela, you and I both know that the burden of living this life is too great a price to pay for any love."

"No, you're wrong!" I started to cry in earnest.

"Look at me, Angela." He held my chin so that I was forced to gaze into his fathomless blue eyes.

"Tell me the truth, from your heart. I know you love me, but do you want to *be* me, to live as I live?"

"Yes!"

He gave his head a tiny shake. "You can't lie to me, Angela. I can see into your heart."

He was right. I couldn't take just the advantages that being a vampire offered—the ability to heal, the chance to be with Eric forever—without taking on the burdens. Eric was strong, as strong as anyone I'd ever met, and the affliction of living the shadow-filled, guilt-ridden existence of a predator was almost too much for him to bear. Certainly it would be too much for me.

"Okay, you're right. I can't imagine being a vampire. But I can't imagine living without you, either."

"Nor I you." He placed a light kiss on my forehead. "I have never felt about anyone the way I feel about you."

"Wow, that's saying a lot."

He laughed. "Yes, I suppose it is." He squeezed onto the narrow bed with me and picked up the hand that wasn't attached to an IV. I turned so that our faces were inches from each other. I still couldn't get used to the clarity of Eric's skin, free of every bump and blemish that marred human flesh.

"I honestly don't know what I can offer you,

Angela," he said sadly. "I cannot marry you, I cannot give you children. I shall not grow old with you."

"I can think of one thing you could do for me."

"What's that?"

I traced the outline of his lips with my finger, and then kissed him slowly, sensuously, until I almost forgot what I was going to say.

"You could make me rich."

"What?"

"Just kidding." I laughed. "But not really. It would be for a good cause. Steve and I have wanted to start our own company for ages. We even have the name already: M&B Public Relations. We would only handle small nonprofits who are doing important work in the community and need help getting the word out. We could do great things if we had some money to get started."

Eric nodded thoughtfully. "Well, that's easy enough. And I can think of something else I could do for you."

I was going to quip that I could think of a few things he could start doing right now, but I sensed the seriousness of his intent, so I just waited for him to continue.

"I could heal your mother."

I was silent for a minute, contemplating his offer. I didn't have to ask him how he would do it, I had witnessed his healing abilities firsthand. But I did wonder about one thing.

"But you'd have to bite her."

He sighed. "Yes."

"And then she'd know what you are."

"I could arrange it so that she would think that it was a dream. She might have some guilty feelings about me afterward, but she would probably keep them to herself. It's not something you would mention at a family dinner." He smiled slightly.

"You're going to be at my family dinners?"

"If you allow me, yes. As long as they're after dark."

We kissed again. A heady swirl of sensation and emotion took me over. The machine behind me began to beep more rapidly. I pulled away before my accelerated heartbeat brought a nurse running.

"I must tell you something, though," Eric said, his voice hesitant.

"Go ahead. I'm feeling strong."

"At some point, I will have to leave." As if to emphasize the point he got out of bed and walked over to the window. He spoke without looking at me.

"I work with a loose network of colleagues, people who feel as I do."

"You mean vampires?"

He nodded. "When we find someone like Barry, an evildoer who must be stopped, the network moves into action. Someone is selected to follow up on the case. It could be anywhere in the world, as we have people on every continent, watching. If I am chosen I must go."

I smoothed the sheets down over my lap. "Fine. When they call, we'll go."

He turned around when he heard that statement. "*We?*"

"Did I help you with Barry or not?"

"Of course, but . . ."

"No buts, you'd be dead if it wasn't for me. And vice versa. We can help each other. You can make me strong without making me into a vampire, and keep me strong."

The red neon light glinted in his eyes, and I could have sworn I saw tears.

"Are you crying?" I asked.

He smiled. "I have never had a partner before."

"Do you want one?"

"Yes, of course, if it's you." In a movement so fast that my eyes couldn't capture it, Eric crossed the room and was back at my bed.

"Good, then it's settled. Now cure me of this concussion, so I can get out of here. We've got work to do."

"It would be my pleasure."

Eric bent over me. At that point I stopped reasoning and let pure feeling take over.